For what seemed a long time, Ryana remained motion-less, her crossbow held ready. There was no sign of movement out beyond their camp, and she could hear nothing but the rustling of the wind in the dry desert grass and the pagafa branches overhead. The fire was almost completely out now. She expelled her breath, suddenly realizing that she had been holding it, put down the crossbow, and reached for some more branches to put on the fire.

A shadow suddenly fell over her, and she felt pow-erful arms closing around her from behind. . . .

TRIBE OF ONE

Simon Hawke

The Seeker

Simon Hawke

TRIBE OF ONE TRILOGY
Book Two

THE SEEKER

Cover art by Brom.

First Printing: April 1994

Printed in the United States of America

Library of Congress Catalog Card Number: 93-61473

9 8 7 6 5 4 3 2 1

ISBN: 1-56076-701-4

TSR, Inc.
P.O. Box 756
Lake Geneva, WI 53147
U.S.A.

TSR Ltd.
120 Church End, Cherry Hinton
Cambridge CB1 3LB
United Kingdom

With best wishes,
FOR ROD AND SHARI

Acknowledgments

With special thanks and acknowledgments to Bruce and Peggy Wiley; Becky Ford; Pat Connors; Robert M. Powers and Sandra West; Pamela Lloyd; Michel Leckband; and the staff and management Acton, Dystel, Leone and Jaffe, Inc. Thanks also to Nancy L. Thompson of Pima Community College, and to all my students, for keeping me fresh and on my toes. And if I forgot anyone, I plead combat fatigue. . . .

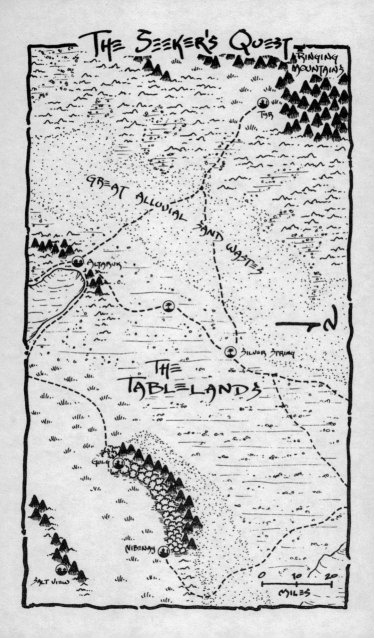

PROLOGUE

The twin moons of Athas flooded the desert with a ghostly light as the dark sun sank on the horizon. The temperature dropped quickly while Ryana sat warming herself by the campfire, relieved at having left the city.

Tyr held nothing for her but bad memories. As a young girl growing up in a villichi convent, she had dreamt of visiting the city at the foot of the Ringing Mountains. Tyr had seemed like an exotic and exciting place then, when she could only imagine its teeming marketplaces and its tantalizing nightlife. She had heard stories of the city from the older priestesses, those who had been on pilgrimages, and she had longed for the day when she could take her own pilgrimage and leave the convent to see the outside world. Now she had seen it, and it was a far cry from the dreams of her youth.

When in her girlish dreams she had imagined the crowded streets and glamorous marketplaces of Tyr, she had pictured them without the pathetic, scrofulous beggars that crouched in the dust and whined plaintively for coppers, holding out their filthy hands in supplication to every passerby. The colorful images of her imagination had not held the stench of urine and manure from all the beasts penned up in the market square, or the human waste produced by the city's residents, who simply threw their refuse out the windows into the streets and alleys. She had imagined a city of grand, imposing buildings, as if all of Tyr were as impressive as the Golden Tower or Kalak's ziggurat. Instead she found mostly aging, blocky, uniformly earth-toned structures of crudely mortared brick covered with cracked and flaking plaster, such as the ramshackle hovels in the warrens. There the poor people of Tyr lived in squalid and pitiful conditions, crowded together like beasts crammed into stinking holding pens.

She had not imagined the vermin and the filth, or the flies and the miasma of decay as garbage rotted in the streets, or the pickpockets and the cutthroats and the vulgar, painted prostitutes, or the rioting mobs of desperate people caught up in the painful transition of a city laboring to shift from a sorcerer-king's tyranny to a more open and democratic form of government. She had not imagined that she would come to Tyr not as a priestess on a pilgrimage, but as a young woman who had broken her sacred vows and fled the convent in the night, in pursuit of the only male she had ever known and loved. Nor had she imagined that before she left the city, she would learn what it meant to kill.

She turned away from the shadowy city in the distance, feeling no regret at leaving it, and gazed across the desert spreading out below. She and Sorak had made camp on the crest of a ridge overlooking the Tyr Valley, just east of the city. Beyond the city, to the west, the foothills rose to meet the Ringing Mountains. To the east, they gradually fell away, almost completely encircling the valley, save for the pass directly to the south, along which the trade route ran from Tyr out across the tablelands. The caravans always took the pass, then headed southeast to Altaruk, or else turned to the northeast toward Silver Spring, before heading north to Urik, or northeast to Raam and Draj. To the east of the oasis known as Silver Spring, there was nothing but rocky, inhospitable desert, a trackless waste known as the Stony Barrens that stretched out for miles before it ended at the Barrier Mountains, beyond which lay the cities of Gulg and Nibenay.

The caravans all have their routes mapped out, Ryana thought, while ours has not yet been determined. She sat alone, huddled in her cloak, her long, silvery white hair blowing gently in the breeze, and wondered when Sorak would return. Or, perhaps more properly, she thought, the Ranger. Shortly before he had left the campsite, Sorak had fallen asleep, and the Ranger had come out to take control of his body. She did not really know the Ranger very well, though she had met him many times before. The Ranger was not much for words. He was a hunter and a tracker, an entity wise in the lore of the mountain forests and desert tablelands.

The Ranger ate flesh, as did the other entities who made up Sorak's inner tribe. Sorak, like the villichi among whom he was raised, was vegetarian. It was one of the many anomalies of his multiplicity. Though, unlike her, Sorak had not been born villichi, he had been raised in the villichi convent and had adopted many of their ways. And, like all villichi, he had sworn to follow the Way of the Druid and the Path of the Preserver.

Ryana recalled the day when Sorak had been brought to the convent by the pyreen elder, who had found him half dead in the desert. He had been cast out of his tribe and left to die because he had been born a half-breed. Though the human and demihuman races of Athas frequently mixed, and half-breeds such as half-dwarves, half-giants, and half-elves were not uncommon, Sorak was an elfling—perhaps the only one of his kind.

Elves and halflings were mortal enemies, and usually killed one another on sight. Yet, somehow, an elf and a halfling had mated to produce Sorak, giving him the characteristics of both races. Halflings were small, though powerfully built, while elves were extremely tall, lean and long-limbed. Sorak's proportions, a mixture of the two, were similar to those of humans. In fact, at first glance, he looked completely human.

The differences were slight, though significant. His long black hair was thick and luxuriant, like a halfling's mane. His eyes were deeply set and dark, with an unsettling, penetrating gaze, and like both elves and halflings, he could see in the dark. His eyes had the same, catlike lambency that halfling eyes had in the darkness. His facial features had an elvish cast, sharply pronounced, with high, prominent cheekbones; a sharp nose; a narrow, almost pointed chin; a wide, sensual mouth; arched eyebrows; and pointed ears. And, like elves, he could grow no facial hair.

But as unique as his physical appearance was, his mental makeup was even more unusual. Sorak was a 'tribe of one.' The condition was exceedingly rare, and so far as Ryana knew, only the villichi truly understood it. She knew of least two cases that had occurred among villichi, though neither during her lifetime. Both priestesses who had been so afflicted had kept extensive journals, and as a girl, Ryana had studied them in the temple library, the better to understand her friend.

She had been only six years old when Sorak had been brought to the villichi convent, and he had been approximately the same age. He had no memory of his past, the time before he was cast out into the desert, so he himself did not know how old he was. The trauma of his experience had not only wiped out his memories, it had divided his mind in such a way that he now possessed at least a dozen different personalities, each with its own unique attributes, not the least of which were powerful psionic powers.

Before Sorak came, there had never been a male in residence at the villichi convent. The villichi were a female sect, not only by choice, but by accident of birth, as well. Villichi, too, were rare, though not as uncommon as tribes of one. Only human females were born villichi, though no one knew why. They were a mutation, marked by such physical characteristics as their unusual height and slenderness, their fairness, and their elongated necks and limbs. In terms of their physical proportions, they had more in common with elves than humans, though elves were taller still. But what truly made them different was that they were born with fully developed psionic abilities. Whereas most humans and many demihumans had a latent potential for at least one psionic power, it usually took many years of training under a psionicist, a master of the Way, to bring it out. Villichi children were born with it in full flower.

Ryana was short for a villichi, though at almost six feet, she was still tall for a human female, and her proportions were closer to the human norm. The only thing that marked her as different was her silvery white hair, like that of an albino. Her eyes were a striking, bright emerald green, and her skin was so fair as to be almost translucent. Like all villichi, she burned easily in the hot Athasian sun if she was not careful.

Her parents were poor and already had four other children when she was born. Things had been hard enough for them without an infant who tossed household objects around with the power of her mind whenever she was feeling hungry or cranky. When a villichi priestess on pilgrimage had come to their small village, they had been relieved to surrender the custody of their troublesome psionic child to an order devoted to the proper care, nurturing, and training of others like her.

Sorak's situation had been different. Not only was he a male, which was bad enough, he was not even human. His arrival at the convent had stirred up a great deal of heated controversy. Varanna, the high mistress of the order, had accepted him because he was both a tribe of one and gifted with incredible psionic powers, the strongest she had ever encountered. The other priestesses, however, had initially resented the presence of a male in their midst, and an elfling male at that.

Even though he was just a child, they had protested. Males sought only to dominate women, they had argued, and elves were notoriously duplicitous. As for halflings, not only were they feral flesh-eaters, they often ate human flesh as well. Even if Sorak did not manifest any of those loathsome traits, the young villichi felt that the mere presence of a male in the convent would be disruptive. Varanna had stood firm, however, insisting that though Sorak had not been born villichi, he was nevertheless gifted with unusual psionic talent, as were they all. He was also a tribe of one, which meant that without villichi training to adapt him to his rare condition, he would have been doomed to a life of suffering and, ultimately, insanity.

On the day Sorak was first brought to Ryana's residence hall, the other young priestesses had all protested vehemently. Ryana, alone, stood up for him. Looking back on it now, she was not sure she could remember why. Perhaps it was because they were roughly the same age, and Ryana had no one else her age to be friends with at the convent. Perhaps it was her own natural willfulness and rebelliousness that had caused her to diverge from the others and stand up for the young elfling, or perhaps it was because she had always felt alone and saw that he was alone, too. Perhaps, even then, she had known somehow, on some deeply intuitive, subconscious level, that the two of them were fated to be together.

He had seemed hurt, lost and alone, and her heart went out to him. He had no memory. He did not even know his own name. The high mistress had named him

Sorak, an elvish word used to describe a nomad who always walked alone. Even then, Ryana had joined herself to him, and they had grown up as brother and sister. Ryana had always thought she understood him better than anybody else. However, there were limits to her own understanding, as she had discovered on the day, not very long ago, when she had announced her love to Sorak—and been rebuffed, because several of Sorak's personalities were female, and could not love another woman.

She had first felt shock, and then humiliation, then anger at his never having told her, and then pain . . . for him and for his loneliness, for the unique and harsh realities of his existence. She had retired to the meditation chamber in the tower of the temple to sort things out in her own mind, and when she came out again, it was only to learn that he had left the convent.

She had blamed herself at first, thinking she had driven him away. But the high mistress had explained that, if anything, she had only been the catalyst for a decision Sorak had been struggling to make for quite some time.

"I have always known that he would leave us one day," Mistress Varanna had said. "Nothing could have held him, not even you, Ryana. Elves and halflings are wanderers. It is in their blood. And Sorak has other forces driving him, as well. There are questions he hungers to have answered, and he cannot find those answers here."

"But I cannot believe that he would simply leave without even saying good-bye," Ryana had said.

Mistress Varanna had smiled. "He is an elfling. His emotions are not the same as ours. You, of all people, ought to know that by now. You cannot expect him to act human."

"I know, but . . . It's just that . . . I had always thought . . ."

"I understand," the high mistress had said in a sympathetic tone. "I have known how you felt about Sorak for quite some time now. I could see it in your eyes. But the sort of partnership you hoped for was never meant to be, Ryana. Sorak is an elfling and a tribe of one. You are villichi, and the villichi do not take mates."

"But there is nothing in our vows that prohibits it," Ryana had protested.

"Strictly speaking, no, there is not," the high mistress had agreed. "I will grant you that the interpretation of the vows we take could certainly be argued on that point. But practically speaking, it would be folly. We cannot bear children. Our psionic abilities and our training, to say nothing of our physical makeup, would threaten most males. It is not for nothing that most of the priestesses choose celibacy."

"But Sorak is different," Ryana had protested, and the high mistress held up her hand to forestall any further comment.

"I know what you are going to say," she said, "and I will not disagree. His psionic powers are the strongest I have yet encountered. Not even I can penetrate his formidable defenses. And since he is a half-breed, he may also be unable to sire offspring. However, Sorak has certain unique problems that he may never be able to overcome. At best, he will only find a way to live with them. His path in life is a solitary one, Ryana. I know that it is hard for you to hear these things right now, and harder still to understand them, but you are young yet, and your best and most productive years are still ahead of you.

"Soon," she had continued, "you will be taking over Sister Tamura's training sessions, and you will discover that there is a great measure of satisfaction to be found in molding the minds and bodies of the younger sisters. In time, you will be departing on your first pilgrimage to seek out others like ourselves and bring them into the fold, and to gather information about the state of things in the outside world. When you return, it will help us in our quest to find a way of reversing all the damage that our world has suffered at the hands of the defilers. Our task here is a holy and a noble one, and its rewards can be ever so much greater than the ephemeral pleasures of love.

"I know these things are hard to hear when one is young," Varanna had said with an indulgent smile. "I was young myself once, so I know, but time brings clarity, Ryana. Time and patience. You gave Sorak what he needed most, your friendship and your understanding. More than anyone else, you helped him gain the strength that he required to go out and find his own way in the world. The time has come for him to do that, and you must respect his choice. You must let him go."

Ryana had tried to tell herself that the high mistress was right, that the best thing she could do for Sorak was to let him go, but she could not make herself believe it. They had known each other for ten years, since they were both small children, and she had never felt as close to any of her villichi sisters as she had to Sorak. Perhaps she had nurtured unreasonable expectations as to the sort of relationship they could have, but while it was now clear to her that they never could be lovers, she still knew that Sorak loved her as much as he could ever love anyone. For her part, she had never wanted anyone else. She had never even known another male.

The priestesses had frequently discussed the different ways in which physical desire could be sublimated. On occasion, a priestess on a pilgrimage might indulge in the pleasures of the flesh, for it was not expressly forbidden by their vows, but even those who had done so had eventually chosen celibacy. Males, they said, left much to be desired when it came to such things as companionship, mutual respect, and spiritual bonding. Ryana was still a virgin, so she had no personal experience from which to judge, but the obvious implication seemed to be that the physical side of love was not all that important. What was important was the bond that she had shared with Sorak from childhood. With his departure, she had felt a void within her that nothing else could fill.

That night, after everyone had gone to sleep, she had quickly packed her rucksack with her few possessions, then stole into the armory where the sisters kept all the weapons used in their training. The villichi had always followed a philosophy that held the development of the body to be as important as the training of the mind. From the time they first came to the convent, the sisters were all trained in the use of the sword, the staff, the dagger, and the crossbow, in addition to such weapons as the cahulaks, the mace and flail, the spear, the sickle, and the widow's knife. A lone villichi priestess on a pilgrimage was not as vulnerable as she appeared.

Ryana had buckled on an iron broadsword and tucked two daggers into the top of each of her high moccasins. She also took a staff and slung a crossbow across her back, along with a quiver of bolts. Perhaps the weapons were not hers to take, but she had put in her share of time in the workshop of the armory, fashioning bows and arrows and working at the forge, making iron swords and daggers, so in a sense, she felt she had earned a right to them. She did not think Sister Tamura would begrudge her. If anyone would understand, Tamura would.

Ryana then had climbed over the wall so as not to alert the old gatekeeper. Sister Dyona might not have prevented her from leaving, but Ryana was sure she would have tried to talk her out of it and insisted that she first discuss it with Mistress Varanna. Ryana was in no mood to argue or try to justify her actions. She had made her decision. Now she was living with the consequences of that decision, and those consequences were that she had absolutely no idea what lay ahead of her.

All she knew was that they had to find a wizard known only as the Sage, something that was a lot easier said than done. Most people believed the Sage was nothing but a myth, a legend for the common people to keep hope alive, hope that one day the power of the defilers would be broken, the last of the dragons would be slain, and the greening of Athas would begin.

According to the story, the Sage was a hermit wizard, a preserver who had embarked upon the arduous path of metamorphosis into an avangion. Ryana had no idea what exactly an avangion was. There had never been an avangion on Athas, but the ancient books of magic spoke of it. Of all the spells of meta-morphosis, the avangion transformation was the most difficult, the most demanding, and the most danger-ous. Aside from dangers inherent in the metamorphsis itself, there were dangers posed by defilers, especially the sorcerer-kings, to whom the avangion would be the greatest threat.

Magic had a cost, and that cost was most dramati-cally visible in the reduction of Athas to a dying, desert planet. The templars and their sorcerer-kings claimed that it was not their magic that had defiled the landscape of Athas. They insisted the destruction of the ecosystem began thousands of years earlier with those who had tried to control nature, and that it was aided by changes in the sun, which no one could control. There may have been some truth to that, but few people believed these claims, for there was noth-ing that argued against them quite so persuasively as the devastation brought about by the practice of defiler magic.

Preservers did not destroy the land the way defilers did, but most people did not bother to differentiate between defiler and preserver magic. Magic of any form was universally despised for being the agency of the planet's ruin. Everyone had heard the legends, and there was no shortage of bards who repeated them. "The Ballad of a Dying Land," "The Dirge of the Dark Sun," "The Druid's Lament," and many others were songs that told the story of how the world had been despoiled.

There had been a time when Athas was green, and the winds blowing across its verdant, flowering plains had carried the song of birds. Once, its dense forests had been rich with game, and the seasons came and went, bringing blankets of virgin snow during the winter and rebirth with every spring. Now, there were only two seasons, as the people said, "summer and the other one."

During most of the year, the Athasian desert was burning hot during the day and freezing cold at night, but for two to three months during the Athasian summer, the nights were warm enough to sleep outside without a blanket and the days brought temperatures like the inside of an oven. Where once the plains were green and fertile, now they were barren, desert tablelands covered merely with brown desert grasses, scrubby ironwood and pagafa trees, a few drought resistant bushes, and a wide variety of spiny cacti and succulents, many of them deadly. The forests had, for the most part, given way to stony hills, where the winds wailed through the rocky crags, making a sound like some giant beast howling in despair. Only in isolated spots, such as the Forest Ridge of the Ringing Mountains, was there any evidence of the world the way it once had been, but with every passing year, the forests died back a little more. And what did not die was destroyed by the defilers.

Magic required energy, and the source of that energy could be the life-force of the spellcaster or that of other living things such as plants. The magic practiced by defilers and preservers was essentially the same, but preservers had a respect for life, and cast their spells conservatively so that any energy borrowed from plant life was taken in such a way as to allow a full recovery.

Preservers did not kill with their magic.

Defilers, on the other hand, practiced the sorcery of death. When a defiler cast a spell, he sought only to absorb as much energy as he could, the better to increase his power and the potency of his spell. When a defiler drew energy from a plant, it withered and died, and the soil where it grew was left completely barren.

The great lure of defiler magic was that it was incredibly addictive. It allowed the sorcerer to increase his power far more quickly than those who followed the Path of the Preserver, which mandated reverence for life. But as with any addictive drug, the defiler's boundless lust for power necessitated ever greater doses. In his relentless quest for power, the defiler eventually reached the limit of what he could absorb and contain, beyond which the power would consume him. . . .

Only the sorcerer-kings could withstand the flood of complete defiling power, and they did so by changing. They transformed themselves through painful, time-consuming rituals and gradual stages of development into creatures whose voracious appetites and capacities for power made them the most dangerous life-forms on the planet. . . . Dragons.

Dragons were hideous perversions, thought Ryana, sorcerous mutations that posed a threat to all life on the planet. Everywhere a dragon passed, it laid waste to the entire countryside and took a fearful toll in the human and demihuman lives that it demanded as a tribute.

Once a sorcerer-king embarked upon the magical path of metamorphosis that would transform him into a dragon, there was no return. Merely to begin the process was to pass beyond redemption. With each successive stage of the transformation, the sorcerer changed physically, gradually losing all human appearance and taking on the aspect of a dragon. By then, the defiler would have ceased to care about its own humanity, or lack of it. The metamorphosis brought with it immortality and a capacity for power beyond anything the defiler had ever experienced before. It would make no difference to a dragon that its very existence threatened all life on the planet; its insatiable appetite could reduce the world to a barren, dried out rock incapable of supporting any life at all. Dragons did not care about such things. Dragons were insane.

There was only one creature capable of standing up to the power of a dragon, and that was an avangion. Or at least, so the legends said. An avangion was the antithesis of a dragon, a metamorphosis achieved through following the Path of the Preserver. The ancient books of magic spoke of it, but there had never been an avangion on Athas, perhaps because the process took far longer than did the dragon metamorphosis. According to the legend, the process of avangion transformation was not powered by absorbed life-force, and so the avangion was stronger than its defiler enemies. While the dragon was the enemy of life, the avangion was the champion of life, and possessed a powerful affinity for every living thing. The avangion could counteract the power of a dragon and defeat it, and help bring about the greening of the world.

According to the legend, one man, a preserver—a hermit wizard known only as the Sage—had embarked upon the arduous and lonely path of metamorphosis that would transform him into an avangion. Because the long, painful, and extremely demanding transformation would take many years, the Sage had gone into seclusion in some secret hiding place, where he could concentrate upon the complicated spells of metamorphosis and keep safe from the defilers who would seek to stop him at all costs. Even his true name was unknown, so that no defiler could ever use it to gain power over him or deduce the location of his hiding place.

The story had many different variations, depending on which bard sang the song, but it had been around for years, and no avangion had been forthcoming. No one had ever seen the Sage or spoken to him or knew anything about him. Ryana, like most people, had always believed the story was nothing but a myth . . . until now.

Sorak had embarked upon a quest to find the Sage, to both discover the truth about his own past and find a purpose for his future. He had first sought out Lyra Al'Kali, the pyreen elder who had found him in the desert and brought him to the convent.

The pyreens, known also as the peace-bringers, were shapechangers and powerful masters of the Way, devoted to the Way of the Druid and the Path of the Preserver. They were the oldest race on Athas, and though their lives spanned centuries, they were dying out. No one knew how many of them were left. It was believed that only a very small number remained. The pyreens were wanderers, mystics who traveled the world and sought to counteract the corrupting influence of the defilers, but they usually kept to themselves and avoided contact with humans and demihumans alike. When the Elder Al'Kali had brought Sorak to the convent, it had been both the first and last time Ryana had ever laid eyes on a pyreen.

Once each year, Elder Al'Kali made a pilgrimage to the summit of the Dragon's Tooth to reaffirm her vows. Sorak had found her there, and she had told him that the leaders of the Veiled Alliance—an underground network of preservers who fought against the sorcerer-kings—maintained some sort of contact with the Sage. Sorak had gone to Tyr to seek them out. In trying to make contact with the Veiled Alliance, he had inadvertently become involved in political intrigue aimed at toppling the government of Tyr, exposing the members of the Veiled Alliance, and restoring the templars to power under a defiler regime. Sorak had helped to foil the plot and, in return, the leaders of the Veiled Alliance had given him a scroll which, they said, contained all they knew about the Sage.

"But why write it down upon a scroll?" Sorak wondered aloud after they had left. "Why not simply tell me?"

"Perhaps because it was too complicated," Ryana had suggested, "and they thought you might forget if it were not written down."

"But they said that I must burn this after I had read it," Sorak said, shaking his head. "If they were so concerned that this information not fall into the wrong hands, why bother to write it down at all? Why take the risk?"

"It does seem puzzling," she had agreed.

He had broken the seal on the scroll and unrolled it.

"What does it say?" Ryana asked, anxiously.

"Very little," Sorak had replied. "It says, 'Climb to the crest of the ridge west of the city. Wait until dawn. At sunrise, cast the scroll into a fire. May the Wanderer guide you on your quest.' And that is all." He shook his head. "It makes no sense."

"Perhaps it does," Ryana had said. "Remember that the members of the Veiled Alliance are sorcerers."

"You mean the scroll itself is magic?" Sorak said. Then he nodded. "Yes, that could be. Or else I have been duped and played for a fool."

"Either way, we shall know at dawn tomorrow," said Ryana.

By nightfall, they had reached the crest of the ridge and made camp. She had slept for a while, then woke to take the watch so that Sorak could sleep. No sooner had he closed his eyes than the Ranger came out and took control. He got up quietly and stalked off into the darkness without a word, his eyes glowing like a cat's. Sorak, she knew, was fast asleep, ducked under, as he called it. When he awoke, he would have no memory of the Ranger going out to hunt.

Ryana had grown accustomed to this unusual behavior back when they were still children at the convent. Sorak, out of respect for the villichi who had raised him, would not eat meat. However, his vegetarian diet went against his elf and halfling natures, and his other personalities did not share his desire to follow the villichi ways. To avoid conflict, his inner tribe had found this unique method of compromise. While Sorak slept, the Ranger would hunt, and the rest of the tribe could enjoy the warm blood of a fresh kill without Sorak's having to participate. He would awaken with a full belly, but no memory of how it got that way. He would know, of course, but since *he* would not have been the one to make the kill and eat the flesh, his conscience would be clear.

It was, Ryana thought, a curious form of logic, but it apparently satisfied Sorak. For her part, she did not really care if he ate flesh or not. He was an elfling, and it was natural for him to do so. For that matter, she thought, one could argue that it was natural for humans to eat flesh, as well. Since she had broken her vows by leaving the convent, perhaps there was nothing left to lose by eating meat, but she had never done so. Just the thought was repellent to her. It was just as well that Sorak's inner tribe went off to make their kill and consume it away from the camp. She grimaced as she pictured Sorak tearing into a hunk of raw, still warm and bloody meat. She decided that she would remain a vegetarian.

It was almost dawn when the Ranger returned. He moved so quietly that even with her trained villichi senses, Ryana didn't hear him until he stepped into the firelight and settled down on the ground beside her, sitting cross-legged. He shut his eyes and lowered his head upon his chest . . . and a moment later, Sorak awoke and looked up at her.

"Did you rest well?" she asked, in a faintly mocking tone.

He merely grunted. He looked up at the sky. "It is almost dawn." He reached into his cloak and pulled out the rolled up scroll. He unrolled it and looked at it once again. " 'At sunrise, cast the scroll into a fire. May the Wanderer guide you on your quest,' " he read.

"It seems simple enough," she said. "We have climbed the ridge and made a fire. In a short while, we shall know the rest . . . whatever there may be to know."

"I have been thinking about that last part," Sorak said. " 'May the Wanderer guide you on your quest.' It is a common sentiment often expressed to wish one well upon a journey, but the word 'quest' is used instead of 'journey' in this case."

"Well, they knew your journey was a quest," Ryana said with a shrug.

"True," said Sorak, "but otherwise, the words written on the scroll are simple and direct, devoid of any sentiment or salutation."

"You mean you think that something else is meant?"

"Perhaps," said Sorak. "It would seem to be a reference to *The Wanderer's Journal*. Sister Dyona gave me her own copy the day I left the convent."

He opened his pack, rummaged in it for a moment, and then pulled out a small, plain, leather-bound book, stitched together with animal gut. It was not something that would have been produced by the villichi, who wrote their knowledge down on scrolls. "You see how she inscribed it?

"A small gift to help guide you on your journey. A more subtle weapon than your sword, but no less powerful, in its own way. Use it wisely.

"A subtle weapon," he repeated, "to be used wisely. And now the scroll from the Veiled Alliance seems to refer to it again."

"It is known that the Veiled Alliance makes copies of the journal and distributes them," Ryana said thoughtfully. "The book is banned because it speaks truthfully of the defilers, but you think there may be something more to it than that?"

"I wonder," Sorak said. "I have been reading through it, but perhaps it merits a more careful study. It is possible that it may contain some sort of hidden meaning." He looked up at the sky again. It was getting light. "The sun will rise in another moment." He rolled the scroll up once again and held it out over the fire, gazing at it thoughtfully. "What do you think will happen when we burn it?"

She shook her head. "I do not know."

"And if we do not?"

"We already know what it contains," she said. "It would seem that there is nothing to be served by holding on to it."

"Sunrise," he said again. "It is most specific about that. And on this ridge. On the crest, it says."

"We have done all else that was required. Why do you hesitate?"

"Because I hold magic in my hand," he said. "I feel certain of it now. What I am not certain of is what spell we may be loosing when we burn it."

"The members of the Veiled Alliance are preservers," she reminded him. "It would not be a defiler spell. That would go against everything that they believe."

He nodded. "I suppose so. But I have an apprehension when it comes to magic. I do not trust it."

"Then trust your instincts," said Ryana. "I will support you in whatever you choose to do."

He looked up at her and smiled. "I am truly sorry that you broke your vows for me," he said, "but I am also very glad you came."

"Sunrise," she said, as the dark sun peeked over the horizon.

"Well . . ." he said, then dropped the scroll into the fire.

It rapidly turned brown, then burst into flame, but it was a flame that burned blue, then green, then blue again. Sparks shot from the scroll as it was consumed, sparks that danced over the fire and flew higher and higher, swirling in the rising, blue-green smoke, going around faster and faster, forming a funnel like an undulating dust devil that hung over the campfire and grew, elongating as it whirled around with ever increasing speed. It sucked the flames from the fire, drawing them up into its vortex, which sparked and crackled with magical energy, raising a wind that plucked at their hair and cloaks and blinded them with dust and ash.

It rose high above the now-extinguished fire, making a rushing, whistling noise over which a voice suddenly seemed to speak, a deep and sonorous voice that came out of the blue-green funnel cloud to speak only one word.

"Nibenaaaay . . ."

Then the glowing funnel cloud rose up and skimmed across the ridge, picking up speed as it swept down toward the desert floor. It whirled off rapidly across the tablelands, heading due east, toward Silver Spring and the desert flats beyond it. They watched it recede into the distance, moving with such amazing speed that it left a trail of blue-green light behind it, as if marking out the way. Then it was gone, and all was quiet once again.

They both stood, gazing after it, and for a moment, neither of them spoke. Then Sorak broke the silence. "Did you hear it?" he asked.

Ryana nodded. "The voice said, 'Nibenay.' Do you think it was the Sage who spoke?"

"I do not know," Sorak replied. "But it went due east. Not southeast, where the trade route runs to Altaruk and from there to Gulg and then to Nibenay, but directly east, toward Silver Spring and then beyond."

"Then that would seem to be the route that we must take," Ryana said.

"Yes," said Sorak, nodding, "but according to *The Wanderer's Journal*, that way leads across the Stony Barrens. No trails, no villages or settlements, and worst of all, no water. Nothing but a rocky waste until we reach the Barrier Mountains, which we must cross if we are to reach Nibenay by that route. The journey will be harsh . . . and very dangerous."

"Then the sooner we begin it, the sooner it will end," Ryana said, picking up her rucksack, her crossbow, and her staff. "But what are we to do when we reach Nibenay?"

"Your guess is as good as mine," said Sorak, "but if we try to cross the Stony Barrens, we may never even reach the Barrier Mountains."

"The desert tried to claim you once before, and it failed," said Ryana. "What makes you think that now it will succeed?"

Sorak smiled. "Well, perhaps it won't, but it is not wise to tempt fate. In any case, there is no need for both of us to make so hazardous a journey. You could return to Tyr and join a caravan bound for Nibenay along the trade route by way of Altaruk and Gulg. I could simply meet you there and—"

"No, we go together," said Ryana, in a tone that

brooked no argument. She slung her crossbow across her back and slipped her arms through the straps of the rucksack. Holding her staff in her right hand, she started off down the western slope. She walked a few paces, then paused, looking back over her shoulder. "Coming?"

Sorak grinned. "Lead on, little sister."

ONE

They traveled due east, moving at a steady but unhurried pace. The oasis at Silver Spring was roughly sixty miles straight across the desert from where they had made camp upon the ridge. Sorak estimated it would take them at least two days to make the journey if they walked eight to ten hours a day. The pace allowed for short, regular rest periods, but did not allow for anything that might slow them down.

Ryana knew that Sorak could have made much better time had he been traveling alone. His elf and halfling ancestry made him much better suited for a journey in the desert. Being villichi, Ryana's physique was superior to most other humans, and her training at the convent had given her superb conditioning. Even so, she could not hope to match Sorak's natural powers of endurance. The dark sun could quickly sap the strength of most travelers, but even in the relentless, searing heat of an Athasian summer, elves could run for miles across the open desert at speeds that would rupture the heart of any human who attempted to keep pace. As for halflings, what they lacked in size and speed, they made up for in brute strength and stamina. In Sorak, the best attributes of both races were combined.

As Ryana had reminded him, the desert had tried to claim him once before, and it failed. A human child abandoned in the desert would have had no hope of surviving more than a few hours, at best. Sorak had survived for days without food or water until he had been rescued. Still, it had been a long time since Sorak had seen the desert, and it held a grim fascination for him. He would always regard the Ringing Mountains as his home, but the desert was where he had been born. And where he had almost died.

As Ryana walked beside him, Sorak remained silent, as if oblivious to her presence. Ryana knew that he was not ignoring her; he was immersed in a silent conversation with his inner tribe. She recognized the signs. At such times, Sorak would seem very distant and preoccupied, as if he were a million miles away. His facial expression was neutral, yet it conveyed a curious impression of detached alertness. If she spoke to him, he would hear her—or, more specifically, the Watcher would hear and redirect Sorak's attention to the external stimulus. She maintained her own silence, however, so as not to interrupt the conversation she was not able to hear.

For as long as she had known Sorak, which had been almost all her life, Ryana had wondered what it must be like for him to have so many different people living inside him. They were a strange and fascinating crew. Some she knew quite well; others she hardly knew at all. And there were some of whom she was not even aware. Sorak had told her he knew of at least a dozen personalities residing within him. Ryana knew of only nine.

There was the Ranger, who was most at home when he was wandering in the mountain forests or hunting in the wild. He had not liked the city and had only come out rarely while Sorak was in Tyr. As children, when Ryana and Sorak had gone out on hikes in the forests of the Ringing Mountains, it was always the Ranger who was in the forefront of Sorak's consciousness. He was the strong and silent type. So far as Ryana knew, the only one of Sorak's inner tribe with whom the Ranger seemed to interact was Lyric, whose playfulness and childlike sense of wonder compensated for the Ranger's dour, introspective pragmatism.

Ryana had met Lyric many times before, but she had liked him much better in her childhood than she did now. While she and Sorak had matured, Lyric had remained essentially a child by nature. When he came out, it was usually to marvel at some wildflower or sing a song or play his wooden flute, which Sorak kept strapped to his pack. The instrument was about the length of his arm and carved from stout, blue pagafa wood. Sorak was unable to play it himself, while Lyric seemed to have the innate ability to play any musical instrument he laid his hands on. Ryana had no idea what Lyric's age was, but apparently he had been "born" sometime after Sorak came to the convent. She thought, perhaps, that he had not existed prior to that time because Sorak had sublimated those qualities within himself. His early childhood must have been terrible. Ryana could not understand what Sorak could possibly regain if he managed to remember it.

Eyron could not understand, either. If Lyric was the child within Sorak, then Eyron was the world-weary and cynical adult who always weighed the conse-

quences of every action taken by the others. For every
reason Sorak had to do something, Eyron could usually
come up with three or four reasons against it. Sorak's
quest was a case in point. Eyron had argued in favor of
Sorak's continued ignorance about his past. What difference would it really make, he had asked, if Sorak
knew which tribe he came from? At best, all he would
learn was which tribe had cast him out. What would it
benefit him to know who his parents were? One was an
elf; the other was a halfling. Was there any pressing
reason to know more? What difference did it make,
Eyron had asked, if Sorak never learned the circumstances leading to his birth? Perhaps his parents had
met, fallen in love, and mated, against all the beliefs
and conventions of their respective tribes and races. If
so, then they may both have been cast out themselves,
or worse. On the other hand, perhaps Sorak's mother
had been raped during an attack on her tribe, and
Sorak had been the issue—not only an unwanted child,
but one that was anathema to both his mother and her
people. Whatever the truth was, Eyron had insisted,
there was really nothing to be gained from knowing it.
Sorak had left the convent, and life was now his to start
anew. He could live it in any manner that he chose.

Sorak disagreed, believing he could never truly find
any meaning or purpose in his life until he found out
who he was and where he came from. Even if he chose
to leave his past behind, he would first have to know
what it was he was leaving.

When Sorak had told Ryana of this discussion, she
had realized that, in a way, he had been arguing with
himself. It had been a debate between two completely
different personalities, but at the same time, it was an

argument between different aspects of the same personality. In Sorak's case, of course, those different aspects had achieved a full development as separate individuals. The Guardian was a prime example, embodying Sorak's nurturing, empathic, and protective aspects, developed into a maternal personality whose role was not only to protect the tribe, but to maintain a balance between them.

When she had read the journals of the two villichi priestesses who had also been tribes of one, Ryana had learned that cooperation between the different personalities was by no means a given. Quite the opposite. Both women had written that in their younger days, they had no real understanding of their condition, and that they had often experienced "lapses," as they called them, during which they were unable to remember periods of time lasting from several hours to several days. During those times, one of their other personalities would come out and take control, often acting in a manner that was completely inconsistent with the behavior of the primary personality. At first, neither of them was aware that they possessed other personalties, and while these other personalties were aware of the primary, they were not always aware of one another. It was, the victims wrote, a very confusing and frightening existence.

As with Sorak, the training the women received at the villichi convent enabled them to become aware of their other personalities and come to terms with them. Training in the Way not only saved their sanity, but opened up new possibilities for them to lead full and productive lives.

In Sorak's case, the Guardian had been the one who

had responded first, serving as a conduit between Sorak and the other members of his inner tribe. She possessed the psionic talents of telepathy and telekinesis, while Sorak, contrary to initial perceptions, appeared to possess no psionic talent whatsoever.

This had frustrated him immensely during his training sessions, and when his frustration had reached a peak, the Guardian would always take over. It was Mistress Varanna who had first realized this and prevailed upon the Guardian to acknowledge herself openly, convincing her that it would not be in Sorak's best interests for her to protect him from the truth about himself. For Sorak, that had been the turning point.

Because the Guardian always spoke with Sorak's voice, Ryana had never realized that she was female. It was not until Ryana told Sorak she desired him that she discovered the truth about the Guardian's gender. No less shocking was the discovery that Sorak had at least two other female personalities within him—the Watcher, who never slept and only rarely spoke, and Kivara, a mischievous and sly young girl of a highly inquisitive and openly sensual temperament. Ryana had never spoken with the Watcher, who never manifested externally, nor had she ever met Kivara. When the Guardian came out, she usually manifested in such a manner that there was no visible change in Sorak's personality or his demeanor. From the way Sorak spoke about Kivara, however, it seemed clear that Kivara could never be that subtle. Ryana could not imagine what Kivara would be like. She was not really sure she wanted to know.

She knew of three other personalities Sorak possessed. Or perhaps it was they who possessed him.

There was Screech, the beastlike entity who was capable of communication only with other wild creatures, and the Shade, a dark, grim, and frightening presence that resided deep within Sorak's subconscious, emerging only when the tribe was facing a threat to its survival. And finally, there was Kether, the single greatest mystery of Sorak's complicated multiplicity.

Ryana had encountered Kether only once, though she had discussed the strange entity with Sorak many times. The one time she had seen him, Kether had displayed powers that seemed almost magical, though they must have been psionic, for Sorak had never received any magical training. Still, that was merely a logical assumption, and when it came to Kether, Ryana was not sure that logic would apply. Even Sorak did not quite know what to make of Kether.

"Unlike the others, Kether is not truly a part of the inner tribe," Sorak told her when she voiced her thoughts. He appeared nervous, attempting to explain the little he understood about the strange, ethereal entity called Kether. "At least, he somehow does not seem to be. The others know of him, but they do not communicate with him, and they do not know where he comes from."

"You speak as if he comes from somewhere *outside* yourself," Ryana said.

"Yes, I know. And yet, that is truly how it seems."

"But . . . I do not understand. How can that be? How is it possible?"

"I simply do not know," Sorak replied with a shrug. "I wish I could explain it better, but I cannot. It was Kether who came out when I was dying in the desert, sending forth a psionic call so powerful that it reached

Elder Al'Kali at the very summit of the Dragon's Tooth. Neither I nor any of the others have ever been able to duplicate that feat. We do not possess such power. Mistress Varanna always believed that the power was within me, but I suspect the power truly lies with Kether and that I am but a conduit through which it sometimes flows. Kether is by far the strongest of us, more powerful even than the Shade, yet he does not truly seem to be a part of us. I cannot *feel* him within me, as I can the others."

"Perhaps you cannot feel him because he resides deep beneath your level of awareness, like the infant core of which you spoke," Ryana said.

"Perhaps," said Sorak, "though I am aware of the infant core, albeit very dimly. I am also aware of others that are deeply buried and do not come out . . . or at least have refrained from coming out thus far. I sense their presence; I can feel them through the Guardian. But with Kether, there is a very different feeling, one that is difficult to describe."

"Try."

"It is . . ." He shook his head. "I do not know if I can properly convey it. There is a profound warmth that seems to spread throughout my entire body and a feeling of . . . dizziness, though perhaps that it not quite the right word. It is a sort of lightness, a spinning sensation, almost as if I am falling from a great height . . . and then I simply fade away. When I return, there is still that sensation of great warmth, which remains present for a while, then slowly fades. And for however long Kether possessed me, I can usually remember nothing."

"When you speak of the others manifesting," said

Ryana, "you simply say they 'come out.' But when you speak of Kether, you speak of being possessed."

"Yes, that is how it feels. It is not as if Kether comes out from *within* me, but as if he . . . *descends* upon me somehow."

"But from where?"

"I only wish I knew. From the spirit world, perhaps."

"You think that Kether is a *fiend?*"

"No, fiends are merely creatures of legend. We know that they do not exist. We know that spirits do exist, however. They are the animating core of every living thing. The Way teaches us that the spirit never truly dies, that it survives corporeal death and unites with the greater life-force of the universe. We are taught that elementals are a lower form of spirit, entities of nature bound to the physical plane. But higher spirits exist upon a higher plane, one we cannot perceive, for our own spirits have not yet ascended to it."

"And you think that Kether is a spirit that has found a way to bridge those planes through you?"

"Perhaps. I cannot say. I only know there is a sense of goodness about Kether, an aura of tranquility and strength. And he does not seem as if he is a part of me, somehow. More like a benevolent visitor, a force from without. I do not know him, but neither do I fear him. When he descends upon me, it is as if I fall asleep, then awake with a pervading sense of calm, and peaceful-ness, and strength. I cannot explain it any more than that. I truly wish I could."

I have known him almost all my life, Ryana thought, and yet, there are ways in which I do not know him at all. For that matter, there are ways in which he does not even know himself.

"A copper for your thoughts," Sorak said, abruptly bringing her back to the present from her reverie.

She smiled. "Can you not read them?"

"The Guardian is the telepath among us," he replied gently, "but she would not presume to read your thoughts unless you gave consent. At least, I do not think she would."

"You mean you are not sure?"

"If she felt it was important to the welfare of the tribe, then perhaps she might do it and not tell me," he said.

"I do not fear having my thoughts read by the Guardian. I have nothing to hide from you," Ryana said. "From any of you. Just now, I was merely thinking how little I truly know you, even after ten years."

"Perhaps because, in many ways, I do not truly know myself," Sorak replied wistfully.

"That is just what I was thinking," said Ryana. "You must have been reading my mind."

"I told you, I would never knowingly consent to—"

"I was only joking, Sorak," said Ryana.

"Ah, I see."

"You really should ask Lyric to loan you his sense of humor. You have always been much too serious."

She had meant it lightly, but Sorak nodded, taking it as a completely serious comment. "Lyric and Kivara seem to possess all of our humor. And also Eyron, I suppose, although his humor is of a somewhat caustic stripe. I have never been very good at being able to tell when people are joking with me. Not even you. It makes me feel . . . insufficient."

Parts of what should have been a complete personality have been distributed among all of the others, thought Ryana with a touch of sadness. When they were younger, she had often played jokes on him because he was always such an easy victim. She wondered whether she should save her jests for Lyric, who could be tiresome because he seemed to have no serious side at all, or try to help Sorak develop the lighter side of his own nature.

"I have never felt that you were insufficient in any way," she told him. "Merely different." She sighed. "It's strange. When we were younger, I simply accepted you the way you were. Now, I find myself struggling to understand you—all of you—more fully. Had I made the effort earlier, perhaps I would have never driven you away."

He frowned. "You thought you drove me away from the convent?" He shook his head. "I had reasons of my own for leaving."

"Can you say with honesty that I was not one of those reasons?" she asked directly.

He hesitated a moment, then replied, "No, I cannot."

"So much for the duplicity of elves," she said.

"I am only part elf," Sorak replied. Then he realized she was teasing him a bit and smiled. "I had my own reasons for leaving, it is true, but I also did not wish to remain a source of emotional distress to you."

"And so you created even more emotional distress by leaving," she said lightly. "I understand. It must be elfling logic."

He gave her a sidelong glance. "Am I to suffer your barbs throughout this entire journey?"

"Perhaps only a part of it," she replied. She held up her hand, thumb, and forefinger about an inch apart. "A small part."

"You are almost as bad as Lyric."

"Well, if you are going to be insulting, then you can just duck under and let Eyron or the Guardian come out. Either one could certainly provide more stimulating conversation."

"I couldn't agree more," Sorak replied, suddenly speaking in an entirely different tone of voice, one that was more clipped, insouciant, and a touch wry. It was no longer Sorak, Ryana realized, but Eyron. Sorak had taken her literally. He had apparently decided that she was annoyed with him, so he had ducked under and allowed Eyron to come forth.

His bearing had undergone a subtle change, as well. His posture went from erect and square-shouldered to slightly slumped and round-shouldered. He altered his pace slightly, taking shorter steps and coming down a bit harder on his heels, the way an older, middle-aged person might walk. A casual observer might not have noticed any difference, but Ryana was villichi, and she had long since become alert to the slightest change in Sorak's bearing and demeanor. She would have recognized Eyron even if he hadn't spoken.

"I was only teasing Sorak a little," she explained. "I was not really insulted."

"I know that," Eyron replied.

"I know you know that," said Ryana. "I meant for you to let Sorak know it. I did not mean for him to go away. I just wish he wouldn't be so somber and serious all the time."

"He will always be somber and serious," said Eyron. "He is somber and serious to the point of pain. You are not going to change him, Ryana. Leave him alone."

"You'd like for me to do that, wouldn't you?" she

said irately. "It would make the rest of you feel more secure."

"Secure?" Eyron repeated. "You think you present any sort of threat to us?"

"I did not mean it quite that way," said Ryana.

"Oh? How did you mean it, then?"

"Why must you always be so disputatious?" she countered.

"Because I enjoy a good argument occasionally, just as you enjoy teasing Sorak from time to time. However, the difference between us is that I enjoy the stimulation of a lively debate, while you tease Sorak because you know that he is hopelessly ill equipped to deal with it."

"That is not true!" she protested.

"Isn't it? I notice that you never try it with me. Why is that, I wonder?"

"Because teasing is a playful pastime, and your humor is all caustic and bitter."

"Ah, so you want playful humor? In that case, I will summon Lyric forth."

"No, wait. . . ."

"Why? I thought that was what you wanted."

"Stop trying to twist my words!"

"I am merely trying to make you see their import," Eyron replied dryly. "You never try to bait me with your wit, not because you fear I am your match, but because you bear me no resentment, as you do Sorak."

She stopped in her tracks suddenly, absolutely astonished at his words. "*What?*"

Eyron glanced back at her. "You are surprised? Truly, it seems you know yourself even less well than Sorak does."

"What are you talking about? I *love* Sorak! I bear no

resentment toward him! He knows that! You *all* know that!"

"Do we, indeed?" Eyron replied, with a wry grimace. "In point of fact, Lyric knows you love Sorak merely because he has heard you say so. But he comprehends nothing of the emotion himself. The Ranger may or may not know it. Either way, it would make no difference to him. Screech? Screech could comprehend the act of mating, certainly, but not the more complex state of love. The Watcher knows and understands, but she is uneasy with the concept of a woman's love. Kivara is rather titillated by the notion, but for reasons having to do with the senses, not the heart. And the Shade is as far removed from love as the night is from the day. Now the Guardian knows you love Sorak, but I doubt she would disagree with me that you also feel resentment toward him. As for Kether . . . well, I would not presume to speak for Kether, as Kether does not condescend to speak with me. Nevertheless, the fact remains that beneath your love for Sorak smolders a resentment that you lack the courage or honesty to acknowledge to yourself."

"That is absurd!" Ryana said, angrily. "If I were to resent anyone, it would be *you*, for being so contentious all the time!"

"On the contrary, that is precisely why you do *not* resent me," Eyron said. "I allow you an outlet for your anger. Deep down, you are angry at Sorak, but you cannot express it. You cannot even admit it to yourself, but it is there, nevertheless."

"I thought the Guardian was the telepath among you," said Ryana sourly. "Or have you developed the gift as well?"

"It does not require a telepath to see where your feelings lie," said Eyron. "The Guardian once called you selfish. Well, you are. I am not saying that is a bad thing, you understand, but by not admitting to yourself that your feelings of anger and resentment stem from your own selfish desires, you are only making matters worse. Perhaps you would prefer to discuss this with the Guardian. You might take it better if you heard it from another female."

"No, you started this, you finish it," Ryana said. "Go on. Explain to me how my own selfish desires led me to break my vows and abandon everything I knew and cherished for Sorak's sake."

"Oh, please," said Eyron. "You did absolutely nothing for Sorak's sake. What you did you did for your *own* sake, because you *wanted* to do it. You may have been born villichi, Ryana, but you always chafed at the restrictive life in the convent. You were always dreaming of adventures in the outside world."

"I left the convent because I wanted to be with Sorak!"

"Precisely," Eyron said, "because you *wanted* to be with Sorak. And because with Sorak gone, there was no compelling reason for you to remain. You sacrificed nothing for his sake that you would not have gladly given up, in any case."

"Well . . . if that is true, and I have only done what I wanted to do, then what reason would I possibly have for being angry with him?"

"Because you want him, and yet you cannot have him," Eyron said simply.

Even after knowing him for all those years, and having seen how his personas shifted, it was difficult for her to hear those words coming from his lips. It was Eyron speaking, and not Sorak, but it was Sorak's face she saw and Sorak's voice she heard, even though the tone was different.

"That has already been settled," she said, looking away. It was difficult to meet his gaze. Eyron's gaze, she reminded herself, but still Sorak's eyes.

"Has it?"

"You were there when we discussed it, were you not?"

"Simply because a matter was discussed does not mean it has been settled," Eyron replied. "You grew up with Sorak, and you came to love him, even knowing that he was a tribe of one. You thought you could accept that, but it was not until you forced the issue that Sorak told you it could never be, because three of us are female. It came as quite a shock to you, and Sorak bears the blame for that because he should have told you. There lies the root of your resentment, Ryana. *He should have told you*. All those years, and you never even suspected, because he kept it from you."

Ryana was forced to admit to herself that it was true. She had thought she understood, and perhaps she did, but despite that, she still felt angry and betrayed.

"I never kept anything from him," she said, looking down at her feet. "I would have given anything, *done* anything. He had but to ask! Yet, he kept from me something that was a vital part of who and what he was. Had I known, perhaps things might have been different. I might not have allowed myself to fall in love with him. I might not have built up my hopes and expectations. . . . *Why*, Eyron? Why couldn't he have told me?"

"Has it not occurred to you that he might have been afraid?" said Eyron.

She glanced up at him with surprise, seeing Sorak's face, his eyes gazing back at her . . . yet it was not him. "Afraid? Sorak was never afraid of anything. Why would he be afraid of me?"

"Because he is male, and he is young, and because to be a young male is to be awash in insecurities and feelings one cannot fully understand," Eyron replied. "I speak from experience, of course. I share his doubts and fears. How could I not?"

"What doubts? What fears?"

"Doubts about himself and his identity," said Eyron. "And a fear that you might think him less of a male for having female aspects."

"But that is absurd!"

"Nevertheless, it is true. Sorak loves you, Ryana. But he can never *make* love with you because our female aspects could not countenance it. You think that is not a source of torment for him?"

"No less than it is for me," she replied. She looked at him, curiously. "What of you, Eyron? You have said nothing of how *you* feel about me."

"I think of you as my friend," said Eyron. "A very close friend. My only friend, in fact."

"What? Do none of the others—?"

"Oh, no, I did not mean that," said Eyron, "that is different. I meant my only friend outside the tribe. I do not make friends easily, it seems."

"Could *you* countenance me as Sorak's lover?"

"Of course. I am male, and I consider you my friend. I cannot say that I love you, but I do have feelings of affection for you. Were the decision mine alone to make—mine and Sorak's, that is—I would have no objections. I think the two of you are good for one another. But, unfortunately, there are others to consider."

"Yes, I know. But I am grateful for your honesty. And your expression of goodwill."

"Oh, it is much more than goodwill, Ryana," Eyron said. "I am very fond of you. I do not know you as well as Sorak does; none of us do, except perhaps the Guardian. And while I must confess that my nature is not the most amenable to love, I think that I could learn to share the love that Sorak feels for you."

"I am glad to hear that," she said.

"Well, then, perhaps I am not quite as disputatious as you think," said Eyron.

She smiled. "Perhaps not. But there are times. . . ."

"When you would like to strangle me," Eyron completed the statement for her.

"I would not go quite that far," she said. "Pummel you a bit, perhaps."

"I am gratified at your restraint, then. I am not much of a fighter."

"Eyron fears a fee-male! Eyron fears a fee-male!"

"Be quiet, Lyric!" Eyron said, in an annoyed tone.

"Nyaah-nyaah-nyahh, nyaah-nyaah-nayahh!"

Ryana had to laugh at the sudden, rapid changes that flickered across Sorak's features. One moment, he was Eyron, the mature and self-possessed, articulate adult; in the next instant, he was Lyric, the taunting and irrepressible child. His facial expressions, his bearing, his body language, everything changed abruptly back and forth as the two different personas alternately manifested themselves.

"I am pleased you find it so amusing," Eyron said to her irritably.

"Nyaah-nyaah-nyaah, nyaah-nyaah-nyaah!" Lyric taunted in a high-pitched, singsong voice.

"Lyric, please," Ryana said. "Eyron and I were having a conversation. It is not polite to interrupt when grown-ups are speaking."

"Oh, all-riiight. . . ." Lyric said dejectedly.

"He never listens to me the way he listens to you," said Eyron, as Lyric's pouting expression was abruptly replaced on Sorak's face by Eyron's wry look of annoyance.

"That is because you are impatient with him," Ryana said with a smile. "Children always recognize the weak points in adults, and they are quick to play on them."

"I grow impatient merely because he delights so in annoying me," said Eyron.

"It is only a ploy to get attention," said Ryana. "If you were to indulge him more, he would feel less need to provoke you."

"Females are better at such things," said Eyron.

"Perhaps. But males could do equally well if they took the time to learn," Ryana said. "Most of them forget too easily what it was like to be a child."

"Sorak was a child," Eyron said. "I never was."

Ryana sighed. "There are some things about you all that I think I shall never understand," she said with resignation.

"It is better simply to accept some things without trying to understand them," replied Eyron.

"I do my best," Ryana said.

They continued talking for a while as they walked, and it helped to pass the time of their journey, but

Eyron soon wearied of the trek and ducked back under, allowing the Guardian to manifest. In a way, however, the Guardian had been there all along. Like the Watcher, she was never very far beneath the surface, always present, even when one of the others had come out. As her name implied, her primary role was to act as the protector of the tribe. She was the strong, maternal figure, sometimes interacting with the others in an active way, sometimes content to remain passive, but always there as a moderating presence, a force for balance in the inner tribe. While she was manifested, Sorak was there too as an underlying presence. If he chose to, he could speak, or else he could simply listen and observe while the Guardian interacted with Ryana.

When any of the others were out, things were often slightly different. If Lyric was at the fore of their personas, he and Sorak could both be out at the same time, like two individuals awake in the same body, as was the case with Sorak and the Guardian, or Screech. But if it was Eyron, or the Ranger, or any of the others that were stronger personalities, Sorak often wasn't there at all. At such times, he faded back into his own subconscious, and his knowledge of what occurred during the times when any of the stronger ones were out depended on the Guardian granting him access to the memories. Kivara seemed to cause him the greatest difficulty. Of all his personalities, she was the most unruly and unpredictable, and the two were frequently in conflict. If Kivara had her way, Sorak had explained, she would come out more often, but the Guardian kept her in line. The Guardian was capable of overriding all the other personalities, Sorak's included, save for Kether and the Shade. And those two appeared only rarely.

It had taken Ryana ten years to become accustomed to the intricacies of the relationships of Sorak's inner tribe. She could imagine how it would be for anyone who met Sorak for the first time. And she could understand why Sorak did not trouble to explain his curious condition to others that he met. It would only frighten people and confuse them. Without training in the Way, it would have frightened and confused him, too. She wondered if there was any way that he could ever become normal.

"Guardian," she said, knowing that the privacy of her own thoughts would be respected unless she invited the Guardian to look into her mind, "I have been wondering about something, but before we speak of it, I wish to make certain you do not take it amiss. It is not my desire to offend."

"I would never think that of you," the Guardian replied. "Speak then, and speak frankly."

"Do you think that there is any chance Sorak could ever become normal?"

"What is normal?" the Guardian replied.

"Well . . . you know what I mean. Like everybody else."

"Everybody else is not the same," the Guardian replied. "What is normal for one person may not be normal for another. But I believe I understand your meaning. You wish to know if Sorak could ever become just Sorak, and not a tribe of one."

"Yes. Not that I wish you did not exist, you understand. Well . . . in a sense, I suppose I do, but it is not because of any feeling that I have against you. Any of you. It is just that . . . if things had been different . . ."

"I understand," the Guardian replied, "and I wish

that I could answer your question, but I cannot. It goes beyond my realm of knowledge."

"Well . . . suppose we find the Sage," Ryana said, "and suppose he can change things with his magic—make it so that Sorak is no longer a tribe of one, but simply Sorak. If that were possible . . ." her voice trailed off.

"How would I feel about that?" the Guardian completed the thought for her. "If it were possible, I suppose it would depend on *how* it were possible."

"What do you mean?"

"It would depend on how it would be achieved, assuming that it could be achieved," the Guardian replied. "Imagine yourself in my place, if you can. You are not simply Ryana, but Ryana is merely one aspect of your self. You share your body and your mind with other aspects, who are equally a part of you, though separate. Let us say that you have found a wizard who can make you the same as everybody else—the same, that is, in the sense you mean. Would you not be concerned about how that would be done?

"If this wizard were to say to you, 'I can make you whole, unite all of your aspects into one harmonious persona,' well, in that case, you might be inclined to accept such a solution. And accept it eagerly. But what if that same wizard were to say to you, 'Ryana, I can make it so that you will be like everybody else. I can make it so that only Ryana will exist, and the others will all disappear'? Would you be so eager to accept such a solution then? Would it not be the same as asking you to agree to the deaths of all the others? And if we assume, for the sake of the discussion, that you could accept such a situation, what would be the outcome? If all the others were separate entities who made up a greater whole, what would be gained, and what would be lost? If they were to die, what sort of person would that leave? One who was complete? Or one who was but a fragment of a balanced individual?"

"I see," Ryana said. "In such a case then, if the choice were mine to make, I would, of course, refuse. But suppose it was the first choice that you mentioned?"

"To unite us all in one persona—Sorak's?" asked the Guardian.

"In a manner that would preserve you all, though as one individual instead of many," said Ryana. "What then?"

"If that were possible," the Guardian replied, "then I think, perhaps, I would have no objection. If it would benefit the tribe to become one instead of many and preserve all those within it as a part of Sorak, then it might indeed be for the best. But again, we must think of what might be gained and what might be lost. What would become of all the powers we have as a tribe? Would they be preserved, or would some be lost as a result? And what would become of Kether? If Kether is, as we suspect, a spirit from another plane, would his ability to manifest through Sorak be preserved? Or would that bridge be forever burned behind us?"

Ryana nodded. "Yes, those are all things that would have to be considered. Still, it was but an idle speculation. Perhaps not even the Sage would have such power."

"We shall not know that until we find him," said the Guardian. "And who is to say how long this quest may take? There is still one more thing to consider, so long as we are discussing possibilities. Something that you may have failed to take into account."

"And that is?"

"Suppose we found the Sage, and he was able to unite us all into one person, with no loss to any of us. Sorak would become the tribe, all blended into one person who was, as you say, 'normal.' And the tribe would become Sorak. All the things that I am, all that is Kivara, and Lyric, the Watcher and the Ranger and the Shade, Screech and Eyron and the others, some of whom still lie deeply buried, all would become a part of Sorak. What, then, would become of the Sorak that you know and love? Would he not become someone very different? Would the Sorak that you know not cease to exist?"

Ryana continued walking silently for a while, mulling that over. The Guardian did not impinge upon her contemplation. Finally, Ryana said, "I had never considered the possibility that Sorak might be changed in a manner that would render him completely different. If that were the case, then I suppose my own thoughts on the matter, my own feelings, would be determined by whether or not such a change would be in his best interests. That is to say, in *all* of your best interests."

"I do not mean to be harsh," the Guardian said, "but consider also that it is Sorak as you know him now who loves you. I understand that love, and am capable of sharing it to some degree, but I could not love you that way that Sorak does. Perhaps it is because I am a female and my nature is such that I could not love another female. If Sorak were to change in the way we are discussing, perhaps that love would change, as well. But you must also consider all the others. Eyron is male, yet he thinks of you as a friend, not as a lover. The Watcher does not love you and never could. The Ranger is indifferent to you, not because of any short-coming on your part, it is just that the Ranger is the Ranger, and he is not given to such emotions. Neither is the Shade. Kivara is fascinated by new sensations and experiences, but while she may not balk at a physical relationship with you, she would be a very fickle and uncaring lover. And there are all the others, whose feelings and modes of thought would all go into creating the new Sorak of whom we speak. It is quite possible that this new Sorak would no longer love you."

Ryana moistened her lips. "If the change would benefit him—would benefit you all—and make him happy, then I would accept that, despite the pain that it would bring me."

"Well, we speak of something that may never come to pass," the Guardian replied. "When we first spoke of your love for Sorak, I called you selfish and accused you of thinking only of yourself. I spoke harshly and I now regret that. I know now that you are nothing of the sort. And what I am about to say, I say not for my sake, but for yours. To long for something that may never be is to build a foundation on a swamp. Your hopes are likely to sink into the quagmire. I know that it is far more easily said than done, but if you could try to learn how to love Sorak as a friend, a brother, then whatever happens in the future, you may save your heart from breaking."

"You are right," Ryana said. "It is far more easily said than done. Would it were not so."

They traveled on throughout the day, stopping occasionally to rest, and their journey was, for the most part, uneventful. As the day wore on, the temperatures climbed steadily, until the dark Athasian sun was beating down on them like a merciless adversary. Sorak came out again and accompanied her for the rest of their journey that day, though the Guardian kept him from remembering the last part of their conversation. They found themselves conversing less and less, conserving their energies for the long trek still ahead of them.

Ryana had never traveled in the Athasian desert before, and as the tablelands stretched out before them seemingly into infinity, she marveled at the land's savage beauty and its eerie stillness. She had always somehow thought of the desert as an empty and desolate place, but it was far from that. It was full of life, though of a sort that had, of necessity, found ways to adapt to the inhospitable climate.

Scrubby pagafa trees dotted the landscape, though in the desert they grew much smaller and more twisted than they did in the forest and around the cities, where more water was available. Here, in the tablelands, they grew no taller than ten or fifteen feet, and their bare and twisted, leafless branches afforded nothing in the way of shade. Their blue-green trunks and branches enabled them to manufacture life-sustaining energy from the sun, and their roots went deep in search of water, spreading wide with numerous feeders. During the brief rainy season, when the monsoons would sweep across the desert, depositing the precious water in brief but furious storms, the branches of the pagafa tree would leaf out in fine, needlelike growth, creating a feathery-looking crown, and additional branches would shoot forth to take advantage of the added

water. Then, when the almost ever-present drought
returned, the needlelike leaves would fall and the new
branches would die back, allowing the tree to conserve
its energy for its next cycle of growth.

The leaves fell, dried out in less than a day, and
made a rust-colored blanket underneath the tree. These
dried leaves made excellent nesting material for desert
rodents, which dug burrows beneath the many forms
of cacti that grew out in the tablelands. Some of the
cacti were very small, no larger than a human fist, covered with a fine growth of silvery pincushion that once
or twice a year—after a rain—exploded into brightly
colored blooms that lasted no more than a day. Some
were large and barrel-shaped, as tall as a full-grown
man and twice as thick around.

The rodents liked to nest among the thick roots at the
pagafa's base, and eventually, their burrowing killed
the plant, though only after many years. Slowly, the
huge tree lost its support and fell from its own weight,
and then dried out, its carcass becoming a temporary
home for kips and scarab beetles, who dined upon its
drying, pulpy meat. The large, thick spines of the cactus were then harvested by desert antloids, whose
worker drones formed long lines across the desert as
they carried back the thick spines to their warrens to
help support the many tunnels that they excavated in
the hard-baked desert ground.

Occasionally, antloid warrens came under attack
from desert drakes, one of the large reptiles that made
its home in the Athasian desert. Part lizard and part
snake, the drake's thick hide, so highly prized for
armor in the cities, rendered it impervious to the
mandibles of antloids. Its long, talonlike claws allowed

it to dig up the warrens, and its thick, twin-pronged, muscular tongue gave it the ability to capture antloids and drag them out to where it could crush their exo-skeletons.

The antloids would come swarming out to fight it, and sometimes, if the colony was large enough, they overwhelmed the drake by the sheer weight of their numbers, piling up their huge bodies on top of it. If the drake prevailed over the antloids, the survivors scattered and abandoned the dug up warren. It then provided a home for hurrums, brightly colored beetles prized in cities for the melodious humming sounds they made, or renks, large desert slugs that dined on the wastes left behind in the antloid warren.

If the antloids managed to defeat the drake, however, they ate its carcass, sharing it with other life forms: jankx, furred and squeaking mammals that lived in townlike burrows on the tablelands; or z'tals, tall, bipedal lizards that lived in small herds out in the desert and laid eggs inside the excavated antloid warren after they had disposed of the carcass of the drake.

The loosened earth left behind after the drake destroyed the antloid warren allowed the seeds of brambleweeds to root, and they grew up around the eggs left behind by the z'tal, their spiny tentacles poking up out of the ground and protecting the eggs from predatory snakes and rodents. All life in the desert was closely interdependent, a mutated yet balanced ecology that had grown up in the devastation left behind by the defilers.

Ryana wondered what the desert had been like before, in the days when Athas was still green. She tried to imagine the barren, scrubby, rolling plain before her when it was covered with tall grasses that rippled in the wind, blooming with wildflowers, and resonating with the song of birds. It was the dream of every druid and of all villichi, of all preservers everywhere, that someday Athas would once again grow green. Chances were that Ryana would never live to see that day, but even so, she was glad that she had left the mountains to truly see the desert—not the vast and empty wasteland it appeared to be, seen from the heights of the Ringing Mountains, but the strangely beautiful and vibrant place it really was.

She knew some of that beauty could be deadly. If the ten-foot antloids attacked, which was especially likely in the season their queen produced young, their fearsome mandibles would make short work of her. The rare and gorgeous burnflowers that grew out in the desert could be as lethal as they were beautiful. Though easily avoided in the light of day because their patches could be seen for miles, they could kill during the early morning if an unwary traveler happened to be near them when the bulb-shaped flowers opened. The shiny, silvery-colored blooms, some as large as two to three feet in diameter, would open toward the sun and track its progress across the sky throughout the day, absorbing its life-giving rays and reflecting them back as deadly beams of energy. It was the plant's protective mechanism, but the sight of those beautiful blooms opening would be the last sight anyone would ever see.

If the burnflowers killed, it was merely an accident of their adaptation to survive in such a hostile climate, but a blossomkiller did so by design. The blossomkiller was carnivorous, and its survival in the desert depended on its ability to trap its prey. It did so with a wide network of rootlike surface vines that, unlike its taproot, radiated out from the body of the plant to a distance of as much as fifty feet. It took but the merest touch on one of these vines to send an impulse to the pistils of the colorful flowers, which would then shoot out a spray of sharp, needlelike quills. These quills were covered with a poison that produced paralysis. Once the hapless victim, whether animal, humanoid or human, was frozen into immobility, the tendrils of the blossomkiller would reach out and wrap themselves around their prey. A small desert rodent or mammal would be digested within a matter of hours. For a human, the process could take days. It was a horrible and agonizing death.

Nor were lethal plants and insects the only dangers in the desert. There was a wide variety of deadly reptiles, from poisonous snakes no longer than a human finger to the deadly drakes, some species of which could grow as long as thirty feet and wider than the trunk of a well-watered agafari tree. Death could come from above, in the form of floaters, creatures with light, translucent bodies composed of a jellylike protoplasm with stinging tendril tentacles that trailed down below them. The merest brush of one such tentacle could produce a large and painful welt that would take weeks to heal, while solid contact could be fatal. And death could also come from underfoot, in the form of dune trappers, sand cacti, or sink worms.

Dune trappers were lifeforms that were neither plant nor animal, but something in between. They lived almost entirely beneath the desert surface in pits they excavated as they grew. The mouth of the dune trapper gradually grew and spread out on the surface, filled with what appeared to be a pool of cool, clear water. Plants would grow up around the mouth of the strange creature, sustained by the moisture it produced, giving the deceptive appearance of a small, welcoming oasis. But to approach that pool in an attempt to drink from it was almost certain death. The mouth of the dune trapper, triggered by a footstep on the soft membrane that lay just beneath the sand, would suck the unsuspecting victim down into the pit the creature occupied, there to be digested by the fluid that had first appeared to be a pool of water.

Sand cacti were no less deadly. Like the dune trapper, the main body of the plant grew beneath the surface of the desert, especially where the soil was sandy. Only the tips of its numerous spines protruded just above the surface, over a wide area, poking up no more than an inch or two, so that they were difficult to spot. Stepping on a spine would trigger a response within the plant that would cause it to shoot that spine up into the victim's foot, where its barbed hook would find firm purchase, and the plant would start to drain the blood out of its prey. Once "hooked," the victim's only chance was to tear loose from the spine, or cut it free, but this could not be accomplished without also tearing loose a lot of flesh, and if any of the spine remained embedded in the victim, it had to be cut out or else infection would set in.

Sink worms posed an even greater danger. A sharp-eyed traveler might detect the shallow depressions left in the sandy soil where they had passed, but to be hunted by a sink worm was a terrifying prospect, for it could detect the footsteps of its prey upon the surface and come up underneath it. A small, young sink worm could take off a foot or an entire leg. An adult could swallow a human being whole.

Nor were those the only dangers of the desert. Back in the villichi temple, Ryana had studied about all the life-forms that dwelled on Athas, and desert predators had filled up an entire stack of scrolls. The Ringing Mountains were not without their dangers, but they paled in comparison to what the desert held in store. It was a place of quiet and ethereal beauty, but it also promised death to the unwary. In the daytime, a vigilant traveler, well versed in the hazards of the desert, could take steps to avoid them. At night, the dangers multiplied as the nocturnal predators awoke.

And night was fast approaching.

TWO

As the sun sank slowly in the sky, it cast a surreal light over the desert, flooding it with an amber-orange glow. The flame-colored Athasian sky took on a blood-red tint after nightfall, gradually fading to dark crimson as the twin moons, Ral and Guthay, began their pilgrimage across the heavens. Sorak and Ryana made camp beneath an ancient pagafa tree, its three gnarled, blue-green trunks spreading out from its base and branching off into twisted, leafless boughs. As the light faded, they broke off some of the smaller branches in order to build a fire. The sparse, dry desert grass they had uprooted easily caught fire from the sparks of their fire stones, and soon a small blaze was crackling in the shallow depression they had hollowed out for the fire pit.

Ryana drank sparely from her water skin, despite her thirst. The long trek had left her feeling very dry, but the water had to last until they reached the oasis at Silver Spring, which was still at least another day's journey to the east. Sorak took only a few drops from his own water skin, and it seemed to be enough for him. Ryana envied him his elfling ability to get by on less water. She thought wistfully of the stream near the convent, where water flowed down from the mountain peaks and cascaded over the rocks in the streambed. It was fresh and cold and good to drink, and she thought longingly of all the times she and her sisters would run down to the lagoon following weapons practice, strip down, and frolic in the bracing pool. She had taken it for granted then, and now it seemed like an incredible luxury to be able to bathe every day and drink her fill.

At such times, Sorak had always wandered away from the others, going farther downstream along the riverbank to where the water flowed over large, flat boulders in the middle of the streambed. He would take his accustomed place upon the largest rock and sit cross-legged in the water that flowed around him, his back to the others at the lagoon, a short distance upstream. The sound of the water would drown out all but the occasional playful cries made by the sisters as they played in the lagoon, and he would sit alone, staring out into the distance or down into the water on the smaller rocks below. Ryana had learned not to accompany him at such times, for he often seemed to have a need to be alone. Alone to sit and brood.

In the beginning, when they had been small children, he used to join the sisters at their play in the lagoon, but as they grew older, he took to going off by himself. Ryana used to wonder if it was because his growing awareness of his male nature made it awkward for him to frolic naked with the others.

As she grew and started to become more aware of her own female sexuality, she would often glance at the bodies of the other sisters and compare them to her own, which had always seemed inadequate. The others were all taller than she, and more slender, with longer and more sinewy limbs and graceful necks. They seemed so beautiful. Compared to them, her own proportions seemed squat and unattractive. Her breasts and hips were larger, her torso was shorter, her legs, though long by human standards, seemed too short compared to theirs. And their hair seemed much more beautiful than hers. Most villichi were born with thick, red hair, either flame-colored or dark red with brighter highlights. Her own silvery white hair seemed drab and lusterless by comparison.

She would look at the other sisters and wonder if Sorak found them as beautiful as she did. Perhaps, she thought, he had taken to absenting himself from their frolics because his male nature was making him become aware of them in the same manner as her own maturing female nature was making her become aware of him.

Of course, she had not known then that Sorak's nature was a great deal more complex than that. She had not known that several of his personalities were female. She knew now that when he had gone off to brood by himself, he had been preoccupied with matters not of the flesh, but of the self. More and more, as he grew older, he had been plagued by questions to which he had no answers. Who was he? What was his tribe? Who were his parents? How did he come to be?

His pressing need to learn the answers to those questions was what had driven him to leave the convent and embark upon his quest to find the Sage. But who was to say how long this quest would take? Athas was a large world with many secret places, and the Sage could be almost anywhere. For years, longer than they both had been alive, the defilers had also sought the Sage with no success, and they had their powerful defiler magic to aid them in their search. Without magic, could they be more successful?

"I cannot banish from my mind the thought that there is something more to *The Wanderer's Journal* than merely advice for travelers," said Sorak as he sat cross-legged on the ground by the fire. The flames gave forth scarcely enough light to read by, but with his elfling eyes, Sorak had no difficulty making out the words. "Listen to this," he said, as he started reading a section of the journal out loud.

> *"On Athas, there are several different types of clerics. Each of them pays homage to one of the four elemental forces—air, earth, fire or water. Of course, the latter are perhaps the most influential on our thirsty world, but all are powerful and worthy of respect.*
>
> *"Another group of people call themselves the druids and, at least by most accounts, are considered to be clerics. Druids are special in that they do not pay tribute to any single elemental force, but rather work to uphold the dying life-force of Athas. They serve nature and the planetary equilibrium. Many people consider it a lost cause, but no druid would ever admit that.*
>
> *"In some cities, the sorcerer-king is glorified as if he were some sort of immortal being. In fact, many such rulers are actually able to bestow spellcasting abilities upon the templars who serve them. Are they truly on a par with the elemental forces worshipped by the clerics? I think not."*

Ryana shook her head. "If there is some hidden meaning in those words, it is not one I can discern," she said.

"Perhaps the meaning is not really hidden so much as it is implied," said Sorak. "Consider what the Wanderer has said here. On the surface, it merely sounds as if he is writing about clerical magic, describing what exists. In this section of the journal, for the most part, he describes what everyone already knows. What would seem to be the necessity for that? Unless he were also saying something else, something that was not quite so readily apparent."

"Such as what?" Ryana asked.

"He mentions the four elemental forces—air, earth, fire, and water," Sorak said. "Well, this is something every child knows, but then he goes on to say that the latter are perhaps the most influential on our thirsty world."

"Well, that makes perfect sense," Ryana said. "Water would naturally be the most important element on a dry world such as ours."

"But he does not say 'the latter *is;*' he says 'the latter *are,*' " said Sorak. "That means the latter *two* he mentions, water *and* fire."

Ryana frowned. "So? Fire is important, too."

"But why?" asked Sorak. "Aside from the obvious reasons, of course, that it provides heat and light, and energy to cook with. We can readily perceive how water might be more important than air and earth, but why fire? Besides, he does not really say that fire and water are more important. He says they are more *influential.*"

"I still do not understand," Ryana said, looking

perplexed. "What is it you see in those words that I do not?"

"Perhaps I am merely reading something into them that is not really there," Sorak replied. "However, I suspect that is not the case. Consider: he addresses himself here to the subject of clerical magic. He also mentions druids. Well, we are both trained in the Druid Way, and we both know that in terms of clerical magic the elements of air and earth are much more significant than fire. Plants require air and earth to grow—and water, of course—but they do not require fire. Quite the opposite. Fire is the enemy of growing things. And clerical magic, especially druid magic, is not chiefly obtained from fire. It draws more on the earth."

"That is true," Ryana said.

"So why, in a section of the journal devoted to describing clerical magic, would he say that fire was more influential than both earth and air? It may be more influential in the lives of people, certainly, but not in clerical magic. There are far more clerics who pay homage to the elemental forces of air and earth than to fire."

"Yet there are some who do," Ryana said. "Especially among the dwarves."

"But do they devote themselves to fire, or to the *sun*?" asked Sorak.

"Well, to the sun," Ryana said with a shrug. "But that is the same thing, is it not?"

"Is it?" Sorak said. "Then why does he not say so? Even if it were, there are far fewer sun clerics than there are those who devote themselves to air and earth. The greatest number devote themselves to earth, and then to air. But in this section about magic, where he speaks of druids in particular, he also speaks of fire as being more influential than either earth or air. Or, at least, that is what he seems to say here. And no druid devotes himself to fire."

"No druid devotes himself to any one elemental force," Ryana said. "He says as much."

"Yes, he does, indeed," said Sorak. "So why, then, does he seem to say that fire and water are more influential than earth and air in terms of clerical magic?"

Ryana shook her head. "I do not know."

"Consider this, too," Sorak said. "He goes on to say that sorcerer-kings are glorified as if they were immortal beings."

"Well, they are immortal," said Ryana. "Their defiler magic makes them so, especially once they have begun the dragon metamorphosis."

"But he does not say they are immortal," Sorak insisted. "He says that they are glorified *as if* they were immortal. He is telling us that they are *not* immortal, that while they may live forever through the power of their magic, they can still be killed.

"And then consider carefully the words he chooses when he writes the following: "'. . . many such rulers are actually able to bestow spellcasting abilities upon the templars who serve them. Are they truly on a par with the elemental forces worshipped by the clerics? I think not.' On the surface, it seems as if the Wanderer is saying here that sorcerer-kings are not as powerful as the elemental forces worshipped by the clerics. Or perhaps he means that their templars are not as powerful. But, of course, everyone knows that. Whether templar or sorcerer-king, no one is more powerful than an elemental force. So why bother to say it?"

"But you think that is not what he is saying?" asked Ryana.

Sorak passed the journal to her. "Read it carefully," he said.

She strained her eyes to see the pages in the firelight. She read the passage once, then twice, then a third time. The fourth time, she slowly read it aloud. "'In fact, many such rulers are actually able to bestow spell-casting abilities upon the templars who serve them. Are they truly on a par with the elemental forces worshipped by the clerics?'"

"Stop there," said Sorak. "Now look at that last sentence once again. When he uses the word 'they,' to whom does he refer? Or, more specifically, to what?"

"To what?" she repeated with a frown. And then comprehension dawned. "Ahh! To *what*, not to whom! It refers not to the templars, but to the spellcasting abilities bestowed upon them!"

"Exactly," said Sorak. "The way it is written, the meaning could be taken either way, but if he means the rulers are not on a par with the elemental forces, then he merely states the obvious, for the sorcerer-kings use those elemental forces for their power, as does any other adept. Read the other way, however, it appears to suggest that elemental forces may be used to defeat the powers bestowed upon the templars, and in particular, the Wanderer is drawing our attention to the element of fire. He cites the influence of water on our thirsty world merely to help conceal his meaning."

"But are you certain that is what he means?" Ryana asked.

"The more I think about it, the more certain of it I become," said Sorak. "Think back to our weapons training at the convent. Do you recall how tiresome it seemed in the beginning and how pointless to practice the forms over and over and over again, to constantly go through the same series of movements?"

Ryana grinned. "Yes, we were all so very eager to actually fight with one another."

"But now we know that ceaseless practice of the forms ingrained those movements in our minds and bodies so that when it came to fighting, they were done by reflex and executed perfectly, with no thought to the execution. When Sister Dyona gave me this journal, she inscribed it with the words, 'A more subtle weapon than your sword, but no less powerful, in its own way.' And now I think I finally understand. *The Wanderer's Journal* is, in its own way, much like a weapons form. To simply read it through once or twice is to become familiar with the basic movements. But to read it through continually, over and over again, is to achieve refinement and perceive its structure, to realize its true content. It *is* a guide, Ryana, and a most subversive one. On its surface, it is a guide to Athas, but in its deeper meaning, it is a guide to the struggle against the defilers. Small wonder its distribution has been banned, and the sorcerer-kings have placed a bounty on the Wanderer's head, whoever he may be."

"Do you think he is still alive?" Ryana asked.

"Perhaps not. The journal first appeared many years ago; no one seems to be sure exactly when or how. It is painstakingly copied and secretly distributed by the Veiled Alliance. The Wanderer was clearly a preserver, perhaps a high-ranking member of the Alliance."

"I wonder if we shall ever know," Ryana said, feeding more wood into the fire. The pagafa wood burned slowly and gave a welcome warmth against the night chill. In the distance, some creature howled. The sound sent a shiver down Ryana's spine.

"You look tired," Sorak said. "You should eat something. You will need your strength tomorrow. We still have a long way to go."

She opened her rucksack and took out her pouch of rations: pine nuts from the forests of the Ringing Mountains, kory seeds, the chewy and succulent leaves from the lotus mint, and sweet, dried fruit from the jumbala tree. She offered him the pouch, but he shook his head.

"You eat," he said. "I am not hungry now."

She knew that meant he would eat later, when the Ranger went out to make a kill, and so she did not press him.

"I will sleep for a short while now," Sorak said, "and then keep watch so you may rest." He lowered his head and closed his eyes, and an instant later, the Ranger opened them and stood, sniffing the air. Wordlessly, he turned and walked out into the moonlit night, moving without making the slightest sound. Moments later, he had disappeared from sight.

Ryana was left alone, sitting by the fire. With Sorak gone, she suddenly felt more vulnerable and exposed. Ral and Guthay cast a ghostly light down on the desert out beyond the firelight, and the shadows seemed to move. A cool breeze blew. The silence was only occasionally punctuated by the distant cry of some wild beast. She had no idea how close the creatures that she heard might be. Sound in the desert carried a long way.

She sighed and munched on her provisions. She ate very sparingly, though she felt quite hungry. The food

would have to last her a long while, for there was no
way to know what they might find on their trek or at
the oasis to supplement their supplies. Perhaps, she
thought, it might become necessary for her to eat
meat. The corners of her mouth turned down at the
thought. It was a possibility she had to seriously consider, however. She was not a priestess anymore. Or
was she? Strictly speaking, she had violated her vows
by leaving the convent, but that did not make her
cease being villichi. And nothing she believed had
really changed.

Was she no longer part of the sisterhood? She had
never heard of a villichi being expelled. What would
Varanna say? How would her sisters react? What had
they thought when they learned that she had run
away? Did they think less of her, or would they try to
understand? She missed them all. She missed the companionship and the comforting routine of life back at
the convent. It had been a good life. Could she ever go
back to it? Would she want to go back to it?

She had no thought of leaving Sorak, but with the
Ranger out hunting somewhere in the night, she felt
suddenly very much alone and lost, even though she
knew that he would soon return. But what if he did not
return? What if something happened to him? There
were many things that could happen to a traveler alone
out in the desert, especially at night, and none of them
were pleasant to contemplate. Sorak was an elfling,
and even though he had grown up in the forests of the
Ringing Mountains, he was naturally suited to this savage country. Still, he was not invulnerable.

She pushed the thought from her mind. The dangers of the desert were not the only perils they would

face upon their journey. If their experience in Tyr was anything to judge by, they would face far greater dangers in the cities—in Nibenay and wherever the road would lead them from there. It was pointless to dwell upon such things. She tried to still herself into a calm, meditative state, quiet and yet still alert to everything around her, just as she had been trained. She felt very tired and was looking forward to when the Ranger would return from his hunt, so she could get some sleep.

Try not think about sleep, she told herself. Relax and find the center of your being. Be still and open your senses to everything around you. Become a part of the cool stillness of the desert night. There were many ways to rest, she thought, and sleep was merely one of them. No, do *not* think about sleep. . . .

She opened her eyes suddenly, startled into wakefulness. It seemed as if no more than a moment had passed, but the fire had burned down low and was almost out. She had fallen asleep, after all. But for how long? And what had awakened her? She remained quiet and motionless, resisting the impulse to throw some more wood onto the fire. She had heard something. But what was it? Everything seemed quiet now, but there was a tingling at the back of her neck, an apprehensive feeling that something was not right. She looked around, scanning for any sign of movement, alert for the slightest sound. Out in the moonlit night beyond the dwindling fire, she could see nothing but shadows. And then one of those shadows moved.

* * * * *

Sorak slumbered as the Ranger moved out into the still night, which was disturbed only by the occasional far-off sounds of nocturnal creatures. To the Ranger, however, even these faint calls were clearly recognizable: the distant cry of the desert razorwing, a smaller species than those found in the mountains, as it swooped down on prey; the howling of a rasclinn as it called out to others in its pack; the squeaking cries of small furry jankx as they came out of their burrows when night fell and began to search for food. The communication of the desert's many inhabitants, whether in low moans or ultrasonic squeaks and barks, would have been indecipherable to human ears, but the Ranger heard them clearly and understood. He possessed a preternatural sensitivity to his surroundings, an awareness Sorak in his waking moments did not fully share.

Unlike Sorak, however, the Ranger did not spend any significant time in contemplating the inner tribe's condition or place in life. On the rare occasions when he gave any thought to it at all, he simply accepted it in his stoic manner and reasoned it went beyond any ready explanation. There was nothing he could do to change or better understand the tribe's origin or destiny, so he accepted that he was the Ranger, that he shared a body with a number of other entities, and that this was simply their reality. Instead of worrying about it or trying to understand it, he would concentrate on more immediate problems. Problems he could solve.

In this case, the immediate problem was food. Red meat, not the seeds and fruit and vegetables Sorak ate. That diet satisfied Sorak, but it did not satisfy the others, nor did it satisfy the Ranger, whose appetites were more carnivorous. Perhaps they could all survive simply on the food Sorak ate, as did the villichi sisters, but the Ranger did not believe that such a diet was beneficial to the body they all shared. He had no desire to convert Sorak to his way of thinking, but neither did he have any desire to fight evolution. He had not clawed his way to the top of the food chain to eat seeds. What he needed now, and what the others hungered for, was the taste of fresh-killed meat, the sensation of warm blood running down his throat.

Although the others hungered, they kept still within the body they all shared. They did not disturb the Ranger or intrude on his thoughts. He was aware of them, dimly, but they kept their peace and distance. He was the hunter among them, skilled at identifying the slightest sights and sounds and smells of nature, adept at tracking and stalking, expert at killing quickly and effectively. They all wanted to share in the taste of fresh-killed meat—all save Sorak, who would sleep through the hunt and the interlude of feeding and awaken with no memory of it. The others all waited with tense anticipation.

Though the Ranger was at the forefront of their consciousness, in control of the body, those of them who were awake all shared his perceptions and experiences. Not all the entities who made up the complex creature that was Sorak were awake this night. Lyric slept, preferring the light of day to come awake and watch with childlike wonder what Sorak and the others did, coming out occasionally to sing or whistle when the others felt the need of the lightness of his being. The fearsome entity known as the Shade slept also, and the others feared to tread around the depths of Sorak's being where he slumbered. He was like a great, hibernating beast, sleeping often, sometimes coming awake to watch like a lurking creature in a cave, coming out only when there was a need to unleash the dark side of Sorak's nature.

Further down within the depths of Sorak's psyche slept a being none of the others really knew, for this particular entity never came awake. They were all aware of him, but only in the sense that they knew that he was there, cocooned in layers of protective mental blocks. This was the Inner Child, the most vulnerable part of them—that from which they all had sprung. The Child was the father of the men and women they became, giving birth to them ten years before in the Athasian desert, when the small and frightened boy he was had been cast out from his tribe to die in the trackless waste. In one final, wrenching cry of abject terror, that child had given birth to them all and fled from that which he could no longer endure. He slept now, deep within the shelter he had constructed for himself, curled up in a sleep almost like death. And, in a way, perhaps, it was a sort of death. The Inner Child would likely never wake again. And, if he did, none of the others knew what would become of them.

The Guardian suspected. They were all born when the Child fled from waking life, which had become a waking nightmare. Now the Child slept. If he awoke again, it could well be the end for all of them. Perhaps even for Sorak; Sorak, in a sense, was not the Child grown. Sorak was the primary, for that was the nature of the agreement they had made among themselves, a compact that had been necessary to preserve their sanity. But Sorak, too, had been born after the fact, after the

Child went to sleep. If the Inner Child awoke, there was a chance—the Guardian did not know how strong a chance—that it might integrate with Sorak, and perhaps with some of them as well. But there was also a chance that Sorak, like the rest of them, would cease to be, and the body they all shared would revert to the Child it had been before. Not physically, but mentally. The Guardian often thought about that, and wondered.

Kivara had no such concerns. She reveled in the night. She often catnapped during the day so that she could be awake at night, especially when the Ranger came to the fore and set out to hunt. Kivara was no hunter. She was purely a creature of the senses, mischievous and inquisitive, a sly young female who lacked the capacity to recognize any limits. Left to her own devices, she would indulge herself in whatever sensual pleasure was presented, or explore whatever fascinating new experience she might encounter, regardless of the risks. In that sense, she could be dangerous, for if the others did not watch her, she could jeopardize all of them—and flee, ducking under to let someone else bear the responsibility of safeguarding their welfare.

Tonight, however, Kivara was content just to remain awake and watch, and feel, and listen. Through the acute senses of the Ranger, the night came vibrantly alive to her. She would not intrude upon the Ranger, in part because she lacked the capability. The Ranger was much stronger, and if she made any such attempt, he would simply brush her abruptly aside and duck her under, the way he might shoo away some annoying desert fly or flick a sand flea off his breeches. But Kivara had no desire to come out when the Ranger manifested because through the Ranger, she could experience sensual pleasures far more sharply than she could when she came to the fore herself. And, of course, she was hungry, too, and none of them would eat until the Ranger made his kill.

Eyron simply waited . . . impatient as always. He wished the Ranger would hurry up and find some game for them. He never understood why it always took so long. His wryly cynical and pessimistic nature made him worry that, perhaps this night, the Ranger would fail in his hunt and they would have to go through one more day of Sorak and his druid food. Eyron found it maddening. Those silly priestesses had muddled Sorak's thinking. He was part elf and part halfling—and both halflings and elves ate meat. Eyron preferred his raw and freshly killed, but any meat would do in place of the roughage Sorak ate during the day. What did he need with seeds and fruit and lotus leaves? That was a diet for a kank, not for an elfling! Each time they were in a city and Sorak passed a stand that sold cooked meat, Eyron would smell it and begin to salivate. Sometimes, Sorak also would begin to salivate from Eyron's hunger, and Eyron would sense the primary's irritation and sullenly withdraw to sulk. He wished the Ranger would be quick about it. He wanted to feed and go to sleep with a full belly.

The Ranger felt Eyron's impatience, but paid no attention to it. He rarely paid much heed to Eyron. Such thoughts as Eyron had were pointless and of no interest to him. Eyron could not hunt. Eyron could not follow a trail. Eyron could not smell game, nor was he observant enough to detect its movement in the desert brush. He could not hear anything save for the sound of his own voice, of which he was inordinately fond. Eyron, thought the Ranger, was a foolish creature. He much preferred the company of Lyric, who was foolish too, but in a pleasant way. During the day, when the Ranger came to the fore, he would often allow Lyric to come out with him and sing a merry tune that he could listen to while he followed a trail. But listening to Eyron was a waste of time. And as the Ranger thought this, Eyron perceived the thought and resentfully kept his peace.

As he walked, his night vision as keen as any mountain cat's, the Ranger kept a sharp eye on the ground around him, alert for any signs of game. All at once, he spotted something and knelt, examining some faint markings on the ground that any of the others would have missed. They were scratchings made by the passing of an erdland, a large, flightless desert bird that walked upright on two long powerful legs ending in sharp talons. The Ranger knew erdlands were related to the erdlus that ran wild in the tablelands, but were also raised by desert herdsmen for sale to the city markets. Erdlus were prized by city dwellers mostly for their eggs, though their meat was often eaten. A wild erdlu could be quite difficult to catch, for they were easily spooked and capable of running at great speeds. Erdlands, however, being larger birds, could not move as quickly. And while their eggs were not as tasty as erdlus', their flesh could make a satisfying meal. An erdland would provide a feast, enough meat to fill their belly full to bursting, with still enough left over to make a meal for the desert scavengers. However, while an erdland did not move as quickly as its smaller relative, bringing one down posed other challenges.

A full-grown erdland stood as tall as fifteen feet and
weighed up to a ton. Its powerful legs delivered lethal
kicks, and its talons inflicted damaging wounds. More-
over, an adult bird, such as this one was judging by its
track, possessed a large wedge-shaped beak, unlike
young birds, whose beaks were small and not as dangerous. A full-grown erdland could peck so hard that it
would shatter bone, and a snap of its powerful beak
could take a hand right off.

The Ranger carefully examined the ground around
the track. Wild erdlands generally roamed in herds, but
this one seemed alone, and the track was fresh. The
Ranger went back to the track and began to follow it,
looking for any signs that might tell him if the bird was
wounded. A few feet farther on, he found what he was
looking for. The bird was missing part of one claw, not
enough to disable it, but enough to slow it down so
that it could not run with the rest of the herd. This one
had been left behind, but it would still be no easy prey.

The Ranger followed the track, moving quickly, but
not making any sounds as he trailed his prey. From
time to time, almost like an animal, he would stop and
sniff the air, not wanting to come suddenly upon the
bird and alert it to his presence. And, after following
the trail for perhaps a mile or so, he caught its scent. A
human's senses would not have been sharp enough to
catch it, but the Ranger smelled the creature's faintly
musky odor on the wind. He quickly judged the way
the breeze was blowing to make sure he was down-
wind of it, then moved forward at a crouch as he began
to stalk.

After covering perhaps a quarter of a mile, he could
hear it. It was moving slowly, its feet making soft,

thudding sounds that would have been inaudible to human ears, but not to the Ranger's. The Ranger checked the ground once more. There were no signs of other predators. Just the same, as he continued to stalk the bird, he took his time to make sure that no other creature hunted it. Erdlands were large enough to discourage attack by all but the largest and the fiercest of the night creatures, but it would not be smart to focus only on the game at hand and neglect another predator that might be stalking it. That could lead to an unpleasant surprise, and competing with another predator for prey would not only be dangerous, but a sure way to give the erdland enough time to make good its escape.

The Ranger felt the eager anticipation of the others and ignored it. A good hunter never rushed his kill. He stalked the erdland carefully and slowly. Gradually, he closed the distance between himself and the large bird. It was fully fourteen feet in height, with a long snake-like neck and a large rounded body from which its two strong legs sprouted like stilts. Its scaly collar, which it flared and expanded when attacked to make its head look bigger and more fearsome, was folded back as it moved slowly, scanning the ground ahead of it for food. The Ranger got down very low and patiently began to circle behind it, taking care not to make the slightest sound. He ignored the eager tension of the others, not wanting anything to distract him. His movements were lithe and catlike as he proceeded on all fours, pausing every now and then to check the wind and make sure it had not shifted.

It took agonizing patience, for the slightest sound would alert his quarry—the merest snapping of a dry twig on some low-growing desert scrub; the slightest crunch of his foot upon some stones; a sudden shift in the breeze. . . . The bird would be alerted to his presence in an instant and either try to run or turn and attack. An erdland was most dangerous when one was meeting it head-on.

Slowly, the Ranger advanced, gradually closing the distance between himself and his prey. The bird was still completely unaware of him, even though he had moved up to within only ten or fifteen feet of it. He was almost close enough, but not yet, not quite. He wanted to make sure.

Only eight or nine feet now. If the bird turned, it could not avoid seeing him. The moonlight on the desert rendered him clearly visible, and it was only by stealth and by keeping directly behind it that he had managed to approach this close.

The bird suddenly stopped in its tracks, its head coming up alertly as its neck straightened.

In that instant, the Ranger made his move.

With a swiftness matched only by that of an elf, he came up from all fours, ran three quick steps, and leaped. As the bird started, he landed on its back, clamping his legs tightly around its body as he seized its neck with both hands.

The bird gave out a piercing cry and jumped forward, leaping high on its powerful legs as it tried to dislodge him, while at the same time, its collar flared out wide, and its strong, muscular neck twisted in his grasp. The Ranger clamped his grip with all his might as the bird tried to twist its head around and peck him with its beak. One blow of that powerful, wedge-shaped beak could break his skull. The Ranger resisted the efforts of the bird to twist its head around. He held on, squeezing hard with his legs, as the erdland hopped around erratically, trying to buck him off.

The bird tried everything to fight free of his grasp. It lunged with its long neck, trying to pull him forward and off balance so that it could fling him off, but the Ranger held on tightly and pulled back, preventing the bird from extending its neck all the way. For a moment, the erdland fought against his pull, then abruptly gave in to it and brought its neck straight back. The Ranger almost lost his balance, but he managed to hold on.

The bird leaped from one leg to the other, doing everything it could to throw him off, and the Ranger felt his muscles burning with the effort of trying to hold on. The bird twisted its head first one way, then the other, but the Ranger would not loosen his grip. As the bird brought its neck sharply back once more to force him off, he went with the motion and used the opportunity to slide his hands up quickly under the erdland's flared out collar, to the point where the skull joined the neck.

The bird screeched as he slowly started trying to bend its head straight up and back. Its leaping redoubled, but the Ranger held on. It tried to extend its neck out once again, but he pulled back against it, straining as he forced its head up farther until the bird's beak was aimed straight up at the sky. It snapped that wedge-shaped beak uselessly and shrieked as he forced its head back, the muscles on his arms standing out like cords. And then, the neck broke.

The bird dropped like a stone, falling heavily to the ground, and the Ranger rolled free of it, landing hard and scrambling to get away from its legs as it thrashed several times, and then lay still. The others exulted in the thrill of it. The Ranger got up and removed the hunting knife from his sheath. He bent down and lifted one of the bird's long legs and slit its soft underbelly open. The blood gushed forth, and the smell of it was heady. The Ranger threw back his head and gave out a triumphant cry. The others felt his joy and sense of accomplishment, the fulfillment of his purpose. They celebrated with him. Then they began to feed.

The Ranger did not hurry as he headed back toward the place where they had camped. They had all eaten their fill and left enough behind to satisfy a hoard of scavengers. Nothing would be wasted. Only the bones of the large bird would be left to bleach slowly in the desert sun, after its scales had dried up and fluttered away upon the wind. After a successful hunt, the Ranger liked to walk and feel the night, savor its sounds and smells, open up his spirit to the vastness of the desert.

Unlike the shelter of the forest on the Ringing Mountains, where he enjoyed the canopy of leaves above him and felt the closeness of the trees, the tablelands were wide and open, a seemingly infinite desert plain that stretched out as far as the eye could see. The Ranger felt a strong affinity for the forest, for it was and would always be his home, but the desert possessed its own sweet and savage beauty. It was as if he could feel himself expanding in a hopeless effort to fill it with his presence. The forest was comfortable and cozy, but here, there was room to breathe. There was a different sort of solitude out on the tablelands. A solitude that filled him with a sense of the vastness of the harsh world that he lived in, the majesty of it. For all the desolation of the desert, there was a serene quality to it that filled one with a sense of peace. It could be a brutal, dangerous, and unforgiving place where violence struck suddenly at the unwary, but to one who did not fight it and who could accept its ways it could be a place of transformation.

The Child had almost died out on the desert once before, many years ago. Instead, the tribe had been born there, and had returned now and learned how to survive in it. And, on the tablelands of Athas, survival was no mean accomplishment. The Ranger dwelled upon these thoughts as he made his way unerringly back to the camp.

Then suddenly he stopped. All his senses were sharp and focused. An instant later, he knew what had alerted him, and he began to run, full speed, back toward the camp.

* * * * *

Ryana reached quickly for her crossbow, but in the instant she had taken her eyes away, the shadow disappeared. Rising to her knees, she quickly pulled the bow back and inserted a bolt from her quiver. She held the bow in front of her, ready to raise it on the instant, her gaze scanning the area around her. Perhaps it had only been her imagination, but she was certain she had seen something moving out there. Whatever that shadow was, it seemed to have slithered away into the night.

Ryana moistened her lips, which suddenly felt very dry. She wished that Sorak would return. She remained perfectly motionless, alert, bow held ready, her ears straining to hear the slightest sound. Off in the distance, the cry of some beast echoed. Something making

a kill, or being killed. It sounded far away. She longed
to throw some fresh wood on the fire, which was
almost out now, but she hesitated to put down the
crossbow. Could it have been only a trick of the moonlight? The chill night breeze ruffled her long hair as she
crouched and waited, listening intently. Was that something moving, or was it just the wind, rustling the
scrub brush?

For what seemed a long time, Ryana remained
motionless, her crossbow held ready. There was no
sign of movement out beyond their camp, and she
could now hear nothing but the rustling of the wind in
the dry desert grass and the pagafa branches overhead.
The fire was almost completely out now. She expelled
her breath, suddenly realizing that she had been holding it, put down the crossbow, and reached for some
more branches to put on the fire.

A shadow suddenly fell over her, and she felt powerful arms closing around her from behind.

With a cry, she raised her arms up and slithered out
of the attacker's grasp, then rolled and kicked out in a
sweeping motion behind her with one leg. She felt her
foot connect with something and heard a deep grunt as
someone or something fell to the ground, then she
rolled to her feet to face whatever it was that had
attacked her.

The dry branches she had dropped onto the fire suddenly burst into flame, and she saw what at first
looked like a man getting to his feet. He was very tall
and powerfully built, with broad shoulders, a narrow
waist, long dark hair, and gaunt features. But the proportions were all wrong somehow. With his exceedingly long arms and legs, he looked almost like a male

villichi, though, of course, that was impossible. She saw his pointed ears and thought he was an elf, and then she saw his hands as he raised them up in front of him, fingers hooked like claws. The hands were very large, more than twice the size of normal human hands, and the fingers were at least three times as long. They seemed to flare out at the tips, and then she suddenly realized what they were. Suckers. With an involuntary shudder, she realized what she was facing. It was neither man nor elf. It was a thrax.

At one point, it must have been a human, but it was not a human anymore. It was a vile creature that had been created by another like itself. The first thraxes were abominations created by defiler magic as a scourge to direct against their enemies. But not even the defilers had been able to control them. They ran wild and escaped into the desert, where they stealthily preyed on travelers. Shifting into shadow form, the thraxes would creep up on their unwary victims and then solidify behind them, grasping them in powerful arms, fastening suckers on them and draining their bodies of moisture. They would inflict such pain that usually their victims could not even struggle, and they would die in agony, reduced to desiccated corpses.

Ryana had never heard of anyone who had survived a thrax attack. Even if the victim broke free somehow, as this one must have done, contact with those suckers would make the vile magic that created the vampiric creatures pass to the victim, and in time, another thrax would be created. The magical mutation would begin with an aching in the hands and feet, then in the arms and legs as the bones started to elongate. The pain would increase, spreading out throughout the entire

body, and then the skin at the fingertips would rupture
and begin to bleed as the flesh sprouted into suckers.
At the same time, the raging thirst would strike, a thirst
that could, perhaps, be initially assuaged by draining
the moisture from small mammals, but that was not
enough. The thirst would grow and grow, driving out
all sanity, and only a victim that was humanoid or
human could provide enough bodily moisture to slake
it . . . and then only for a short time.

As the thrax crouched across the fire from her, its
long, sucker-tipped fingers extended and waggling
obscenely, the puckered mouth of the vile creature
twitched with thirst. Ryana knew that there was only
once chance to escape death, or a fate even worse than
death, and that was to strike a mortal blow while the
thrax was still solidified. Her crossbow was out of
reach, on the other side of the fire. Her sword was still
in its leather scabbard, beside the rucksack where she
had left it. She had only her knives. Moving quickly,
she reached down and drew one of the blades from the
top of her high moccasin and, in one smooth motion,
hurled it at the creature. The thrax immediately shifted
into shadow form and the blade passed through it
harmlessly, striking one of the thick trunks of the
pagafa tree, where it stuck. The vile shadow solidified
once more as the thrax crouched, preparing to leap.

Without taking her eyes off the creature, Ryana
quickly reached down and drew her other boot knife.
She held the long stiletto blade out before her and
crouched slightly, feet spread wide apart. The thrax
saw the second blade and hesitated. In that instant of
momentary hesitation, Ryana reached out with the
power of her mind, and, with psionic force, flung the

burning branches in the fire directly at the thrax's face. Instinctively, the thrax recoiled and raised its hands, and Ryana lunged toward the creature. But the beast recovered quickly, much more quickly than she had anticipated, and as she stabbed out with her blade, it passed through shadow.

The shadow leapt back, away from her, and the thrax solidified once more, more wary this time, circling and watching her intently. It feinted toward her once or twice, attempting to bait her into throwing the knife, but Ryana already knew that would not work. Instead, she drew another knife, the large, wide-bladed one in the sheath fastened to her belt. These blades were the only weapons she had left—along with her psionic power and her ingenuity. The thrax knew now that she was not an easy victim, a solitary woman who would fall prey to her own fear. But the creature was thirsty, and she was the only drink for miles around.

They circled warily, neither committing to an attack. The thrax tried to bait her into throwing one of her weapons, but she resisted the temptation. She, meanwhile, remained alert for any opportunity to strike, but each time she made a move toward the deadly creature, it shifted into shadow once again and faded back, attempting to lose itself in the other shadows and come around behind her. Ryana could not allow her vigilance to relax even for an instant. That instant would be fatal.

She knew she could not keep it up. Sooner or later, the thrax would fool her and slither around in shadow form behind her, or else its thirst would drive it into a direct frontal attack, in shadow form, enveloping her and passing through her, wrapping its shadowy appendages around her, and then solidifying into death.

Even as she thought of it, the thrax shifted into shadow and leapt toward her. Instead of recoiling, as it had expected, Ryana lunged to meet it, passing through the creature in its shadow state before it could solidify its grasp around her. She fought the gorge rising in her throat as she forced her way through the shadow, feeling its foul chill permeate her. Once beyond it, she turned to face the thrax again as it solidified, too late to trap her, but ready for another try. How long could she keep this up? Time favored the thrax. She was tired, and the creature knew it. One slip, one misstep, and it would be all over.

Their positions now were almost identical to what they were when the thrax had first attacked. The crossbow was still out of her reach, as was the sword, and she could spare no time to grab for them.

But she was villichi, schooled in the Way, and it was only that, if anything, that gave her the advantage. As she watched the thrax, not taking her gaze from it for a second, she reached out with the power of her mind, focusing upon the knife she had thrown earlier, now embedded in the pagafa tree. Slowly, it began to pull free behind the thrax. As she felt it coming loose, she kept her focus on the knife, and at the same time threw one of the other blades she held. The thrax quickly shifted into shadow form and the blade passed through it harmlessly. As it solidified again, Ryana quickly threw her second knife, purely by reflex, all the while keeping her psionic focus on the knife that she was working free from the pagafa trunk.

The thrax shifted into shadow form once more, and the second knife passed through it, and now, seeing her weaponless, the creature solidified once more, ready to leap. Behind it, the knife in the pagafa tree pulled free, pivoted around its axis, and flew forward, directed by psionic force, squarely into the creature's back, between its shoulder blades.

The thrax howled and shifted into shadow once again. The blade that had stuck in its back dropped to the ground, but in that instant, Ryana threw her focus to her sword, lying at the foot of the pagafa tree, beside her rucksack. The iron blade leapt from its scabbard and flew across the fire hilt-first, directly into Ryana's outstretched hand.

As the thrax solidified and leapt, Ryana quickly side-stepped and brought her sword down in a sweeping arc, decapitating the creature with one blow. It fell to the ground, dark blood bubbling up out of its neck, and its severed head rolled toward the fire. The long and oily hair burst into flame, and the odor of charred flesh assailed Ryana's nostrils. She backed away and retched.

Suddenly, she felt that tingling sensation at the back of her neck again and spun around, her sword held ready before her. The Ranger stood there, watching her with a dispassionate gaze. She sighed with enormous relief and, exhausted, lowered her sword.

The Ranger stepped forward and looked down at the decapitated corpse of the creature, its blood staining the sand. "Thrax," he said simply. Then he looked at her and nodded with approval. Without another word, he went over to the fire, where the thrax's head was burning, its charred flesh sending out a nauseating odor as it was consumed. The Ranger tossed on some more wood. He sat down, cross-legged, on the ground, lowered his head onto his chest, and slept. A moment later, the head came up again and Sorak gazed at her.

"You seem to have had a busy night," he said. "You can sleep now, if you like. I will keep watch until dawn."

"When did you come back?" she asked, still breathing heavily from her exertions.

"I only awoke just this moment," Sorak said.

"I meant the Ranger," she said.

"Ah. One moment, I will ask him." His face took on a distant, preoccupied expression for a moment, then his attention focused on her once again. "It seems he arrived a few moments before you killed the thrax," he said.

"And it did not occur to him to help?" she asked with astonishment.

"You seemed to have the situation well in hand," said Sorak. "He did not wish to interfere with your kill."

"With my kill?" she said, with disbelief. "I was fighting for my life!"

"Successfully, it would appear," said Sorak, with a glance toward the thrax's headless body.

"Damn you, Sorak! You could have helped me!"

"Ryana," he said apologetically, "forgive me, but I slept through the whole thing."

Her shoulders slumped as she sighed and tossed her sword down on the ground beside him. "Right," she said, with a grimace. "Of course."

"You are angry with me."

"No," she said, with resignation, "but I would certainly like to give the Ranger a piece of my mind!"

"Go ahead, if it will make you feel better," Sorak said. "He will hear you."

She sank down to the ground beside him. "Oh, what's the point?" she said. "Doubtless, it would only puzzle him."

"I fear that's true," said Sorak. "But still, if it would help. . . ."

"Just go and get my knives," she said, curling up on the ground and wrapping her cloak around her. "I'm tired, and all I want to do is sleep."

She pillowed her head upon her rucksack and closed her eyes. She could not remember when she had ever felt so thoroughly exhausted. The next thing she knew, it was dawn.

THREE

With Sorak keeping watch, the rest of the night passed uneventfully, and Ryana awoke shortly after sunrise, feeling more rested but still tired and sore. When she opened her eyes and sat up, she saw that the body of the thrax was gone, and for a moment, the alarming thought occurred to her that one of Sorak's more carnivorous personalities had eaten it.

"I dragged it off into those scrub bushes over there last night," he said, as if reading her mind. "I did not think it would be a very pleasant sight for you to see first thing in the morning. The scavenger beetles were already at it."

She sighed inwardly with relief.

"You cried out in your sleep last night," he said.

She nodded, repressing a shudder. "I dreamt about the thrax. It was not a very pleasant dream."

"Understandable, considering the circumstances," Sorak said. "Still, how many people can boast of vanquishing a thrax single-handedly? You acquitted yourself well, little sister. Tamura would be proud of you."

She thought of their weapons training instructor back at the convent and was grateful now that Tamura had been such a relentless taskmaster. Ryana had cursed her on more than one occasion. Now, she blessed her. If not for Tamura's training, it would have been her corpse that would now be lying in the bushes.

"We still have a long way to go," said Sorak, gathering his things. He looked remarkably fresh, and Ryana envied him not only his amazing elfling powers of endurance, but also his ability to duck under and sleep while one of his other personalities took control of his body. She would not wish to trade places with him, but she was forced to admit that there were certain unique advantages to his condition.

"How far do you think we have come?" she asked him.

"I would estimate a little more than halfway to the spring," he said. "The thrax would not have wandered very far from the trail. They like to stay within striking distance of the caravan routes and keep watch for vulnerable stragglers. I think that we should reach the trail before midday. The traveling should be easier after that."

"Well, I'm all for that," she said, gathering her belongings.

"I retrieved your knives last night, as you requested," said Sorak, with a smile, recalling her curt command to him to get her knives. He handed her the blades.

"Thank you."

"I had to do some searching to find this one," he said, as he gave her back one of the stilettos. "I was surprised to see how far it flew. You have a strong arm."

"Fear induces strength," she said wryly.

"Were you afraid?"

"Yes. Very much so."

"But you did not let your fear paralyze you," he replied. "That is good. You have learned well. Few things can be more frightening than a thrax."

"Well, whatever those few things are, I can do without meeting them," she said.

They shouldered their packs and headed east, toward the rising sun, moving at a steady, yet comfortable pace. Ryana was in excellent physical condition, yet still her legs felt sore from walking all the previous day. The fight with the thrax had taken a lot out of her, as well. She felt the effects not only of the previous night's exertions, but of the stress, too. She noticed Sorak slowing his pace slightly, so as not to make her work to keep up. I'm slowing him down, she thought. He could easily make twice the time or more by running. Yet he knew that if he did so, she would never be able to keep pace with him.

"I am sorry that I cannot move faster," she said, feeling woefully inadequate.

"There is no hurry," Sorak replied. "No one is chasing us. We have all the time in the world to reach Nibenay. For that matter, we do not even know what we are supposed to do when we get there."

"Try to make contact with the Veiled Alliance," she said. "That seems the obvious course."

"Perhaps, but it will not be easy," he said. "Strangers are always looked upon with suspicion in the cities. I remember how it was in Tyr. Neither of us have ever been to Nibenay, and unlike Tyr, Nibenay is still ruled by a defiler. The templars of the Shadow King will control all the power in the city, and they will have many informants. We shall have to be very circumspect in our inquiries."

"We know the necessary signals for making contact with the Veiled Alliance," said Ryana.

"Yes, but the templars doubtless know them, too. I fear that will not be enough. Long before we are aware of the Alliance in Nibenay, they shall be aware of us, which means that the templars will probably be aware of us, as well. In a city ruled by a defiler, the Veiled Alliance will want to take our measure carefully before attempting to make contact with us. We shall have to prove ourselves to them somehow."

"Then we shall simply have to judge our opportunities as they arise," Ryana replied. "Making any further plans at this point would serve little purpose. Remember, we still have to get there in one piece."

Sorak grinned. "After seeing how you dealt with that thrax, I have few worries on that score."

"I would have fewer worries still if we did not have so far to walk," Ryana said dryly.

"Would you prefer to ride?" asked Sorak.

She glanced at him with surprise. He was always so serious, it seemed out of character for him to tease her.

"You have not been paying very close attention," Sorak explained. He indicated the ground in front of them. "I had thought you would be more observant."

She looked down where he pointed. "Kank spoor," she said.

"We have been following it for the past hour," Sorak said. "There is a small herd of kank somewhere just ahead of us. This spoor is fresh. They should be within sight before too long."

"How many do think there are?" she said.

"Judging from the spoor, I should say at least a

dozen or more," Sorak said.

"We have seen no signs of any herdsman's camp," she said.

"No, which means these kanks are wild," he replied. "They have all kept fairly close together while they have been on the move, so it is not a foraging party. They have broken off from a larger herd to form a hive and are searching for a place to build it."

"That means they have a brood queen," said Ryana.

"Yes, a young one, I should think, as the herd is still quite small."

"So the soldiers will be quite aggressive," she said. She glanced at him dubiously. "Do you think that you can handle them?"

"I could not, but Screech may be able to."

"*May?*" she said uneasily.

Sorak shrugged. "Screech has never faced wild kanks before," he said, "only tame ones raised by herdsmen."

"And he has never faced wild soldier kanks defending a young brood queen," Ryana added. "Do you think he will be up to the task?"

"There is only one way to find out," said Sorak. "Kanks do not move very quickly."

"Neither do I, compared to you," she said.

"Would you rather walk?"

She took a deep breath and exhaled heavily. "Villichi priestesses always walk when they take pilgrimages. But then, I am no longer a priestess. It would be nice to ride to Nibenay."

"Well, then we shall have to see what Screech can do," said Sorak.

Within a short while, they topped a small rise and

came within sight of the kanks. They heard them first. The clicking of their large mandibles made sounds like sticks being struck together. There were perhaps thirteen or fourteen of the creatures, spread out over a small area, their shiny, black, chitinous exoskeletons gleaming darkly in the sun. Ordinarily, kanks were docile insects, which was fortunate because of their very large size. Adults grew up to eight feet in length and stood as much as four feet high, weighing between three and four hundred pounds. Their segmented bodies consisted of a large, triangular-shaped head, an oval thorax and a round, bulbous abdomen, all of which were covered with a hard, chitinous exoskeleton. Their six multiple-jointed legs sprouted from the thorax, and each leg ended in a strong claw, which allowed the kank to grip uneven surfaces or prey.

Kanks were omnivorous creatures, but they gener-ally did not attack people. They foraged for their food, or else subsisted on small desert mammals and reptiles. The exception was when they were on the move to establish a new hive and had a brood queen with them. In an established colony, the brood queen stayed in the hive, tended to by the food-producing kanks, who always remained in or near the hive, and by the soldiers, whose task it was to bring forage to the hive and provide protection to the food produc-ers and the queen. A young brood queen was gener-ally about the same size as the soldiers, who were smaller than the food producers and had larger pin-cers. Once the hive had been established, however, the brood queen took her permanent place in her nest in the large, central chamber of the hive, where she was fed constantly until she reached maturity and grew to almost three times her original size. She then started laying eggs, in batches of twenty to fifty, and she continued laying eggs in cycles until the day she died, functioning as nothing more than a reproductive machine.

The food producers nourished the hatchlings with a green honey they manufactured in melon-sized globules covered with a thick membrane that grew out of their abdomens. Kank honey was very sweet and nourishing, and was regarded as a major food source in the cities and villages of Athas, one of the reasons kanks were raised by herdsmen on the tablelands. Kanks raised in this fashion could also be trained as beasts of burden, and commanded a good price in the city marketplaces. Herdsmen also sold their exoskeletons for use in the manufacture of inexpensive armor. Kank armor was functional, but too brittle to stand up to a lot of damage, and had to be frequently replaced. For these reasons, kanks had become a vital part of the economy of Athas.

Wild kanks, on the other hand, though docile for the most part, could be dangerous when migrating to establish a new hive. With their young brood queen exposed and vulnerable, the soldier kanks became very aggressive and would attack anything that ventured near the herd. Kanks had many natural enemies, such as drakes, erdlus, pterrax, thri-kreen, and antloids, which would descend upon their hives in voracious swarms. As a result, the soldier kanks always attacked together, while the food producers would gather round their queen to shield her with their bodies. If humans happened to chance upon a migrating kank herd, they too would be attacked, and the powerful pincers of the soldiers could not only rend flesh and snap off limbs, they also injected a paralyzing poison.

Though kanks did not hunt humanoids or humans, someone bitten by a soldier kank would be recognized as carrion and dragged off to the main body of the herd and used as food. Kanks did not move very quickly, and they ate at a leisurely pace. Being paralyzed and eaten alive by kanks was a process that could take hours, especially if the herd was small. Ryana regarded it as a distinctly unpleasant prospect.

Kanks had poor eyesight and no sense of smell, but they were acutely sensitive to motion and vibrations in the ground. A soft footstep on the desert sand could be detected by them from hundreds of yards away. Halflings, who could move across the desert without making any sounds at all, could come to within a few yards of a kank without being detected, but even with her villichi training, Ryana knew that she could never step so softly. These kanks had become aware of them when they were a little less than two hundred yards away, and the soldiers immediately became highly agitated.

"Perhaps you had better wait here," said Sorak, motioning to her to remain where she was.

"And let you go face them all alone?" she said, though at that particular moment, she was not anxious to venture any closer.

"It is not I who shall be facing them, but Screech," said Sorak. "And if Screech proves unable to deal with them, remember I can run much faster than you."

"I will not argue the point," she said. "But if they get

close enough, there may not be time to run."

"Which is why I intend to keep well away from them until we find out if they will respond to Screech. The tribe is strong, but not too proud to run if necessary. If we should be separated, circle round them widely and head due east. The Ranger will pick up your trail."

He started moving toward them at a steady pace, his cloak billowing out behind him in the desert wind.

"Good luck!" she called out after him. "Be careful!"

As he moved toward them, the kanks began to act like an opposing army. The soldiers moved forward en masse, interposing themselves between Sorak and the food producers clustered around their brood queen. They began to click their mandibles together rapidly in warning, making a sound like a child rattling a stick upon a fence, only much louder.

Sorak slowed as he approached them. Ryana watched the attitude of his body change in a subtle manner and realized that Screech had come to the fore. She had seen it happen before and so recognized the signs, though most people would have perceived no difference in the elfling. His movements altered subtly, and the way he held his body also changed, though not in any dramatically noticeable degree. But to Ryana's practiced eye, Sorak had begun to move in a more animal-like manner. His walk became more flowing, his tread lighter, his entire body took on a sinuous attitude. There was something catlike in his motions at first, and then that attitude underwent a change, as well, this time in a more noticeable way.

As Screech approached the soldier kanks, his movements became jerky and exaggerated, and he hunched over, holding his elbows out from his sides, his arms

sharply bent, his palms flat toward the ground. He
started moving his arms up and down in that curious,
angular attitude, and Ryana watched for several
moments, utterly mystified as to what he was doing. It
appeared as if he were performing some sort of strange,
ritual dance. Almost as if he were trying to imitate the
way a spider moved, or else . . . and then it dawned on
her. Screech was exhibiting the behavior of a kank. She
heard curious sounds coming from his throat, and realized that he was imitating, as closely as his elfling
anatomy would allow, the sounds produced by the
kanks' mandibles.

The soldier kanks, which had been moving toward
him rapidly, suddenly stopped, hesitating. Screech
stopped as well. Ryana saw the large heads of the
kanks swiveling back and forth in puzzlement. She
held her breath, watching with intense fascination.

The kanks were confronted with something that
obviously was not a kank, and yet its movements were
distinctly kanklike. The sounds coming from its throat
were not really the same sounds they made, but their
pattern was similar, and instead of a rapid, challenging
signal, it was a calm indication of recognition.

Ryana saw several of the soldier kanks start forward
once again, and then stop and back away a little. Screech
remained exactly where he was. She watched as he
moved his legs up and down, up and down repeatedly
in a bizarre, jerky, spastic manner, as if he were doing
some sort of stamping dance, synchronizing his arms
with the movements of his legs. She had absolutely
no idea what he was doing, but it looked fascinating. Then, as she watched in astonishment, several of
the soldier kanks began to make similar movements,

moving their multiple-jointed legs up and down
repeatedly, as if running in place. It seemed they were
imitating Screech.

One of them made a series of the curious stamping
movements, then stopped. Next, Screech made a series
of stamping movements and stopped. Then several of
the other kanks did so, and Screech once again repeated
the motions, taking turns doing the odd dance.

As she watched, utterly absorbed in this bizarre pantomime, Ryana suddenly realized what they were
doing. They were communicating through the vibrations created by stamping their legs on the ground. She
had seen penned up, herd-raised kanks making similar
motions in the beast markets of Tyr, and had merely
thought the creatures were restive from being confined
in such close quarters, but now she realized that it was
how they talked to one another. Screech and the soldier
kanks were having a conversation.

As she watched, the aggressive attitude of the soldier
kanks changed noticeably. The rapid, rattling, clicking
sounds they were making with their mandibles died
down and several of them actually turned away and
went back to the food producers and the brood queen.
Those who remained turned so that they were no
longer facing Screech and then started doing the
stamping dance. They're talking it over among themselves, Ryana thought with wonder.

She was sure no other human had seen such a man-
beast conversation before. Kanks could be controlled
by psionic handlers, and herd-raised kanks could be
trained to respond to handling prods, but no one had
ever actually spoken to one before.

After a while, several of the soldiers that had gone

back to the brood queen returned, bringing one of the food producing kanks with them. Ryana could recognize it at a distance because it was slightly larger than the soldiers, with a bigger and more rounded abdomen. There was some more of the stamping pantomime, and then Screech turned and started walking back toward her. The food producer followed, like a pet trailing its master, while the other kanks went back to their brood queen. Ryana had never seen anything like it. She had seen Screech commune with animals before, but never with anything like a kank. As he came back toward her, Screech straightened up, and his pace changed slightly. It was Sorak who reached her, smiling, with the food producing kank following at his heels.

"Your mount awaits, my lady," he said, with a mock bow.

"If I had not seen it, I would not have believed it," she replied, shaking her head with amazement. "What did Screech . . . say to them?"

"Ah, well," said Sorak, "he more or less explained that he had a young brood queen with him and no food producer to help care for her. Kanks do not communicate in quite the same manner as we do, but in essence, that was the substance of the interaction."

"And they simply *gave* you one of their food producers?" Ryana said with disbelief.

"Well, 'gave' would not quite be the right word," he said. "Soldiers kanks are motivated by instinct to protect a brood queen. And food producers are likewise motivated to care for them. They recognized Screech as a fellow soldier kank, although a rather odd one, to be sure, and while their primary responses were to protect their own queen, the idea of another queen with only one soldier to protect and care for her struck them as clearly wrong. In a colony with two brood queens, the soldiers and the food producers divide to make certain both queens have adequate care and protection, and when the younger brood queen starts to mature, the colony divides, as this one did, and some of them go off with the younger queen to construct another hive. The situation Screech presented them with activated that instinctual response. At the same time, however, because this herd is rather small, all the soldiers were strongly motivated to remain with their own queen. They settled on a compromise. The second queen, meaning you, already had one soldier, meaning Screech, but no food producer, so this food producer came with us to help us start our hive."

She simply stared at him, then looked toward the kank, which waited behind him obediently, then back at him again. "But I am not a brood queen," she said. "And you are no soldier kank."

Sorak simply shrugged. "This one thinks we are," he said.

She moistened her lips nervously, as she stared at the kank again. "But I cannot imitate a kank, the way Screech can," she replied. "This kank can surely see the difference."

"Actually, it cannot see very much of anything," said Sorak. "Kanks have very poor eyesight, food producers in particular. Anyway, it does not matter. This kank has already accepted us as fellow creatures. Its bonding response has already been engaged. Kanks do not second guess themselves. They are not very bright."

"Then it will not hurt me?" said Ryana, still dubious.

"The kank would never think of hurting you," Sorak said. "It thinks you are a brood queen. It would be contrary to all the years of kank evolution for this food producer to do anything but care for you."

"What do you mean, care for me?"

"Provide you with food," said Sorak, indicating the blisterlike, membranous globes covering the food producer's abdomen. "You can ride to Nibenay *and* drink your fill of kank honey." He brought his fingertips to his forehead and bowed his head in salute. "It is the very least that I could do for such a valiant thrax killer."

Ryana smiled. But she still looked at the kank a little dubiously. "Brood queens do not ride upon food producers," she said. "Will this one allow me to mount it?"

"Lowly food producers do not question their queens; they merely serve them," Sorak said. "Aside from which, as we walked over here, Screech effected a psionic link with this kank. It would have been dangerous to attempt it with all of them, especially with the soldiers in an agitated state, but controlling this one will pose no difficulty now. It will be as tame as one raised by a herdsman, but it will have a closer bond with us."

He went over to the kank and slapped it several times on its chitinous thorax. The creature lowered itself to the ground, and Sorak held his hand out to Ryana. She glanced uncertainly at the creature's mandibles, smaller than a soldier's but no less intimidating in appearance, then put her foot onto one of the ridges of the kank's armor, stepped up, and swung her leg over the creature's thorax. Sorak climbed up behind her. The kank's rounded carapace made a firm, smooth, and slightly slippery perch, but by relaxing and settling her weight between the rounded ridges on the creature's back, Ryana found the ride comfortable enough. And it certainly beat walking. The kank rose up on its legs, turned, and began to move forward, heading directly to the east on a diagonal course away from its old herd.

Its six-legged gait was remarkably smooth, with only a slight rolling action, and Ryana had no difficulty getting accustomed to it. This was traveling across the desert in style, and riding on the kank had the added advantage of reducing some of the dangers they might have faced. They were now well out of reach of snakes they might have stepped on without noticing them, and sink worms would no longer be a hazard. It would be a rare sink worm that would be large enough to swallow a kank whole, and they did not eat kanks, in any case. The giant, armored ants of the desert were not digestible by sink worms. The kank's sensitivity to ground vibrations also effectively eliminated any potential danger from dune trappers or other creatures that lurked just beneath the surface of the loose sand, though this area of the tablelands was mostly hard-packed scrub desert. Still, the kank would sense approaching danger long before they would have been aware of it themselves.

As they continued their gradual descent along the gently rolling terrain, subtle changes began to occur in the environment around them. The scrubby desert growth gradually became more sparse, and wider patches of sun-baked ground were visible. The isolated stands of pagafa trees became more sparse, as well, and grew lower and more twisted than those they had seen before. The terrain grew flatter and the vistas stretching out before them possessed an openness that made Ryana feel very isolated and exposed. They were now well into the tablelands, and the Ringing Mountains, rising in the distance behind them, seemed very far away.

Ryana felt a disquieting sense of apprehension as they rode along. For miles, as far as she could see, there was absolutely no landmark. With the city of Tyr far behind them in the valley, there was no sign of civilization anywhere. That, in itself, did not disturb Ryana quite so much as the vast openness of the terrain. Growing up as she did in the Ringing Mountains, she had never been surrounded by civilization. However, there was the convent, and that was home, and the tall, dense, ancient forests of the mountains had an embracing closeness. Here, in the tablelands, she suddenly felt as if she were adrift on some vast, dried sea. Nothing in her experience had prepared her for the rather nerve-wracking experience of seeing so far . . . and seeing nothing everywhere she looked.

All around her, the tablelands stretched out into infinity, a panoramic vista broken only by a vague, barely perceptible, uneven line of grayness in the distance to the east. She was looking at all she could see of the Barrier Mountains, which lay on the far side of the tablelands and beyond which lay their destination, Nibenay. All that way, she thought with a distinct sense of unease. We still have to go all that way. . . .

But the desert was not empty. Far from it. When she wearied of looking out into the vast flat plain ahead of them, she began to pay attention to the terrain immediately around them, looking closer at the desert at her feet. It was harsh, inhospitable country, but it teemed with life, life that she only began to notice when she focused her attention on it.

That anything at all could grow here seemed a miracle, but the years had evolved plant life that was capable of thriving in the desert. It was not yet summer, but the short and violent rainy season was approaching, and in anticipation of it, the desert wildflowers had already begun to bloom so that they would be able to deposit their seeds during the brief time when there would be some moisture on the surface. The blooms were, for the most part, very small and not visible for any appreciable distance, but from close up, they imparted tiny yet spectacular splashes of color to the desert. The sparse and trailing claw vine bloomed bright, cerulean blue, and the wild desert moonflowers developed globe-shaped, yellow blossoms that almost seemed to glow. The scrubby false agafari bush, which grew no taller than about knee height, blossomed with small sprays of wispy, feathery pink flowers that looked as fine as ice crystals, and some varieties bloomed bright crimson. The nomad brush, a small shrub that grew no more than two feet high, sent out long, trailing, hirsute vines that gathered moisture from the morning air and grew along the surface until they found purchase in loose soil. They would then take root, and new plants would form while the parent plant died back. In this time of approaching spring, the nomad brush would bloom with the bright orange, brush-shaped thistle that gave it its name.

From the distance, the desert appeared flat and fea-
tureless, a vast, empty, and desolate place. Yet up
close, it possessed a striking beauty. The hardy,
sparse vegetation that grew here, storing moisture for
long periods of time in its wide-branching roots and
succulent flesh, supported a wide variety of small
insects and desert rodents, which in turn supported
reptiles and larger mammals and airborne predators
like razorwings, which rode upon the desert ther-
mals. It was a place vastly different from the forests
of the Ringing Mountains where Ryana had grown
up, but for all that it looked like another world, it was
just as full of life.

For a long time as they rode, Sorak remained silent.
Since he was sitting behind her on the kank's back,
Ryana initially thought he was absorbed in conversation with his inner tribe. When he had remained silent
for a long time, she turned around to glance at him and
saw him quietly looking around at their surroundings.
His facial expression was alert, not vaguely distant, as
it was when he was engaged in internal conversation
with his other personalities. However, he still looked
preoccupied.

"I was merely thinking," he said when he saw her
glance around to look at him.

"About what?"

"It feels very strange to be here. I was born here,
somewhere in the desert, and this is where I almost
died."

"You are thinking about your parents?"

He nodded in a distracted manner. "I was wondering who they were, if they are still even alive, and what
became of them. I was wondering if I was cast out into

the desert because my tribe would not accept me, or because my mother would not accept me. If the former, then did my mother share my fate? And if the latter, then was ridding herself of me the only way that she could maintain her status in the tribe? Thoughts such as that, and others, dwell upon me heavily today. It must be the desert. It has a strange effect on one."

"I have noticed," she said. "It has a strange effect on me, as well, though perhaps not the same effect it has on you."

"What does it make you feel?" he asked.

Ryana thought a moment before replying. "It makes me feel very small," she said at last. "Until we came here, I do not think it ever truly occurred to me how vast a place our world is and how insignificant we are by comparison. It is both an alarming feeling, in a way . . . all this openness and distance . . . and yet, at the same time, it imparts a sense of one's proper place in the scheme of things."

Sorak nodded. "Back in Tyr, when I was working in the gaming house, desert herdsmen would often come in for some recreation after they had sold their beasts to the traders in the market. They had a saying about the tablelands. They would say, 'The distance gets into your eye.' I never quite knew what they meant until now. For all the diversions the city had to offer them, for all that it was a much more comfortable and convenient life, they never lingered very long. They were always anxious to get back to the desert.

"The city, they said, made them feel 'closed in.' I see now what they meant. The distance of the desert gets into your eye. You grow accustomed to the vastness of it, to the openness, and you come to feel that there is room for you to breathe. Cities are crowded, and one becomes merely a part of the throng. Here, one has a sharper sense of self." He smiled. "Or *selves*, as in my case. One does not become caught up in the frenetic rhythms of the city. The soul finds its own pace. Out here, in the vast silence, with only the gentle sighing of the wind to break the stillness, one's very spirit seems to open up. For all the hazards to be found here, the desert imparts a sense of clarity and peace."

She glanced at him with surprise. "That was quite a speech," she said. "You are always so sparing with your words and to the point. Yet that was actually . . . poetic. A bard could not have sung it better."

"Perhaps I have a bit of bard in me, as well," said Sorak with a grin. "Or perhaps it is just my elfling blood warming in its natural environment." He shrugged. "Who is to say? I only know that I feel strangely content here. The forests of the Ringing Mountains are my home, yet it feels somehow as if this is the place where I belong."

"Perhaps it is," she said.

"I do not really know that yet," he replied. "I know that I feel an affinity for these open spaces, and for the quiet solitude they offer—which is not to say that I am not grateful for your company, of course—but at the same time, I shall never truly know where I belong until I learn the story of my past."

They rode a while in silence after that, each of them preoccupied with inner thoughts. Ryana wondered if Sorak ever would learn the truth about his past, and if he did, how would it change him? Would he seek out the tribe that he had come from, the people who had cast him out? And if he found them, what would he do? When Sorak finally tracked down the mysterious adept known as the Sage—if he did—would the reclusive wizard grant his desire? And if so, what would be his price? And what if he was doomed to disappointment in his search? The defilers had sought for the mysterious preserver for as long as bards sang songs about him. Could Sorak, without magic to aid him in his quest, hope to succeed where powerful sorcerer-kings had failed?

How long, Ryana wondered, would Sorak search before he gave up on his quest? He had yearned to discover the truth of his origin for as long as she had known him, and he had never been one to discourage easily. She hoped they would succeed, for his sake, no matter how long their search would take. It was not the life that she had hoped for when she first realized she was in love with Sorak, but at least they were together, sharing as much as it was possible for them to share. She might have longed for more, but she was satisfied with what she had.

Sorak, on the other hand, never would be satisfied until he found the answers to the questions that had tormented him since childhood. Nibenay was still a long journey away, and it was but the next destination in their quest. There was no way of knowing where the path would lead from there. Or, for that matter, if it would lead anywhere. They were both sworn followers of the Path of the Preserver, and though Ryana had forsaken her oath as a villichi priestess, the vow she swore as a preserver was one that she would keep until the day she died. She and Sorak were two preservers headed for the domain of a defiler, the realm of the dreaded Shadow King. The gates of Nibenay would

easily open to admit them, but getting out again might
prove more difficult.

They made much better time riding on the kank than
they would have on foot, and by midday, they had
reached the point where the caravan route from Tyr
came up from the southwest to intersect their path. The
traveling was easier after that, following the wide,
well-worn and hard-packed trail.

Lyric came out for a time and sang a song, one of
the songs the sisters used to sing when they worked
together back at the convent. Ryana joined him, taking pleasure in the singing for old times' sake, and
Lyric instantly shifted key to harmonize his voice
with hers. Ryana knew she was, at best, merely an
average singer, but Lyric's voice was beautiful. Sorak
did not like to sing. His nature was too somber for it,
and he felt his voice left much to be desired, but
Lyric, using the same throat Sorak used, possessed no
such inhibitions and allowed his voice to soar. He
was adroit enough to harmonize with her in such a
manner that they both sounded good, and Ryana
found her spirits lightening as she sang. Even the
kank seemed to respond, matching its gait to the
rhythms of the song.

When they were finished, Ryana laughed with
sheer exhilaration. The desert seemed a far less
oppressive place now, and her worries had been banished, if only for the moment. At the beginning of the
day, with the vastness of the desert stretching out
before them, Ryana had felt intimidated by it—
lonely, small, and insignificant. Now, having seen the
desert through Sorak's eyes and filled it with her
song, she no longer felt diminished by it. She allowed

herself to breathe in the dry desert wind and feel it
filling her with its tranquility. She felt marvelously
free and basked in the wide open spaces of the tablelands, no longer frightened by its endless vistas, but
invigorated by them. Perhaps it was merely a delayed
aftereffect of her battle with the thrax, of having
faced her fear and conquered it; perhaps it was the
gently rolling motion of their mount that had lulled
her into a calm, receptive state; perhaps it was the
joyfulness of song; or perhaps it was all of those
things—or something else, something indefinable.
But the desert had won her over. She felt at peace
with it and with herself.

As the dark sun began to sink over the horizon, they
saw an oasis in the distance, marked by tall and spindly
desert palms and large, spreading pagafa trees, their
wide, majestic crowns—lush and full in the presence of
water—silhouetted black against the orange sky. They
were approaching Silver Spring.

"We are going to have company at the oasis," Sorak
said.

She glanced at him, raising her eyebrows.

He smiled and pointed at the trail ahead of them.
"You have been lost in reverie again, and were not pay-
ing attention. A caravan has passed by here recently.
The tracks are still fresh."

"It is hardly fair for you to chide me for not noticing
such things," she said, "when you can drift with your
thoughts as much as you like while the Watcher misses
nothing."

"True," said Sorak. "That is, indeed, an unfair advantage. I apologize."

"It will be good to see some other people," she said.

"The caravan will have supplies, and we can trade them kank honey to replenish our provisions."

"I was thinking more about hearing news of Nibenay," said Sorak.

"But this caravan is on the route from Tyr," Ryana said.

"Or else it came up from Altaruk, which means it may have originated in Gulg. In either case, the merchant houses have extensive interests, and their caravans range far and wide. Their drivers will have all the latest news from other cities."

As the sun was setting and they drew closer, they could hear the sound of music coming from the spring, and smell the odor of cooking meat. Their mount began to pick up its pace, sensing the herd-raised kanks used by the caravan to haul its cargo. As the kank gathered speed, Ryana remembered what Sorak had said about how kanks were "slow-moving" creatures. Perhaps they were to an elfling, who could run like the wind, but Ryana was now glad she had stayed behind while Screech had gone ahead to meet the wild soldier kanks. She could never have outrun the creatures had they charged.

Soon, they could make out the shapes of people moving up ahead and see the flames of their camp fires. As they approached, the mercenaries hired to protect the caravan and its valuable trade goods came out to meet them. They seemed wary, and with good cause. For all they knew, Sorak and Ryana could have been advance scouts for a raiding party. Marauding bands had been known to infiltrate caravans by posing as simple pilgrims or travelers. In fact, Sorak had foiled just such a plot in Tyr, and saved one of the caravans of a large merchant house from being ambushed by a band of marauders from the Mekillot Mountains. Tribes of nomadic elves were also known to attack caravans from time to time, so the mercenaries hired to guard them took no chances.

"Hold where you are and identify yourselves!" one of the mercenaries cried out as they approached.

Sorak halted the kank and called back, "We are merely two pilgrims on our way to Nibenay."

"Dismount, then, and come forward," the mercenary said. The others stood with their weapons held ready, alert for any sign of treachery.

Ryana noticed that they had spread out and were looking not only at them, but at the trail beyond them and in all surrounding directions in case their arrival was meant as a diversion for an attack by an armed party. These men were well trained, she thought, but that only made sense. The rich merchant houses could easily afford to hire the finest mercenaries. The merchant houses depended on the caravans for their livelihood, and so they were not known to spare any expense when it came to protecting them.

Caravans fell into one of two basic categories: slow-moving and fast-moving. The advantages to a fast-moving caravan, such as this one, were that the journeys took less time, and therefore were more profitable. Berths were sold to passengers traveling from one city to another, and the fees usually included the rent of a tame kank for a mount as well as basic necessities such as food and water for the journey. A first-class berth with a caravan offered a few more luxuries, but for an extra charge, of course. The slow-moving caravans were usually much more heavily laden, and since their pace made them more vulnerable to attack, they employed huge armored wagons drawn by mekillot lizards. With the exception of the mercenary outriders and the wagon handlers, the entire caravan was contained inside the huge, armored enclosures. This practice had its own advantages and disadvantages. It was a slow and lazy way to travel, in that the passengers simply rode inside the wagons. At the same time, the interiors of these wagons quickly became oppressively hot despite the open ventilation ports, and the frequently cramped quarters were not very amenable to those whose nostrils were easily offended. Because the mekillots were huge, slow-moving creatures and sluggish in their temperament, the drivers did not like to stop, and rest periods were few and far between. The giant mekillots were also difficult to control. Even their psionic handlers were sometimes eaten if they carelessly strayed within reach of the mekillots' long tongues. Most travelers preferred to book passage with the fast-moving caravans, even if it meant being exposed to the elements throughout most of their journey.

As Sorak and Ryana approached the mercenary captain, they were able to get a better look at the company, and the mercenaries were able to get a better look at them. It was a mixed group, composed primarily of humans, with a few demihuman half-breeds. They were all well armed and in prime physical condition. Ryana knew that this group was not the entire force. Some would be posted as pickets around the perimeter of the oasis, while others would either be guarding the caravan goods against the potential of light-fingered passengers or taking their rest in the camp.

It was a large caravan, composed not only of a train of loaded kanks and those employed as mounts, but a number of light, partially enclosed carriages drawn by one or two kanks in harness. This meant that there were some important personages traveling with the caravan.

Looking beyond the mercenaries to the camp in the oasis, Ryana's suspicion was confirmed when she saw several large and comfortable tents set up beneath the palms, with guards posted outside them. As she looked toward the tents, a man in robes came out of one of them, glanced in their direction, and started walking toward them at an unhurried pace. A cluster of guards fell in beside him.

"You wear a handsome sword, pilgrim," said the mercenary guard captain, looking Sorak over carefully.

"Even a pilgrim must protect himself," said Sorak.

His gaze flicking back to the sword, the mercenary captain said, "That seems like quite a full measure of protection. From the shape of the scabbard, it appears to be a rather unusual blade."

It was, indeed, Ryana thought, and if the mercenary captain were an elf and not a human, he might have recognized it as Galdra, the legendary sword of the ancient elvish kings.

"May I see it?" asked the captain.

Sorak reached for the hilt, then hesitated slightly when he saw the other mercenaries tense. He drew Galdra slowly. The sight of it produced an immediate reaction among the mercenaries.

"Steel!" said the captain, staring at the wickedly

curved blade. "It must be worth a fortune. Now what would a simple pilgrim be doing with such a blade?"

"It was a gift from a very wise old friend," said Sorak.

"Indeed? And who would that friend be?"

"High Mistress Varanna of the villichi convent."

This, too, provoked a reaction of great interest among the mercenaries, and they murmured among themselves.

"Be silent!" their captain commanded, and they obeyed at once. He never took his gaze off Sorak. "The villichi are a female order," he said. "It is a well-known fact that the priestesses do not admit males to their convent."

"Nevertheless, Sorak was raised there," said Ryana.

"Sorak?" The man with the robes came up behind the mercenary captain. The guards on either side of him rested their hands lightly on the pommels of their obsidian-bladed swords. "I know that name. Are you the one whose warning prevented the attack on the recent caravan from Tyr?"

"I am," said Sorak.

"It would be to his advantage to claim that, whether it was true or not," the captain said. "How do we know he is the one?"

"There is one way of knowing," said the robed man. And turning to Sorak, he said, "Would you be so kind as to pull back the hood of your cloak?"

Sorak sheathed the blade and did as he was asked. At the sight of his features, and his pointed ears, there was once again an excited murmuring among the mercenaries.

"An elf!" said one of them.

"No, he is not tall enough," another said.

"A half-elf, then."

"Neither," said the robed man. "He is an elfling."

"An elfling?" said the captain with a frown.

"Part elf, part halfling," said the robed man.

"But there is no such thing, my lord," the captain protested. "Everyone knows that elves and halflings are mortal enemies."

"Nevertheless, that is what he is," the robed man said. "And he is who he claims to be. We have met before."

"You were at the Crystal Spider," Sorak said, suddenly placing the man.

"And lost heavily, as I recall," the robed man said with a smile. "But my losses would have been far greater had you not exposed the cardsharp who was cheating me. I do not fault you for not remembering me at once. You, on the other hand, are rather more memorable." He turned to the mercenary leader. "The elfling is a friend to the merchant houses, Captain. Besides, much as I respect your fighting prowess, you would not wish to try your blade against his. I have seen what it can do. In fact, even all this company would be hard pressed against these two, or have you failed to note that his companion is a villichi priestess?"

The captain, who had been concentrating his attention on Sorak, looked more carefully at Ryana. "Your pardon, my lady," he said, inclining his head in a small bow of respect. "And yours, elfling. If the Lord Ankhor speaks for you, then my blade is at your service. Allow me to escort you personally into the camp." He snapped his fingers at one of the others. "See to the kank."

One of the mercenaries hurried forward to comply, but Sorak caught his arm as he went past. "I would not do that, if I were you," he said.

"I can handle the dumb beast," the mercenary said confidently, disengaging himself and moving toward the kank. He jumped back with a yelp of surprise, barely in the nick of time as the kank snapped at him with its pincers.

"I warned you," Sorak said. "This kank is wild."

"*Wild?*" said the mercenary with surprise.

Sorak allowed Screech to come to the fore momentarily, long enough to direct a psionic command at the kank to join the others in the train. As the large beetle moved off toward the tame kanks, Sorak came back to the fore again and said, "Just see to it that food is set out within its reach. But advise your handlers to keep clear of it."

"You are full of surprises," said Lord Ankhor. "Come. Join me in my tent. And, of course, the invitation includes you, as well, priestess."

"You are of the House of Ankhor then?" said Sorak.

"I *am* the House of Ankhor," their host replied as they walked back toward his tent, escorted by the two mercenary guards and their captain. "My father, Lord Ankhor the Elder, is the patriarch of our house, but he is growing infirm and advanced in years. I have been directing all the affairs of the house for the past two years, and I had a small fortune in trade goods on that caravan you saved from the marauders. I did not hear of it until after I had met you at the Crystal Spider. I had hoped for a chance to show my gratitude, but by then, you had already left the city. And left it buzzing, I might add."

"Buzzing?" Sorak said.

"The people talk of nothing but how you upset the templars' plans to seize control of the city. You shall not be forgotten in Tyr for a long time. Everyone speaks of Sorak, the nomad. I think you have created the beginnings of a legend."

"Then you left Tyr after we did?" asked Ryana with a frown. "How is it the caravan made so much better time than we, and by a longer route?"

"Because this caravan did not come from Tyr," said Lord Ankhor. "It has come from Gulg by way of Altaruk and is now on its way to Urik. I rode out to meet it at the spring, with part of this company of mercenaries for an escort. Those are my carriages you see there. I had them specially designed. They are light and built for speed. One must move quickly these days to outpace the competition."

"You have business in Urik?" said Sorak. "Is that not dangerous at this time?"

"You mean because King Hamanu covets Tyr?" said Lord Ankhor. He made a dismissive wave with his hand. "The merchant houses are not political. And Hamanu cannot afford to allow political considerations to interfere with trade. His economy depends upon our houses. We have an old saying in the merchant guild: 'Sooner or later, everyone does business with everyone.' Even during times of war, the houses prosper. In some ways, we are more powerful than kings. Of course, it behooves us not to say so."

As they walked through the camp, the people gathered round the cookfires turned to stare at them. The handsome, young Lord Ankhor, with his fine, embroidered robes, was an imposing presence, but Ryana realized that it was she and Sorak who really drew the attention. Most of the people gathered around the fires were employees of the merchant house, veteran mercenaries and hardened caravan drivers, but there were also some passengers on the long journey, and encountering other travelers out in the desert, especially two people traveling alone, was an uncommon occurrence.

Ryana, for her part, tried to ignore their prying eyes. She wrinkled her nose at the odor of roasting animal flesh coming from the spits over the fires. But at the same time, she found with some surprise that it awakened an appetite in her.

They reached Lord Ankhor's spacious tent, which was larger than some of the houses in the warrens of Tyr, and one of the sentries pulled aside the entry flap for them. The interior of the tent was divided into two chambers, separated by a fine tapestry hung between them. The outer chamber housed a table and some chairs along with lamps, writing materials, and ledger scrolls.

"My office on the trail, such as it is," Ankhor explained, conducting them toward the larger, rear chamber of the tent. He pulled aside the tapestry. "Please, come in and make yourselves comfortable. We were about to dine. You would do us an honor if you joined us."

As Sorak and Ryana ducked under the flap of tapestry that Ankhor held aside, they both stopped and stared with amazement at what awaited them. The rear section of the tent was much larger than the front antechamber, and the ground was covered with fine, thick Drajian carpets that were exquisitely worked. Several burning braziers placed around the chamber gave off a warm, intimate glow, the smoke from them curling up through a vent in the tent's roof. The sweet, pungent odor of burning moon-flower leaves came from the braziers, not only per-fuming the air inside the tent, but also serving to keep away annoying insects. Finely worked, comfort-able cushions were scattered about the interior and the long, low table in the center, which stood only about a foot above the tent floor. The table itself was covered with an array of dishes that would have rivaled those served in a sorcerer-king's palace. There were bottles of wine, carafes of water, jars of kank honey, and pots of steaming hot tea made from desert herbs, as well. Lord Ankhor clearly liked to travel in considerable luxury. However, as opulent as the sur-roundings were, it was the other occupants of the tent that drew their immediate attention. Sitting on cushions at the table were two men and a woman.

One of the men was considerably older than the others, with shoulder-length gray hair and a long, though well-groomed beard. His features were lined and gaunt, but his bright blue eyes were alert and energetic in their gaze. He was dressed in a robe every bit as fine as Ankhor's, though much more understated, and on his head he wore a thin chaplet of hammered silver, inscribed with the sign of the House of Ankhor.

The other man was much younger, perhaps in his early- to midtwenties, with dark hair worn to just below the shoulders, and a small, well-trimmed, nar-row black moustache and goatee, no doubt cultivated to make himself look older. He wore a vest of erdlu skin over his bare, well-muscled chest; matching arm guards; soft, striped, kirre skin breeches; and high boots. His jewelry, if not his bearing, revealed him as a young man of considerable social rank, as did the jeweled dagger he wore at his belt.

But the woman was the most striking of the three. She was young, approximately the same age as Ryana, and very fair, with long, extremely fine blond hair that cascaded down her shoulders. Her eyes were a startling indigo, and the beauty of her face was only matched by the perfection of her body. She was clothed in little save a halter of fine blue silk ornamented with gold links and a matching skirt that rode low on her full hips and was slashed deeply up each side, giving maximum freedom of movement and revealing her long, exquisite legs. Her bare feet were smooth and clean, showing no calluses, and her delicate ankles were circled by gold bracelets, as were her wrists and arms.

"We have guests for dinner tonight, my friends," Lord Ankhor said. "Allow me to present Sorak the Nomad, of whom I spoke to you, and his companion, the Priestess . . . forgive me, my lady, but I foolishly neglected to inquire your name."

"Ryana."

"The Priestess Ryana," Ankhor said with a slight bow toward her. "My apologies. Permit me to introduce Lyanus, Minister of Accounts for the House of Ankhor—" the older man nodded toward them as Ankor proceeded with the introductions "—the Viscount Torian, of the first noble family of Gulg—" the dark, bearded, young man acknowledged their bows with a barely perceptible motion of his head "—and last, but by no means the least, Her Highness, the Princess Korahna, youngest daughter of the youngest Queen Consort of His Most Royal Majesty, the Shadow King of Nibenay."

FOUR

As impressive as the assembled company was, the latter introduction took Ryana's breath away. A royal princess of Nibenay, and the daughter of a sorcerer-king, traveling with a merchant caravan! It was absolutely unheard of. The members of the Athasian royal houses rarely left their opulent and well-protected palace compounds, much less their cities, and for this delicate, pampered noble flower to be found on a long journey with a caravan across the entire width of the Athasian tablelands was totally unprecedented. Her presence here not only was shocking, but it also broke with all tradition, and Ryana could not imagine what possible reason the princess could have for being here, or why her family would have allowed it in the first place.

"Please, sit down and join us," said Lord Ankhor.

In her complete surprise and amazement, Ryana was about to comply with the invitation, but Sorak spoke and broke the spell.

"My sincere apologies, Lord Ankhor. I mean no offense against your generous hospitality, but my vows prevent me from breaking bread with a defiler." He avoided looking at the princess, though it was clear to all present that it was she to whom he was referring.

Ryana caught her breath. Her own vows, of course, also abjured her from accepting hospitality from a defiler, though she reminded herself that she had already compromised her vows as a villichi priestess by leaving the convent without permission from Mistress Varanna. Sorak had not taken the villichi vows, but they had both sworn to follow the Way of the Druid and the Path of the Preserver, and those were vows Ryana was determined not to break. Nevertheless, by speaking so, Sorak had pronounced an unutterable insult against the Royal House of Nibenay. It was an unforgivable offense.

Surprisingly, the Viscount Torian chuckled. "Well, the elfling certainly has nerve—I will grant him that."

Of course, Ryana thought, it was not his house that had been insulted. The noble families of Gulg, like those of other cities, were merely aristocrats, not royalty, and if any of them were students or practitioners of the defiler arts, they knew well enough to keep it secret. She looked to the princess for her response, fully expecting outraged fury and a demand that Sorak's offending tongue, if not his life, be forfeit. Instead, the princess stunned her even more by her reply.

"Lord Ankhor is too well versed in the intricacies of diplomacy and social intercourse to commit such a blunder as inviting followers of the Way to break bread with a defiler," she said smoothly, her voice as silky as her fine, revealing garments. "Doubtless, you have been wondering what a Royal Princess of Nibenay is

doing on a journey with a caravan. I have been exiled
from my homeland for committing the unpardonable
offense of taking an oath to follow the Druid Way. It
would be no breach of your vows to break bread at this
table. I, too, am a follower."

"*You?*" said Ryana. "But you are the daughter of a
sorcerer-king! How is that possible?"

"My mother gave birth to me when she was very
young," Princess Korahna replied, "and her disposition was such that she could not be bothered with the
raising of a child. Indeed, such is often the way in
royal families, I am told. I was given to a nurse to
raise—one of the palace templars—and quite against
tradition, she taught me how to read. Although the
templars work for defilers, they keep within their
libraries copies of the writings of preservers, the better to understand their opposition. At the age of thirteen, I found some of those writings in the library and
began to study them in secret, out of curiosity at first.
In the end, I was converted."

"But the oath of the Path of the Preserver must be
administered by a preserver," said Ryana, fascinated.

"And so it was," the princess replied. "I had taken
to disguising myself and stealing out of the palace
grounds late at night in hopes of finding a mentor for
my studies. I managed to make contact with the
Veiled Alliance. After their initial shock upon learning my identity, they were quick to realize the value
in having the converted daughter of a sorcerer-king
as a member. Still, they were suspicious, and it took a
long time for me to gain their trust. In time, they
came to realize I was sincere and administered the
oath to me.

"But quite by accident, my mother discovered my secret life. For teaching me to read, my templar nurse was executed. When I learned of this, I made plans to publicly renounce my family and announce myself a preserver, but before I was able to do so, my mother had me placed under arrest and exiled from the city."

"And your father?" Sorak asked. "What was his response?"

"I do not know," Korahna said. "I am certain that my mother has not even told him, but once they have learned of my fate, the members of the Veiled Alliance are sure to make it public. Nibenay does not concern himself much with his family these days, but he is certain to hear of it. I do not envy my mother when he finds out."

"Where will you go now?" Ryana asked.

"Wherever Lord Ankhor sees fit to conduct me," she replied simply. "In a manner of speaking, he is my jailor for the duration of this journey."

"Now, Your Highness, you do me a grave injustice. You know that is not so," protested Ankhor. "You will give our guests the wrong impression." Turning to Sorak and Ryana, he explained, "The House of Ankhor was employed, through intermediaries, by the queen consort herself to escort her daughter on this journey and give her safe conduct. I am by no means her jailor and, as you can see if you only look around you, this is hardly a jail cell."

"Are you not afraid of what the Shadow King will do when he learns of your involvement?" Sorak asked.

Ankhor merely shrugged. "I have committed no crime," he said. "In fact, I really had no choice in the matter. The House of Ankhor was hardly in a position

to refuse a commission from one of the queen consorts. That would have been a grievous insult to the
Royal House of Nibenay. To the best of my knowledge, I was merely acting in accordance with the
Shadow King's desires, expressed through his youngest
queen."

"You know very well that is not so!" Korahna said.

"Ah, but do I really know that, Your Highness?"
Ankhor replied. "My representatives in Nibenay
accepted the commission in good faith on behalf of our
house from your mother, the queen consort. They saw
to it that you were safely conducted to Gulg and
received a first-class berth with this caravan. Viscount
Torian himself chose to escort you, in token of the long-
standing relationship between his family and our merchant house. I, myself, have only just met you for the
first time."

"And you know how the situation stands, because I
have told you," the princess said.

"You have also told me that you are a self-avowed
preserver and an exile from your own kingdom as a
result," Ankhor said calmly. "Under the circumstances,
surely I could hardly be blamed for thinking that those
were your father's wishes."

"As I have said, Lord Ankhor is well versed in the
intricacies of diplomacy," Korahna said. "Especially
when it comes to turning those skills to his own
ends. I trust my mother paid the House of Ankhor
well."

"Very well, indeed," Viscount Torian said. "I fail to
see the reason for your bitterness, Your Highness.
Doubtless, your mother was afraid of what the Shadow
King would do when he learned of your treachery, for

that is how he would see it, surely. A mother's first instinct is to protect her child. She merely wanted to see you out of harm's way."

"And so she cast my fate upon the winds," Korahna said bitterly.

"With all due respect, Your Highness," Torian replied, "you did that yourself when you first made contact with the Veiled Alliance. In Nibenay, as it is in Gulg, that is a crime punishable by death. You stuck your own head in the noose. You should be grateful to your mother, for it was she who saved your life. Or did you think your father would simply wink at such activities on his daughter's part? The Shadow King has more children by his many consorts than my entire family has servants. I doubt the loss of one errant daughter, especially one who has become a profound embarrassment to the Royal House, would concern him greatly."

Ryana followed this conversation with fascination. Sorak merely kept quiet, listening in what appeared to be a distracted manner. She strongly suspected, however, that he was not merely listening. Undoubtedly, he allowed the Guardian to probe the minds of Ankhor, Torian, and Korahna so that he could ascertain the truth. What truly amazed her, however, was Ankhor's offhandedness about the whole thing. He was not in the least bit concerned about this discussion taking place in front of them. But then again, she thought, why should he be? His position is secure. His house had accepted a commission from the queen consort. To refuse it would have been an insult. Insofar as that went, he was right. He, or Torian and his representatives, truly had no choice.

And if his conduct was called into question, he had no need to concern himself about their bearing witness to it. They were both preservers, and knew what their fate would be if they fell into the hands of a defiler king.

"Must we speak of such depressing matters?" Ankhor said. "We will merely bore our guests. Come, we have a fine dinner set before us, and the wine is of an excellent vintage. Let us enjoy ourselves."

"Indeed," Torian agreed. He turned to Sorak. "So you are the one who foiled the marauder plot to sack the caravan from Tyr. I would be most anxious to hear the details of that story."

"There is little to tell," Sorak replied. "I merely stumbled on the plot and reported my discovery to the Tyrian Council of Advisors."

"Surely there is more to it than that," Torian said. He glanced at Ryana. "I suspect, Priestess, that your friend is being overly modest."

"He has never been much given to conversation," Ryana replied.

"An admirable trait," Torian replied. "Though it does make things a bit one-sided over dinner. What of yourself? Where are you bound on your pilgrimage?"

Ryana hesitated slightly and glanced at the princess, who had fallen into a sullen silence. "Nibenay," she said.

At that, Korahna glanced up briefly, then quickly averted her gaze.

"Indeed? That is a long journey," Torian replied. "A pity we cannot accommodate you. This caravan is on its way to Urik."

"So Lord Ankhor told us," said Ryana. "However,

we are grateful for your hospitality. We shall be resuming our journey in the morning."

"Nibenay is far less hospitable to preservers than is the House of Ankhor," Torian said.

"True enough," Lord Ankhor agreed, "but villichi priestesses do not practice magic, and while their order is devoted to the Druid Way, they are not political. Which is to say, my lady, that while you may not find a ready welcome there, it is unlikely that you shall be molested."

Ryana did not bother to tell him that she was not really on a pilgrimage, at least, not in the way he thought, and that in seeking the Sage, they were embarked upon a quest that was very "political," indeed.

"I am surprised you chose the northern route around the mountains," Torian said. "The southern route, by way of Altaruk and Gulg, would have been shorter."

"The route across the Stony Barrens and over the Barrier Mountains will be shorter still," she said.

Ankhor and Torian both sat up straighter and stared at her with astonishment. "You plan to cross the barrens?" Ankhor said. "With all due respect, my lady, that would be most unwise."

"It would be worse than unwise," said Torian. "It would be insane."

"What my young friend means . . ." began Ankhor, in an effort to soften Torian's remarks, but Torian interrupted him.

"I said precisely what I meant," he said. He glanced at Sorak. "If you plan to take the priestess through the barrens, then you take her to her death. No man who has attempted to cross the barrens has ever lived to tell the tale."

"But I am not a man, my lord," Ryana said. "And neither is my friend. He is an elfling."

"We do not question your abilities, my lady," said Lord Ankhor. "It is well known that priestesses of the villichi order are trained from childhood to deal with all manner of adversities, and Sorak here, beyond a doubt, is quite capable and possesses great powers of endurance. But consider the terrain you plan to cross. There is no more rugged and dangerous ground in all of Athas than the Stony Barrens. You will find no forage for yourselves or for your mount. There is no water. The ground is very rocky and difficult to traverse. It is impossible to move quickly. During the day, the sun bakes the barrens until the heat will roast your feet right through your shoes. And that is to say nothing of the predators that lurk there."

"And even if, by some miracle, you should survive the barrens, you will still need to cross the mountains on the other side," Torian added. "And take it from one who has traveled in those mountains—it is no easy journey. Nor is it a safe one. Of course, if you try to cross the barrens, you need not worry about crossing the mountains safely. You shall never reach them."

"He is right," said Ankhor. "On a map, it is true, the journey may appear much shorter, but a map does not tell the entire story. And no one has ever mapped out the barrens. I urge you, in the strongest terms, to reconsider."

Ryana was about to reply, but Sorak spoke first. "Doubtless, you and my lord Torian are much more familiar with the country in these parts than we are, and we are grateful for your warning. What route would you advise we take instead?"

Ryana glanced at him with surprise, but said nothing.

"Well, from here, whether you travel by the northern or the southern route, the distance would be about the same," said Ankhor. "However, if you took the southern route, you would be able to stop at Altaruk and rest for a few days until you continued on your journey. The village of Altaruk is the seat of our merchant empire. Mention my name and you will find a warm welcome at the house of my father for as long as you may care to stay."

"And you may break your journey once again at Gulg," said Torian, "where you would receive a welcome at my family's estate, as well."

"You are both most kind and generous," said Sorak. "We shall take the southern route, then, and do as you suggest."

"Well, that is a relief," said Ankhor. "To think, if Torian had not asked about your route . . . We shall not think of what might have transpired."

"It was fortunate for us, then, that we met you," Sorak said. "Whatever debt you may have felt you owed me, consider it repaid."

Ankhor smiled. "Excellent. I do so like it when accounts are balanced. You plan to leave first thing in the morning, then?"

"Yes, since we are to take a longer route, it would be best if we started early," Sorak said.

"Well, I am not an early riser, myself," said Ankhor, "so I shall not take offense if you have already departed when I wake. We shall say our farewells tonight, then, and I shall see to it that fresh packs of provisions are prepared for you. May I offer you the use of one of my tents for your accommodations tonight?"

"Thank you," said Sorak, "but you have already been gracious enough. It is a warm night, and we prefer to sleep under the stars, in the druid manner. We shall make our camp on the far side of the spring, where our early departure will not disturb the others."

"As you wish," said Ankhor. "And now, Torian, I really must tell you how our friend, here, saved me from losing my shirt to a devilishly clever cardsharp in a Tyrian gaming house known as the Crystal Spider. . . ."

As they left Lord Ankhor's tent, carrying the packs he had prepared for them, they circled round the pool of the oasis, heading toward the area where the kanks had been staked down. Ryana glanced at Sorak and said, "You were disingenuous with our host. The Guardian found him to be untrustworthy?"

"I found that Lord Ankhor can be trusted to look after his own interests," the Guardian replied, coming to the fore to reply to her directly.

"And the Viscount Torian?"

"The Viscount Torian possesses a great deal of self-confidence," the Guardian said. "He had anticipated the possibility of having his thoughts probed, although he had expected you to be the one to probe them. Telepathy is not one of your talents, of course, but Torian knew that villichi sometimes manifest telepathy as one of their psionic gifts. He did not know if yours was such a gift, but he was prepared for that eventuality."

"You mean he was able to shield himself?" Ryana asked.

"Quite the contrary," the Guardian replied. "He kept his thoughts unguarded to show his confidence and display his forthrightness. A most interesting young man. Few people feel so secure with themselves."

"And what did you find when you looked into his thoughts?"

"Self-interest and a pride born of a sense of his own worth, as well as a strong sense of patriotism for his city. The Viscount Torian is an ambitious man, but he knows how to temper that ambition with a strong dose of practicality and realism. In Princess Korahna, he sees a valuable opportunity. That is why he chose to escort her personally on this journey."

"What sort of opportunity?"

"The cities of Gulg and Nibenay have a long-standing rivalry, in part born of a conflict over the resources of the Barrier Mountains, and in part as a result of the antipathy of their respective rulers. If Torian were to marry Korahna, he would then have a princess of the Royal House of Nibenay to strengthen his standing not only in Gulg, but in Nibenay, as well. In the past, the Shadow King has not allowed any male children borne by his wives to live, to ensure that none of them could ever threaten his throne. His female children, when they reached the age Korahna is right now, were all taken into the ranks of his templars. Torian knows that since the Shadow King embarked upon his dragon metamorphosis, he has shown no interest in any of his wives. Korahna is the last child he will ever sire. Should Korahna bear a male child by Torian, he would be the only rightful heir to the throne of Nibenay."

"I see," Ryana said. "And what of the princess? Or do her desires not count in Torian's plans?"

They bent down to fill their water bags at the oasis pool. "Torian is confident that he can win the princess by making her come to feel dependent on him. She is a plum that has fallen into his outstretched hand. She has never been away from home before, and now she has been exiled by her own mother. The nurse who raised her has been executed, and she has been separated from her friends in the Alliance. She has no one. Torian intends to take advantage of that fact to insinuate himself into her affections. Once he has done so, he plans to wed her and return with her to Gulg, where as his wife, she can bear him a son to claim succession to the throne of Nibenay."

"And what of Korahna's taking the vows of a preserver?" asked Ryana.

"He does not see that as an impediment," the Guardian replied. "He suspects that it may be no more than a youthful indiscretion, but if not, it is something he can still turn to his advantage. A successor to the throne who is raised as a preserver would win ready support among the downtrodden people of the Shadow King. And such an heir would receive the backing of the Veiled Alliance, as well."

Ryana nodded. "Yes, I can see that. The Viscount Torian is, indeed, ambitious. Clever, too."

"And utterly unscrupulous," the Guardian added. "Torian has no sympathies for either preservers or defilers. He would follow whichever path gave him the most advantage. Torian cares only about Torian."

"Poor Korahna," Ryana said. "Though she has been raised in pampered luxury, I still feel sorry for her. It

seems not even princesses are immune to the machina-
tions of ambitious men."

As they made their way to a stand of palm trees
where they would bed down for the night, Sorak
came to the fore once again. "Korahna has no intention of allowing herself to become a pawn in Torian's
game. She is perceptive, and knows just what his
intentions are."

"What will she do?"

"Escape," said Sorak. "In fact, she plans to do it
tonight."

"But how?" Ryana asked. "Where would she go, in
the middle of the desert?"

"With us," said Sorak, "across the Stony Barrens."

"*What?*" said Ryana with disbelief.

"Torian would never suspect a pampered princess of
planning to escape into the desert," Sorak said. "There
are but two guards at the entrance to her tent. She
plans to cut her way out the back and come to us
tonight."

"What makes her think that we shall take her with
us?"

"We are fellow preservers," Sorak said. "She cannot
believe we would refuse, especially after we have seen
how the situation stands. And even if we did refuse,
she could accuse us of trying to steal her away."

"Then we must leave at once," Ryana said, gathering
her things.

"No," said Sorak. "We shall wait and take her with
us."

Ryana stared at him with astonishment. "Have you
lost your mind? Ankhor's mercenaries would be on
our trail in an instant!"

"But they would seek us on the southern route, to Altaruk," said Sorak. "After taking pains to tell us of the dangers we would face if we tried to cross the Stony Barrens, they would never think that we had gone that way, especially with the princess."

"This is madness!" said Ryana. "That pampered palace flower could not survive a trek across the barrens. She would only slow us down, and doubtless burden us with her complaints every step of the way."

"I thought you felt sorry for her," Sorak said.

"Perhaps, but she would be far better off with Torian than with us on a trek across the barrens. What purpose would be served in taking her with us? Or is it that you have become taken with her beauty?"

"Jealousy does not become you, Ryana," Sorak said. "If I were capable of being smitten by a woman, that woman would be you. But you know that could never be, however I may wish it. It is not Korahna's beauty I desire, but her connections with the Veiled Alliance in Nibenay. She could make our task much easier."

"So instead of being Torian's pawn, she will be ours," said Ryana.

"That, too, is unjust," said Sorak. "She longs to return home, to her friends in the Alliance, the only friends she has ever truly known. They can protect her and provide her a home. We shall take her to them. In return, we ask only for an introduction. That is more than a fair exchange, and no one shall be used."

Ryana took a deep breath and expelled it in a heavy sigh. "I cannot argue with your logic," she said. "But I do not relish the prospect of dragging a spoiled princess

across the Stony Barrens. The journey shall be hazardous enough without her."

"True," Sorak agreed. "But quite aside from the fact
that bringing her along will serve our purpose, you
know as well as I that it is the proper thing to do.
Spoiled or not, pampered or not, princess or not, she is
a fellow preserver, and we cannot turn a deaf ear to her
request for aid."

"No, we cannot," Ryana admitted sullenly. "She
knows it, too. But what if she is caught trying to escape?"

"Then we can do nothing," Sorak said. "It is up to
her to make her bid for freedom. After that, she will
have ample opportunity to test her commitment to her
preserver vow. We shall wait until an hour before first
light. If she has not joined us by then, we shall be on
our way. Lie down and get some rest. The Watcher will
remain on the alert."

They did not have long to wait. The campfires
burned low as the caravan bedded down for the
night and silence descended upon the oasis. Shortly
after midnight, Ryana awoke to Sorak's hand gently
squeezing her arm. She came awake immediately,
sitting up quickly, and saw him press a finger to his
lips. A moment later, she heard the soft sound of
light footsteps approaching. A shadowy, hunched
figure in a dark cloak moved across the ground,
searching the area.

"Korahna," Sorak said, softly, as she drew near.

She froze for a moment, then saw them and quickly
made her way toward the stand of palm trees.

"You *expected* me?" she said, with surprise. Then an
expression of sudden comprehension flickered across
her hooded features. "Of course," she said, looking at

Ryana. "You read my thoughts."

Before Ryana could correct her, Sorak said, "We must not lose any time. We shall depart at once. I will get the kank." He moved off quickly into the darkness.

"I am profoundly grateful to you for your aid," Korahna said. "And I can understand the reason for haste. Ankhor's mercenaries will give chase when they learn that I am gone. We must gain time to outdistance their pursuit."

Ryana said nothing. She merely looked at the princess, who had brought nothing with her in the way of provisions, not even a water bag. The jeweled dagger she wore at her waist was clearly more an ornament than a weapon. It was doubtful that she knew how to use it. She wore a light cloak and the same silky costume she had worn to dinner, and on her delicate feet she wore merely a pair of light sandals. Walking in the desert, those sandals would not last even a day. In the barrens, they would be shredded in no time at all. They did not need this added burden. Perhaps Sorak was right and the princess would be of help to them in contacting the Alliance once they reached Nibenay, but looking at her, Ryana had grave doubts that Korahna would last out the journey. She would be an enormous handicap to them.

Sorak returned shortly with the kank following behind. There was a soft thump as something landed in the dirt at Korahna's feet. "Put these on," said Sorak.

Korahna looked down and saw a pair of thick, hide moccasins lying at her feet.

"Those flimsy sandals will not last an hour in the desert," Sorak said. "I took these off a guard watching the pack beasts. By the time he is discovered, bound and gagged, we shall be long gone."

Korahna looked up at Sorak with disbelief. "You expect me to wear the footgear of a caravan guard?" she said with disgust. "Once his filthy feet have soiled them?"

"You will find it preferable to going barefoot in the barrens," Sorak said.

"The barrens?" she said. "But . . . I thought. . . . Surely, you do not still plan to go that way?"

"If we were to take the southern route, the mercenaries would run us down by midday, at the latest," Sorak said. "This way, we stand a chance of eluding them."

"But . . . no one has ever crossed the barrens and lived!" Korahna said.

"Then we shall be the first," said Sorak. "Or you can remain behind with Torian, marry him, and bear his child so that he will have a claim on Nibenay. The choice is yours. But decide now. We are going."

A look of panic came into Korahna's eyes. "Wait! At least give me time enough to lace up these moccasins!"

She crouched, removed her sandals, tied them to her gold link belt, and, wrinkling her nose, proceeded to lace up the moccasins Sorak had taken from the guard. Sorak had already started to move off with the kank. Ryana lingered a moment, looking at the princess, then followed him. Moments later, Korahna came running to catch up with them. They headed away from the oasis, due east.

"Will we not ride?" Korahna said.

"When we have gone some distance from the spring," said Sorak. "In the meantime, keep to the loose, sandy ground. The wind will cover our tracks completely in an hour or so, and by then we should

have reached the outskirts of the barrens. Avoid stepping on anything that grows, lest you break a twig that
could give away our trail to a tracker."

"These moccasins are too big," Korahna said.

"Did you lace them tightly?" Sorak asked.

"Yes, but what if I get blisters on my heels?"

"Then you shall have to walk upon your toes," said
Sorak.

"How dare you take such a tone with me? You will
address me as Your Highness!"

"Why? I am not your subject."

"But I am a princess!"

"One without a kingdom, at the moment," Sorak
reminded her. "I am not Torian, and have no pressing
need to curry favor with you. Remember, it is you who
came to us to ask a boon. We have granted it because
you took a vow as a preserver. To me, that is all that
matters."

Korahna turned to Ryana and asked, "What have I
done that he must treat me so rudely?"

"You have become an unnecessary burden to us,"
said Ryana. "And a source of annoyance, besides. If I
were you, I would cease complaining and conserve my
energy. You will need all you have for the journey still
ahead of us."

Korahna gazed at Ryana helplessly, surprised to find
support lacking from another woman, and a fellow
preserver, at that. She fell silent and walked along
behind them, taking care to watch where she stepped,
so that she would leave no broken plants to give away
their trail, as Sorak had cautioned her.

It was not long before she began to fall behind. Sorak
slowed his pace somewhat, but did not stop for her.

Ryana grew more and more impatient. Torian was no fool, and Ankhor's mercenaries knew their trade. Doubtless, there were good trackers among them, and though they would undoubtedly assume that they had taken the southern trail to Altaruk, it probably would not be very long before they realized their error. However, even mercenaries would hesitate to follow them into the barrens, and the sooner they reached them, the safer they would be. Safe from pursuit, at least, Ryana reminded herself, for there would be little safety in the barrens.

After a little over an hour's time, they had reached the outskirts of the barrens, where the ground gradually became more broken and irregular. They still had at least four hours or so before dawn. Ryana glanced back to see how well the princess was keeping up. Not very well. As Korahna hurried to catch up with them, she suddenly saw Ryana unlimbering her crossbow and quickly fitting a bolt. She stopped, and her eyes grew wide as she saw Ryana draw back the bow and raise it in one smooth motion.

"What are you doing? *No! Don't!*"

The crossbow bolt flew through the air with a whizzing sound, passing inches from Korahna's head as she cried out and, with a soft *thwok*, struck something just behind her. Korahna turned just in time to see a medium-sized drake falling over onto its side, the bolt from Ryana's crossbow embedded deep in its reptilian brain. It was about six feet long and as thick in the body as a man. It spasmed on the rock-strewn ground, its tail thrashing behind it in death reflex. Korahna cried out and recoiled from the creature, throwing her hands up to her face.

"If I had not thought to turn around, that would have been the end of you, Your Highness," Ryana said, stressing her title in a sarcastic tone. "Do try to keep up, won't you?"

"That horrible beast!" Korahna said. "You saved my life!"

"Can we proceed now?" Sorak said.

He saw that Korahna was already limping slightly as she came up. The moccasins were thick, but her delicate feet were clearly unaccustomed to the task of walking in the desert. He crouched before her and unlaced the left moccasin. She rested a hand lightly on his shoulder to balance herself as he raised her left foot to examine it. There was a large blister on her heel that had ruptured. It had to be quite painful for her, yet she had not uttered one word of complaint.

"Perhaps you had better ride for a while," he said, as he laced the moccasin back up. "I will examine your foot later in case the wound should fester, but it is better not to stop now."

Korahna glanced at the kank with trepidation. "I have never ridden on a kank," she said. "Torian had a carriage for me. . . ."

"Ryana," Sorak said. "Put her up behind you."

Ryana mounted the kank, then helped Korahna up. "Just settle your weight and hold onto my waist until you become accustomed to the gait," she said. She looked at Sorak. "What about you?"

"There is no point in overburdening the kank," he said. "I will go on foot. The kank cannot move quickly across this broken ground. It will be no hardship to keep up."

They continued on. The ground became more irregular

and rocky as they traveled, heading east and going deeper into the barrens. The kank did not move much more quickly than they had when they were walking and being slowed down by Korahna. The giant beetle had to pick its way carefully over the rock-strewn terrain, which only grew worse. At some time in the distant past of Athas, a glacier must have moved across the desert, and here it stopped, depositing the rocks it had torn up from the soil in its slow advance. Before long, following a straight course became impossible, and they had to wind their way among the boulders in a serpentine manner.

Ryana had to give the princess credit. She had expected ceaseless whining and complaining, but Korahna kept silent, even though her foot must have pained her, and her rounded buttocks, more accustomed to soft litter cushions and thick beds than the hard, ridged armor of a kank's thorax, must have been quite sore. Before long, the sky began to lighten as the sun's rays started to tint the horizon.

"How long before they discover you are missing, assuming they did not find you gone during the night?" Ryana asked.

"I have never been disturbed after I retired to my tent," Korahna said. "Torian gave strict orders on that account. And Ankhor said that he is not an early riser. Still, the caravan drivers were all awake and at their cookfires by the time I dressed and joined the others. Torian always came to see that I had risen, though he would merely call my name from outside the tent. And that was perhaps two hours after dawn."

"Then we still have a few hours before they discover

you are missing," said Ryana, calculating mentally. "Assuming that they mount a quick pursuit and send a party down the southern route in an attempt to over-take us, that should add perhaps another few hours before they realize their mistake. The caravan is not likely to depart without you, so they will wait back at the spring until the pursuing party has returned. That will add a few hours more. With luck, we shall have almost a full day's start on them if they decide to fol-low us into the barrens."

"Do you think they shall?" Korahna asked.

"Perhaps not," Ryana said, "but if I were Torian, I would. You are too valuable a prize for him to give up so easily, and he struck me as an ambitious and deter-mined man."

"I knew what he wanted," said Korahna. "I never would have given it to him."

"Then when he wearied of employing patience, he would have taken it by force," Ryana said. "That is what men do. At least, so I have heard."

"Sorak seems different," said Korahna, watching him as he walked ahead of them.

"That is because he *is* different," said Ryana.

"He is not your mate?"

"Villichi do not take mates."

"And yet you love him."

"What makes you think so?"

"I can hear it in your voice when you speak of him. And I can see it your eyes when you look upon him. I may be young, but I am a woman, and a woman knows such things. I have not lived so sheltered a life as you may suppose. At least, not in recent years."

"Sorak is like my brother. We grew up together."

"You do not look at him as if he were your brother."

"And if that is so, then what concern is it of yours?" Ryana asked sharply.

"It is no concern of mine," Korahna said softly. "I was merely trying to know you better. I did not intend to give offense."

Ryana said nothing.

"What have I done to cause you to dislike me?" asked Korahna.

"It is not you so much as what you are," Ryana said.

"A princess," said Korahna. "An aristocrat?"

"A woman who has never learned to take care of herself," Ryana said. "One who has lived in idle, pampered luxury all her life, supported in her comforts by the toil of others, her wants and needs secured at the expense of those less fortunate than herself."

"That is all too true," Korahna said, "and yet my fate was not of my own choosing. I could not help the manner in which I was born. I chose neither my father nor my mother. And for much of my life, I was ignorant of how others lived. I thought that everyone lived much the same as I did. I was fifteen years old before I ever set foot outside the palace compound, and that in stealth, at no small risk to myself. When I saw how most of the people really lived, I was deeply shocked and moved to tears. I had never realized. . . . I knew then that things were wrong in Nibenay and vowed that if it was in my power to change them, I would do everything I could to try. But I knew that I was ill equipped for such an effort. In that regard, you are so much more fortunate than I."

"I?" Ryana said. "More fortunate than you?"

"I would give anything to have been born with your

gifts," Korahna said. "The villichi reside in the Ringing Mountains, do they not?"

"Yes," Ryana said.

"To live free in the mountains, to walk in the forest and sit by a stream, listening to the water over the rocks . . . I have never even seen a stream, only a spring in an oasis. I was taught nothing of the land or of the wild beasts. I was never taught to cook, or sew, or weave. Such things are beneath a princess, I was told, though I would have loved to learn them. And if a princess cannot even cook or sew, then she surely cannot fight. My body is soft and weak, while yours is strong and firm. I could not even draw that crossbow that you wield so expertly, and I would probably lack the strength even to lift your sword. I despise the life that I have lived, and I envy yours. I would trade places with you in an instant. Would you be so quick to take my place?"

Ryana did not answer for a moment, studying her companion. Then, after a pause, she replied simply and cooly, "Of course not."

"You think I want to go back so that I may resume my former life?" Korahna said. "So that I may beg forgiveness from my mother and renounce the vow I took? No. I would rather die out here in the desert, which I yet may do. But if I survive this journey, I return to Nibenay not to resume my former life, but to begin a new one, not as a princess, but a preserver in the service of the Veiled Alliance. I know no magic, that is true, but I may yet be of some value to them because of who I am. And if my only use to them is as a symbol, then so be it. It is better than being of no use whatsoever."

Again, Ryana did not respond immediately. In spite of herself, she was warming to the princess. "I may have misjudged you," she said at last.

"I could not blame you if you did," Korahna said. "In truth, I do not know if anyone could truly judge her life as harshly as I have judged my own."

"Perhaps not," Ryana said. "But it is never too late to begin anew. One can always learn, if the desire is there."

"I have that desire. Would you teach me?"

"Teach you what?"

"Everything! How to be more like you."

Ryana had to smile. "That would take quite a bit of teaching."

"Then teach me what you say I lack the most," Korahna said. "Teach me how to take care of myself. Show me how to fight!"

Ryana laughed. "And this from a woman who moments earlier said she could not even lift a sword!"

"If you will show me how, then I shall make the effort," said Korahna.

"You say that now," Ryana said, "but when it comes time to make the effort, you may sing a different tune."

"I won't."

"Truly?"

"Truly."

Ryana drew her sword. "Very well," she said. "Take this." She handed it over her shoulder, to Korahna. "We will have our first lesson."

"*On the back of a kank?*"

"It will serve as well as any other place. You said you wished to learn."

"I do."

"Fine, then. Hold the sword out away from your body, at arm's length."

She heard Korahna grunt softly as she complied, holding it in her right hand. "It is heavier than it appears."

"It will grow heavier still."

"Now what?"

"Just hold it there."

"For how long?"

"Until I say that you can put it down."

They rode awhile that way, with Korahna holding the sword out away from her body, and Ryana glancing over her shoulder every now and then to check on her. Little by little, the sword began to drop as Korahna's arm wearied of the effort, but each time Ryana glanced at her, she gamely raised it once again, gritting her teeth with the effort. Finally, when her arm could take the strain no more, the sword began to waver in her grasp and it dropped lower and lower as her arm bent, unable to keep it up any longer. Ryana glanced over her shoulder to see Korahna's eyes squeezed tightly shut, her lips compressed, her face turning red as she struggled to hold the sword up.

"All right, you may lower it," she said.

Expelling her breath heavily, Korahna lowered the sword, resting it against the kank's hard shell. She took a deep breath and exhaled heavily once more. "My arm feels as if it is on fire!" she said, with a soft moan.

"Sore?" asked Ryana.

"Exceedingly so."

"Good. Now take the sword in your other hand and raise it with your left arm."

"My . . . left arm?"

"The proper response is, 'Yes, Sister,'" Ryana said. "Come, come." She snapped her fingers sharply.

Korahna sighed heavily. "Yes, Sister," she said, with resignation and raised the sword with her left arm.

Ryana smiled. Pampered, maybe, she thought. But spoiled? Perhaps not. Time would tell.

FIVE

By midday, they were well into the barrens. The terrain was difficult, and the going slow. Though the kank was surefooted and able to negotiate the rocky ground, its distress was clearly evident to Sorak, if not to Ryana and the princess. The Stony Barrens had been aptly named. Nothing grew here. At first, they had seen the occasional clumps of scraggly vegetation, but by now, they were traveling over terrain that was completely bare, and the kank knew that it would find no forage. All they could see for miles and miles was broken rock.

Sorak picked his way among the larger boulders, but even where he found ground that wasn't rocky, there was barely any soil visible at all. Where there wasn't jagged rock, his feet crunched down on gravel. And as the day wore on, the merciless dark sun beat down upon the rocks until Sorak could feel the heat through his thick hide moccasins. He did not wish to overburden the kank, which was already carrying two riders. At the same time, he knew it would not be long before his footgear was completely shredded by the rocky ground. Though his feet were hard and callused, he did not relish the thought of going across the barrens barefoot.

The temperature had climbed steadily throughout the morning until now, with the sun at its zenith, it seemed to Sorak as if his perspiration would boil away into steam as it dripped down his cheeks onto the ground. The heat was truly oppressive. Ryana rode the kank in silence, her body rocking slightly with the movements of the beast, while the princess leaned against her back, her head turned to one side, her eyes closed, her breathing slow and labored. Sorak had to give Korahna her due. She was clearly suffering in the sweltering heat, yet she had not uttered one word of complaint.

"It was foolish of us to come this way," said Eyron. "There is no end in sight to this hellish field of broken rock. We should have gone around it."

"The spell of the scroll indicated that we must follow this direction," Sorak replied, speaking to Eyron internally.

"Why?" Eyron persisted. "What is to be served by it? What will be gained if we suffocate from heat and die out here in this desolate wasteland?"

"We shall not die," Sorak replied. "The Sage would not have shown this way to us without a purpose. Perhaps that purpose was a test of our abilities and our resolve. We must not fail it."

"Perhaps the Sage does not wish to be found," said Eyron. "Have you ever thought of that? Perhaps this is merely his way of ensuring that you cannot seek him out. Perhaps he means for us to die here in these barrens."

"I cannot believe that," Sorak said. "If the Sage is unwilling to be found, then there seems little point to his discouraging our efforts in such a drastic manner. The defilers have been seeking the Sage for years, and yet they have never found him."

"So then what makes you think you will succeed?" asked Eyron.

"We shall succeed because the Sage will want us to succeed," said Sorak. "He shall guide our way, as he is doing even now."

"But how do you know it is the Sage who is our guide?" said Eyron. "The scroll came from the Alliance. What proof have you that it is genuine? It may be some plan of theirs to mislead us."

"I suppose that is possible," admitted Sorak, "but I believe it most unlikely. If there was some reason why the Alliance did not wish us to succeed in our quest for the Sage, they needed only to claim ignorance. There was no need for them to give us the scroll."

"Unless they wanted to dispose of us obligingly in the Stony Barrens," Eyron said.

"Enough, Eyron," said the Guardian. "You have made your point, and there is no need to belabor it. Besides, it is too late to turn back now."

"She's right," said Sorak. "If we were to turn back now, all this would have been for nothing, and we would only encounter Torian and his mercenaries, who are doubtless searching for the princess."

"There's another thing," said Eyron. "Why did we need to drag that useless baggage along with us? She is only an unnecessary burden. She did not even bring food or water with her. She will merely deplete our supplies."

"She will be necessary when we reach Nibenay," said Sorak. "Besides, she is not nearly as much of a burden at the moment as are you. I had expected complaints from Korahna, being as she had lived in pampered luxury all of her life and knows nothing of hardship, but she has not complained at all, whereas I have to listen to your pathetic whining. Look to *the princess for your example, Eyron. She is not afraid."*

"Eyron is af-ray-aid, Eyron is af-ray-aid," Lyric taunted in a singsong voice.

"Be silent, you miserable whelp!"

"Eyron is a cow-ard, Eyron is a cow-ard!"

"Will you two stop?" Kivara's shout echoed through Sorak's mind. "I am trying to sleep, and you are giving me a headache!"

"That will be quite enough from everyone," the Guardian said, exerting firm control as the other voices all fell silent. "Sorak needs his energy for the journey ahead. He does not need all of you adding to his troubles."

"Thank you," Sorak said.

"You are welcome," said the Guardian. "If you are growing tired, perhaps you should rest for a while and allow the Ranger the fore."

"I will rest later," Sorak said. "Besides, I have much thinking to do."

"You are concerned about Torian."

"Yes. By now, he surely will have realized we went across the barrens, if he did not see through our plan from the very start."

"You think he will follow?"

"I am sure of it. I did not tell Ryana and the princess, for I saw no point in worrying them any further, but I would be very much surprised if Torian did not embark upon our trail as soon as he realized which way we had gone. He did not strike me as the sort who would discourage easily."

"Nor me," the Guardian agreed. "The question remains, would the mercenaries follow him across the barrens?"

"Given enough incentive, they probably would," said Sorak. "And Torian has more than enough money to provide that. If not, Ankhor will undoubtedly back him."

"*Undoubtedly,*" the Guardian agreed again. "*Still, we have a good start on them. They may not be able to catch up.*"

"*I was wondering about that,*" Sorak said. "*It would depend upon whether or not Torian believed we had taken the southern route. If so, and the pursuit was sent in that direction, then chances are we have placed enough miles between us to outdistance pursuit. But if not. . . .*"

"*Then Torian may catch us?*"

"*It is possible. We still have at least five or six hours' start on them if they did not pursue us down the southern route. It would depend on how hard he drove his mercenaries. There is no way of knowing how long it will take us to cross the barrens. The maps do not give an exact distance. If Torian's men were to travel all night, or most of the night, they could make up the time within a day or two. Three, at the very most.*"

"*Then perhaps we should travel through the night, as well,*" the Guardian suggested.

"*There is much to argue for that,*" Sorak said. "*However, while it poses no great hardship to the tribe, Ryana and the princess would wear out quickly, especially Korahna. She already seems at the limits of her powers of endurance, which are not great.*"

"*Then let them rest in shifts,*" the Guardian suggested. "*The kank need not be driven. Its instinct will be to follow you. The princess can sleep while Ryana remains awake, to make sure she does not slip off and injure herself. Then, after the princess has slept, Ryana can take her turn.*"

Sorak nodded. "*That is a sensible suggestion. We shall have enough to worry about just making it safely across the barrens without having to deal with Torian. And by traveling at night, when it is cooler, we can make better time.*"

"*It will also be more dangerous,*" the Guardian reminded him. "*We shall all have to stay alert.*"

"*The Watcher has never failed us before,*" said Sorak.

"*There has never been so much at stake before,*" the Guardian replied. "*The Watcher misses nothing, but do not let dependence on the Watcher lull you into a false sense of security. We all shall have to remain vigilant.*"

Sorak glanced over his shoulder at Ryana and the princess, riding atop the kank. Ryana looked tired. The unaccustomed heat was getting to her. The princess lolled against her back, holding her around the waist. They were both doubtless looking forward to the coolness of the night, and rest. He did not relish having to tell them that they would be traveling all night. They would have to make at least a short stop when the sun began to set, to rest for perhaps an hour or two before continuing on their way, but the Guardian was right. If Torian chose to press on after them, they could not afford to stop for the night.

Soon, at least, the hottest part of the day would be over. Traveling at night would be easier, if not safer. But then they would have to press on throughout the following day. And there was no way of knowing how many days it would take for them to cross the barrens. It would be hard on Ryana. As for the princess . . . he did not think she could take many more such days. Perhaps Eyron was right, and they should not have taken her along. She had agreed to go willingly enough, but she had not really known what to expect. If she died of exposure out here in the barrens, her life would be on his conscience.

His thoughts turned once again to the Sage, the object of their quest. Why had the mysterious wizard sent them this way? Was it merely a test of their resolve, or was there some other purpose to sending them across the barrens? He recalled what Torian and Ankhor had said. No one had ever made it across the barrens alive. Was it possible the Sage was actually hiding somewhere amidst all this desolation? What better place for a preserver wizard to conceal himself than in a searing, rock-strewn, lethal stretch of desert that no one dared to enter? But then, the voice in the flames had told them to go to Nibenay. The barrens were merely an obstacle they had to overcome on their way there. Over and over again, as he picked his way among the rocks, Sorak asked himself the question, "Why? Why the barrens?" And as the sun began to sink lower in the sky, he looked out ahead of him and saw nothing but jagged rocks, boulders, and outcroppings stretching out as far as the eye could see. The dim gray line on the horizon, the Barrier Mountains, seemed no closer than when they had started out.

* * * * *

"This is pointless," said the mercenary captain, reining in his kank. "They will never make it across this stony waste alive. If we go on, we shall only die out here, as they will. My men will go no farther."

Torian wheeled his mount to face him. He glanced at the other mercenaries, eight of them in all, not counting himself and the captain. Their sullen faces told him they felt as their captain did.

"You will do as you are told," said Torian firmly.

"We did not sign on for this," the captain protested. "We were hired to protect the caravan along the trade route, not go chasing off into the barrens on some fool's errand."

Torian drew his dagger and threw it with such speed that the motion seemed little more than a blur. The knife flew through the air with unerring accuracy and plunged into the soft hollow of the mercenary captain's throat. The captain made a coughing, gagging sound, and his hands went up to the blade as blood spurted from his mouth. He fell from the kank to land in a heap upon the rocky ground, his blood staining the stones. Before any of the others could react, Torian had drawn his sword. Like his knife, it was made of steel, rare and almost priceless, the sort of weapon only a very wealthy noble could afford, assuming he was fortunate enough to find one.

"Does anyone *else* think this is a fool's errand?" Torian said. "Then come try your hand against this fool."

The mercenaries glanced at one another, then at their dead captain, lying at their feet. Torian knew just what they were thinking. There were eight of them, and he was only one. But though the odds favored them, he had a steel blade, and they all knew what that meant. Their own obsidian blades would shatter against his, and he had already given them a lethal demonstration of his abilities. Nobles were not generally known as fighters, but Torian had learned the blades from early childhood with the finest weapons master in Gulg, and he was confident not only of his skills, but of his ability to intimidate the soldiers. They were merely peasant mercenaries, after all, and a lifetime of subservience to the upper classes had conditioned them against even the thought of raising their weapons to an aristocrat.

Still, to guard against that possibility, Torian prudently chose to drive his point home a bit more forcibly. "Your captain was a fine tracker," he said. "His abilities were almost the equal of my own. Perhaps one of you has similar skills. Perhaps you will find your way back out of the barrens on your own, without me. On the other hand, perhaps not. Either way, choose and choose now. But I tell you this, the only way that any of you will go back is if I am lying there, beside your captain."

The mercenaries exchanged nervous glances once more. Even before they replied to him, Torian knew he had already won.

"We shall follow you, my lord," one of the men said.

"Good," said Torian. "You are now captain. Your pay shall reflect your new status. Additionally, each of you shall be awarded the sum of fifty gold pieces when we return with the Princess Korahna."

He smiled at the greedy fire in their eyes. Fifty gold pieces was an unheard of king's ransom to these men. They could serve for the remainder of their lives and never see such a sum. To Torian, it was a mere pittance. His was one of the richest families on Athas, with extensive holdings and close business ties to the House of Ankhor, one of the most powerful of the merchant guilds. And once he had Korahna for his wife, he would be one of the most politically powerful aristocrats on Athas, as well, allied to not one, but two royal houses. For that, he would crawl across the barrens, if he had to.

"My knife, captain," he said.

The newly promoted mercenary captain pulled the steel blade from the throat of his predecessor, wiped it off on his body, and handed it up to Torian.

"We ride," said Torian, turning his mount and heading west. The mercenaries followed. Any one of them, he knew, could easily strike at him once his back was turned, but he also knew none of them would. Not now. Strike at a man's fear, he thought, and then appeal to his greed, and he is yours forever. He knew what tools to use for manipulating men.

But what tools had Korahna used to manipulate the elfling? Had she appealed to his masculine instincts as a woman in distress? That was certainly possible, but then Sorak was not a man. He was an elfling, and neither elves nor halflings were known for placing the interests of others ahead of their own. How had she convinced Sorak to help her escape? Had she promised him wealth? Had she promised him her body? He did not think it was the latter. A desperate woman might well turn to the last resort of offering sexual favors, but then the elfling had a traveling companion who, while a priestess, was no less desirable than the princess. And villichi priestesses, though often celibate, were not always vowed to chastity.

Wealth, then. A reward from the Veiled Alliance for her safe return. Yes, he thought, that would make the most sense. The Veiled Alliance would, indeed, pay handsomely to have her back. A daughter of a sorcerer-king who had taken the preserver vows would be a powerful weapon in their hands. And elves had a love of money that surpassed that of even the greediest humans. As for the priestess, she would, of course, be strongly motivated to come to the aid of a fellow preserver, provided Korahna was able to convince her that she was sincere. Yes, now that he understood their motives, he felt better. It was always helpful to understand one's enemy, and Sorak, in stealing Korahna from him, had declared himself Torian's lifelong enemy. He would soon realize exactly what that meant, thought Torian, and he would come to regret it bitterly.

He turned his attention once more to the ground ahead of him. He soon picked up the trail. There had not been much of a trail to follow from the spring. He had risen early, as he always did, to practice in the still-cool morning air with his blades, and as he stepped outside his tent, he heard a curious noise. A short distance from his tent, he had discovered the guard Sorak had tied up. The man had painstakingly inched his way back toward the tents, crawling like a caterpillar. When Torian cut his bonds, the man had told him what had happened. Torian immediately ran to Korahna's tent.

The sentries on duty outside had told him that the princess was still asleep inside, and that no one had been by since they had taken up their posts. Torian had thrown aside the tent flap, gone inside, and found no trace of Korahna. But he found the slit she had made with her knife in the back wall of the tent. He had personally killed both sentries, then, before raising the alarm, he carefully followed the trail Korahna had left behind. The sand blown by the desert wind had covered up any footprints she had made, but he found broken twigs on a scrub brush she had brushed past, and the trampled new shoots where she had stepped. He had already known where her trail would lead. He saw where the elfling and the villichi priestess had camped the previous night, and he realized that she had fled with them. He surmised

that Sorak had stolen the guard's footgear to replace
Korahna's dainty sandals. That, and the fact that they
had not stolen any of the other kanks, told him which
way they must have gone.

Had they taken the southern route, it would have
made sense for them to steal two of the kanks in addition to their own so that they could make quick time to
outdistance the pursuit they had to know would follow. But kanks would make no better time across the
rocky barrens than a man traveling on foot, and with
no forage to be found, they would have to feed their
mounts from their supplies. Three kanks would deplete
them quickly. With one, perhaps, they stood a chance.
But it would be a very slim chance, indeed.

Torian had never heard of anyone surviving a trek
across the barrens. Of all the races of Athas, elves and
halflings possessed the greatest powers of endurance.
Perhaps, against all odds, the elfling would make it.
It was even possible the priestess would, as well,
with the elfling's aid. The villichi were rigorously
trained to deal with all kinds of hardship. But Torian
had no illusions about Korahna's surviving such a
journey. The little fool would die out there in the barrens, even if they did not fall prey to the creatures
who roamed there.

Korahna would also slow them down. He could not
imagine her making the journey on foot. She would
have to ride. Probably the priestess would, as well. For
all the training the villichi priestesses received, they
were still human, and walking for days in the searing
heat of the Stony Barrens would be beyond even their
considerable capabilities. So that meant the kank
would be burdened with at least two riders, if the

elfling chose to go on foot. And their kank had been a food producer, not a soldier. It would not move as quickly as their own mounts.

How much of a head start could they possibly have? Five hours, maybe six? Certainly no more than that. They could be caught. At some point, they would have to stop and rest. As Torian carefully watched the ground ahead of him, he saw the occasional signs of the kank's passage. Small stones dislodged from depressions in the ground, scratches upon larger stones made by the kank's claws. He was grateful that his father had insisted on his training, and had not raised him as a pampered nobleman. His father had believed that training in the warrior's art built character. His father had been right. A lesser man would have given up rather than risk pursuing his quarry into the barrens. Undoubtedly, that was precisely what the elfling was counting on. Well, thought Torian, he was due for a very unpleasant surprise.

* * * * *

As the sun started to sink on the horizon, Sorak decided to call a brief halt. The kank needed to be fed and they could use some nourishment, as well. Ryana looked exhausted and Korahna looked utterly done in. He helped them both down from the back of the giant beetle, and they practically collapsed with their backs against a large boulder. He passed the water skin to them and cautioned them to drink but sparingly, then watched to make sure they did not succumb to the temptation to drink in large gulps.

"Well, at least it is no longer quite so hot," Ryana

said with a wan smile.

Sorak used his knife blade to pry loose one of the honey globules from the kank's abdomen and brought it over to them. He pierced the membrane with the point of his knife and gave it to Korahna. She squeezed out a little, then passed it to Ryana and leaned back against the boulder, her eyes closed. Sorak hated to have to tell them, but it was best not to delay the unpleasant news any longer.

"At least it will be cooler for the remainder of the night's journey," he said.

Korahna opened her eyes. "We are going *on?* You mean we are not stopping for the night?"

"We will only rest here for a short while," Sorak replied. "The sooner we proceed on our way, the sooner we will reach the mountains."

"You believe that we are being followed," said Ryana flatly.

Sorak nodded. "Yes. And I believe that Torian will drive his mercenaries all night in an attempt to catch us. We cannot allow him to make up the time we have gained."

"But you do not know for a fact that Torian is on our trail," Korahna protested.

"No, I do not," Sorak admitted. "But we cannot afford to assume that he is not. Either way, traveling at night will be easier for the absence of the scorching heat."

"Also more dangerous," Ryana said.

"Perhaps," said Sorak, "but making camp here would not be any safer. We have nothing with which to build a fire. The night predators can attack us here as easily as while we are moving."

"Are you not tired?" Korahna asked him, with wonder. "We have suffered from the heat, but at least we have been riding, while you have walked all day."

"I am an elfling," Sorak said, taking his seat across from them on the rocky ground. He stretched out his legs and flexed them. "I do not tire as easily as do humans. Nevertheless, the day's journey has not been without its effect. It is good to sit, if only for a short while."

Though he was capable of resting while the Ranger or one of the others came to the fore and took over, it was still the same body that made the exertions. And his elfling body, superbly conditioned though it was, did not possess infinite reserves of energy.

"How many more days' journey do you think lie ahead of us?" Korahna asked.

Sorak merely shrugged. "I do not know. Distances appear deceptive in the desert. It could be three or four more days, if we make good progress, or it could be a week or more. I can see the mountains in the distance, but I cannot tell for sure how far away they are."

Ryana made some quick mental calculations. "If it is more than three or four more days, we will run out of water," she said flatly.

"We have the kank honey," Sorak said. "We can add it to the water to extend our supply."

"Kank honey is sweet," Ryana said. "It will only increase our thirst."

"Not if we add it in small amounts," said Sorak.

"Even so," Ryana said, "we have enough to last at most five or six days."

"All the more reason to travel at night and make the crossing as speedily as possible," said Sorak.

"Torian will be facing the same problems," said Korahna. "Surely, he will turn back."

"I do not think he is the sort to give up on a task once he has set his mind to it," said Sorak. "He will probably be carrying more water, and his men will be mounted on soldier kanks, which can travel more quickly than our own beast."

"So then you think he has a chance to catch us?" said Ryana.

"It would depend on when he started his pursuit, and whether or not he realized which way we had gone. And it would depend on the skill of his trackers."

"Torian is a skilled tracker, himself," Korahna said. "He often boasted of it. His father raised him as a warrior. He claims to have studied with the finest weapons master in Gulg. I saw him train one morning. He was easily able to best Lord Ankhor's finest swordsmen."

"Well, that's certainly encouraging news," said Ryana dryly.

"It is all my fault," Korahna said. "Had I not come with you, there would have been no need for you to come this way, or fear pursuit."

"We would have come this way regardless," Sorak said. "And the journey would have been no easier to bear for your absence."

"But why?" Korahna asked. "You could have taken the southern route, and without me along, you could have gone your way unmolested."

"No," said Sorak, "this is the way that we were meant to come."

"*Meant* to come?" Korahna said, looking at him without comprehension. "Why? For what reason?"

"This was the way shown us by a spell," said Sorak.

"A spell released by the burning of a scroll that we obtained from the Veiled Alliance in Tyr."

"The burning of a scroll?" said Korahna, sitting up suddenly and leaning forward. "And was there a specific time and place at which you were to burn it?"

Sorak frowned. "Yes. But how did you know that?"

"Because that is how the Veiled Alliance receives communications from the Sage," Korahna said excitedly. "I have never seen such a scroll myself, but I have heard that these scrolls appear by magic to certain individuals, and that they are useless unless burned in a certain place and at a certain time. And that knowledge is said to come in dreams or visions perceived within a crystal. But it is said that only the secret masters of the Veiled Alliance ever see such scrolls. I had never known whether to believe such tales or not, until today. Why did you not tell me you were members of the Veiled Alliance? Was it that you did not trust the daughter of a defiler king?"

"No, it was because we are *not* members of the Veiled Alliance," Sorak replied. "We had performed a service for them back in Tyr, and they had given us the scroll to aid us in our quest."

"What quest?"

"To find the Sage," said Sorak.

Korahna simply stared at him. "But no one has ever found the Sage!"

"Then I suppose we shall be the first," said Sorak. He stood. "We had best be on our way."

The weary women mounted up, and they moved off once again as the sun slowly disappeared beyond the horizon. For a while, the desert was plunged into total darkness, and then the first of the twin moons rose, followed a short while later by the second, and the Stony Barrens were illuminated in a ghostly, bluish light.

"I know now why you brought me with you," said Korahna as they slowly rode along behind Sorak, who picked his way among the rocks ahead of them. "I thought that you had merely taken pity on a fellow preserver, but you needed me to make contact with the Veiled Alliance in Nibenay."

"That was Sorak's idea," said Ryana. "If you must know, I was against bringing you along. I knew the hardships you would face upon this journey, and I did not think you would survive it."

"I see," Korahna said, softly. "And do you still believe so?"

Ryana gave a small snort. "I am not yet convinced that any of us shall survive it. But you have shown more mettle than I gave you credit for. Who knows? We shall see."

"You do not sound very confident."

"Your spirit is strong, Korahna, but your body is weak," Ryana replied. "I do not say that to condemn you, it merely happens to be the way things are. A strong spirit can often compensate for a body's weakness, but we have been only one day on this journey, and already you are at the limits of your endurance. Do not mistake my meaning. I give you credit for your courage, but I do not know if it shall be enough to see you through this."

"Better to die out here in the barrens, attempting to control my fate, than live with Torian and be controlled," Korahna said. "Thus far, my life has been of little worth, and the strength of my beliefs has not been truly tested. If I must die, then at least I shall die as a preserver and not some rich man's trophy. Hand me your sword."

"Better you should save your strength," Ryana said.

"No, better I should build it," said Korahna. "And holding it will give me something upon which to focus my mind."

"As you wish," Ryana said, handing her the sword.

"It does not feel quite so heavy now," the princess said, holding it out away from her body.

Ryana smiled. "Do not exhaust yourself," she said. "There is more to learning how to use a sword than merely strengthening your arms. And even that does not come quickly."

"But at least this is a beginning," said Korahna.

"Yes, it is a beginning. But only a beginning. It takes many years of training to become proficient with a blade."

"I have the rest of my life to learn," Korahna said.

Indeed, Ryana thought to herself. Let us hope that the rest of your life lasts longer than the next few days.

SIX

Five days, thought Torian with both fury and astonishment. Five miserable days they had traveled through this scorching, stony wasteland without a single night's rest, and still they had not caught up with them. How the elfling and the priestess could keep up this relentless pace, encumbered as they were with the princess, was utterly beyond him. He had pushed his men as hard as it was possible to push them. The first day out, they had ridden hard and kept right on going through the night. He had been certain then that he would catch up with them the very next day, but the next day passed and still their quarry was not in sight. Since then, they had paused only for short rest periods during the day and he allowed his men to sleep no more than three or four hours each night. He did not see how they could have failed to catch them by now. It simply defied belief.

The elfling and the priestess had but one kank with them. His soldier kanks were faster, but then, most of their advantage in speed had been canceled out by the difficult terrain. Still, the elfling could not have been carrying much in the way of supplies. Surely, they must have run out by now. Torian knew that elves and halflings were both well adapted to travel in the desert. The elfling would doubtless have inherited those traits. The villichi priestess had her training to see her through, but Korahna? How could she possibly survive such an ordeal? He had half expected to come across her corpse by now. He would not have thought that she could have survived more than a few hours in the barrens, much less five days of traveling at a forced pace. It just did not seem possible.

The sun's rays, beating down relentlessly upon the rocks, heated them until it seemed as if the party were riding through a blacksmith's furnace. From time to time as they rode, they would hear sharp, cracking reports, a sound that had mystified him and alarmed the mercenaries until they realized it was the sound of stones shattering from the intense heat. It seemed beyond belief that anyone could last so long in this sun-baked inferno.

His throat was parched and his lungs burned from breathing in the heated air. His lips were dry and cracked even though he moistened them constantly, and his skin seemed to feel as if it would crackle when he touched it, like the flesh of a well-roasted fowl. His men, seasoned mercenaries all, were barely able to remain astride their mounts. They were down to six, not counting himself.

The second night out, they had lost one man to a fire drake. The creature had hidden itself among the rocks, its pebbly-grained hide camouflaging it from view, and as the unfortunate man passed, the drake leapt, bringing him down from his mount and fastening its powerful fangs in his shoulder. The other kanks shied away from the creature, and crossbow bolts loosed by the other mercenaries merely glanced off the drake's thick hide. The kanks bolted, and by the time they were able to bring the beasts back under control, the drake had disappeared, dragging its hapless victim away with it. His frenzied screams faded into the distance until they were cut off abruptly.

The next day, they lost another man to an agony beetle. The creature had flown up and landed gently on his back so that he had not felt it. It crawled lightly down his cloak and underneath it to the base of his spine, where it sent out the long, fine, tendril stinger from its snout to penetrate his skin and worm its way deep into his spinal column. The deadly stinger was coated with a substance that numbed the skin so that the victim could not feel the beetle's bite until it was too late. Once the tendril stinger was firmly embedded and wrapped around the nerve endings in the spine, the agony beetle began to live up to its name.

Its victim suddenly started to scream at the top of his lungs and claw at his back as waves of incandescent pain shot up his spine and into his brain. The creature fed on the psionic energy produced by pain, and once its stinger was inserted, removing it without killing the victim was almost impossible. The mercenary fell from his mount to land, writhing and screaming like a banshee, on the rocky ground.

The others simply stared, frightened and astonished, unable to see the source of their comrade's torment. It was Torian who surmised what the cause must be, and he leapt down from his mount and ran over to the fallen man, drawing his knife. With one sweep of his blade, he cut away the thrashing mercenary's cloak and saw the insect, its chitinous black shell gleaming in the sun as it clung to its victim's spine, torturing him unimaginably. Torian and several of the others tried to hold the man down, but the pain-maddened mercenary flung them off and leapt to his feet.

The pain had driven out all rationality. He threw himself repeatedly against the boulders in a futile effort to dislodge the insect, all the while screaming horribly, and then in a desperate effort to drive out the pain, he began smashing his head against a rock. The others could only watch in horror as the rock turned red with his blood. Several of them covered their ears in an effort to shut out the man's screams and the dull, wet, smacking sounds made as he pounded his head against the rock.

Torian snatched a crossbow from one of the other men and quickly fitted a bolt, but before he could shoot the pathetic wretch and put him out of his misery, the man fell silent and slumped to the ground, his head pounded to a gory pulp. He had beaten out his own brains rather than suffer the agonizing torment. As the beetle detached its tendril stinger, Torian picked up a rock and smashed it, pounding away until nothing was left of the loathsome insect but a wet spot on the rocky ground.

The rest of the mercenaries had been badly unnerved by the gruesome spectacle of their comrade's death. Coupled with the earlier death of the man killed by the drake, this loss had left them shaken. They had said nothing, but their faces had been sullen, and Torian did not need to be a mind reader to know what they were thinking. It could happen just as easily to any one of them, and the longer they remained in the barrens, the greater the odds were that none would make it back alive.

Torian now chose to call a brief halt to rest their kanks and feed them. He had brought along two spare, riderless kanks to carry their supplies. As the men pulled even with him, he suddenly noticed that two of them were missing, and along with them, the two pack beasts.

"Where are Dankro and Livak?" Torian demanded.

The others looked around, apparently noticing for the first time that two of them were missing.

"They were bringing up the rear with the pack beasts," one of the men said. And then his eyes grew wide as comprehension dawned. "The miserable bastards have turned back! And they have taken our supplies with them!"

The other three exchanged alarmed glances. They all knew what that meant. All their food, all their fuel for fire, and all their spare water, save for the skins they carried with them, were now gone with the deserters.

"When was the last time any of you saw them?" Torian asked.

They exchanged glances again. "This morning, after our rest break," one of them said.

"They were right behind me when we started off," another said. "But I never thought to turn around. After what happened with the others, we were all watching one another's backs, and I had thought . . ." His voice trailed off as he realized that, probably for much of the day, he had been riding alone at the rear, with no one to watch his back.

"We must turn around at once and go after them," said Rovik, the new captain.

"And lose more time?" said Torian grimly. "No. Let them fend for themselves. We will go on."

"But, my lord, they have taken all our food and water!" Rovik protested. "We have only our own water skins, and they shall not last out the day!"

"I am aware of that," said Torian. "My situation is no different than yours. We shall have to drink but sparingly, and make the water last as long as possible."

"And then what?" one of the others said. "At most, we can make the water last another day or two. Then we shall all die of thirst. We must turn back! Our only chance now is to catch Dankro and Livak!"

"And how much of a head start do you think they have?" asked Torian. "None of you has seen them since this morning. They must have held back as we started off, then turned and bolted at the first opportunity. They will travel at full speed for fear of pursuit, and they shall not stop unless something out here stops them. Then the pack beasts will simply wander off, and we will be no better off than we are now. It is five days back, if we travel without rest. Our water will run out long before then."

"Then either way, we are all dead," one of the mercenaries said.

"Look there," Torian said, turning and pointing toward the mountains, rising up ahead of them in the distance. "The Barrier Mountains are at most another three or four days' ride. I grew up in those mountains, and know them like the back of my hand. Once there, we will find plenty of game and water. We must go forward. It is our only chance."

"What is the use?" said the mercenary who had just spoken. "We shall merely die within a day or two's ride of the mountains, our salvation within sight, but out of reach. It is hopeless. We are finished, Torian. Your pointless, mad pursuit has killed us all. We are dead men."

Torian drew his sword. "Dead men need no water," he said, and plunged his blade into the man's chest. The mercenary cried out and stared at him, incredulous, then his eyes glazed over as he clutched at his wound and toppled from his mount.

Torian turned his kank to face the others, still holding the bloody sword in his hand. "Does anyone else believe there is no hope?" The others simply stared at him in stony silence. "Good. Then we can divide his water among us," Torian said. "If we are sparing with its use, it should extend our supply another day or two. From now on, I will carry all the water and ration it out as I see fit. Any objections?"

No one spoke.

"Then it is settled," Torian said. "Pass me your water skins. From now on, we do not stop until we reach the Barrier Mountains."

* * * * *

On the fourth day of their trek across the barrens, they had run out of food. They had stretched their supply as far as possible, feeding most of it to the kank. The beast had a voracious appetite and could not survive on its honey alone. They had been eating the honey, and there were only several globules left. The kank needed to supplement its diet with forage, and there was none in the barrens. They had fed the remaining honey to the kank, but it was not enough. By the fifth day, the beast was starting to grow weak. But that was not the worst of it. They had also run out of water.

Ryana felt completely drained. She could only imagine how the princess must feel. Korahna had not spoken a word in hours. She merely clung weakly to Ryana, with her arms around her waist, her head lolling against her back. Ryana saw that even Sorak was showing the strain of their ordeal. At least she and Korahna had been able to sleep during their journey. They had taken turns, one of them holding the other to prevent a fall, while the kank had simply followed Sorak obediently.

Sorak had been on foot throughout their journey, and though he had ducked under to sleep while the Ranger or Screech came to the fore, their body had neither slept nor rested, save for the brief stops they made. Ryana could see by Sorak's bearing, each time he surfaced to take over his body once again, that he felt the physical effects of his exertions. His elfling body could take far more punishment than human bodies could, but even he was tired now.

Ryana felt Korahna's grip slipping and turned just in time to catch her as she started to fall. "Sorak!" she called out.

He stopped and turned, looking at her wearily.

"Korahna has swooned," she said.

He walked back to the kank. "Let her down," he said.

He took the princess in his arms as Ryana gently eased her off the back of the kank, then dismounted to stand beside him as he laid her out gently on the ground.

"I never thought that she would even make it this

far," said Ryana. "I can barely stand myself."

Sorak nodded. "It was selfish of me to bring her along," he said. "She would have been better off with Torian."

"She said that she would rather die," Ryana said.

"I fear she will," said Sorak. "She has no strength left. She has come this far on pluck alone. And that is no longer enough. She will be dead by nightfall."

Ryana looked over her shoulder toward the mountains. "Another three or four days' ride and we would have reached the end of this wasteland." She sighed with resignation. "If Torian has not long since turned back, he will find only our corpses."

"We are not dead yet," said Sorak.

"It will be night soon," said Ryana, looking toward the mountains. "Up 'til now, Screech has kept us safe by communing with the creatures that approach us, but Screech cannot make water out of stone. And when our bodies fail us, we shall make a fine meal for some hungry beast. It seems the Sage has merely lured us to our deaths."

There was no reply from Sorak. She turned and saw him sitting cross-legged on the ground beside the princess, who lay motionless, her chest barely moving as she breathed weakly. She looked as if the pallor of death was already stealing over her. Sorak had his eyes closed. He breathed slowly, deeply, and regularly. Then Ryana began to feel warm.

It was a warmth that did not come from the sun, which was already sinking slowly over the horizon. It did not come from the sun-baked rocks, which still felt hot beneath her feet. It did not come from within her. It came from Sorak.

As she watched, she could see heat waves shimmering around him, and his face took on a completely different expression. It was more than merely an apparent change. His mouth, which usually looked harsh and cruel and sensual, had softened, and his lips appeared more full. His normally dour expression became beatific and serene. And when he opened his eyes and looked at her, she saw that the color of his irises had changed from dark brown to an azure blue.

"Kether," Ryana said softly.

He reached out his hand to her. She took it and felt revitalizing warmth flowing into her. She closed her eyes as the energy surged through her arms.

Then, still holding her hand, Kether reached out and lightly placed the fingertips of his other hand on Korahna's forehead. The princess parted her lips and breathed in deeply, uttering a soft moan.

As the princess inhaled deeply, a slight dizziness came over Ryana, and though her eyes were closed, she seemed to "see" the interior of a library, similar to the one at the villichi temple, only much more ornate, with scrolls stored in rows of cubicles carved from polished obsidian set with hammered silver. It was, she realized, the templar library in the palace compound of the Shadow King, where Korahna had first discovered the preserver writings.

Next, she saw the streets of Nibenay at night, with beggars huddled in the doorways and bedraggled prostitutes lounging in the entrances to darkened alleys. She heard the cries of hungry infants coming from the windows up above, and she saw old women searching through the refuse in the streets for some scrap of food to eat. A profound sadness overwhelmed her, seeing the state to which these people were reduced, and she felt tears start flowing down her cheeks, though she herself was not weeping. Images whirled through her consciousness, faces in taverns as Korahna sought to make contact with the Veiled Alliance, hooded figures accosting her in some darkened room, sneaking out of the palace compound at night to attend clandestine meetings, faster and faster the memories flowed through her, and she experienced Korahna's life in one kaleidoscopic surge of thoughts, senses, and impressions. . . .

Then, just as abruptly as it had begun, it ended, and Ryana felt Kether's hand release her own.

She opened her eyes and found herself flushed with perspiration, her entire body tingling. She felt lightheaded, and yet, at the same time, she was no longer tired. She still felt hungry and thirsty, but it was as if a second wind had come upon her and given her new strength. And she saw Korahna's eyelids flicker open and heard her sharp intake of breath as she sat up and said, "I have had the most amazing dream. . . ."

Sorak's head was lowered to his chest, and he was breathing heavily. The warmth was gone now, though Ryana still felt its residual effects. The sun, which had started sinking over the horizon what seemed only a moment ago, had long since set. The twin moons, Ral and Guthay, cast their ghostly light upon the barrens. Sorak raised his head, his eyes still closed, and breathed in deeply, then exhaled slowly.

He opened his eyes and said, "I think we can go on now."

Ryana and the princess were staring at each other. Something incredibly profound had passed between them, and they both knew that somehow a bond had been forged that could never be broken. It suddenly felt as if they had known each other all their lives. They were like sisters, only more than sisters, for through Kether, they had shared an intimacy deeper than even most siblings could achieve.

"I do not understand what just happened," said Korahna slowly. "It seemed like a curious dream, and yet it was not a dream, was it?"

"No," Ryana said. "It was not a dream."

The princess stared at Sorak. "But how . . . ?" Her voice trailed off. She could not think of how to frame the question.

"It is not something we could even begin to understand, Korahna," Ryana told her. "We can do no more than accept it. Kether gave us strength, and more than that. Much more."

"Kether?" said Korahna. And then she looked at Sorak and realized she knew, because Ryana had known. For the first time, she understand who and what Sorak truly was. "A tribe of one," she whispered. It was not something she had even heard of before, but she suddenly knew what it meant.

"Sorak," said Ryana sharply. "Look!"

A mile or so away, directly to the east, where the ground began to rise, a fire burned.

"Torian!" Korahna said. "He has circled round us!"

"No," said Sorak. "That is not the light of a campfire. There is nothing here to burn, and even if Torian had brought torches or wood to build a fire, it would not give off such light. It burns blue, then green, then blue again."

"Like the fire of the spell scroll," said Ryana.

"The Sage?" Korahna said.

"Is it possible that we have found his sanctuary?" asked Ryana.

"Perhaps," said Sorak. "We shall know when we get there. Come, let us make haste."

The two women mounted up, and the kank reluctantly rose and moved off to follow Sorak. The creature was tired and weak, and Ryana did not think it would be able to travel much farther. They had only a mile or so to go to reach the place where the flame burned. But what would they find when they got there?

The ground had started to rise, sloping up in stages toward the mountains, still several days' ride distant. The boulders here were larger, and there were more rock outcroppings through which they had to wind their way. Several times, they lost sight of the flame as they made slow progress toward it. Even so, they slowly but steadily drew closer, winding their way through a maze of rocky rills, almost like the walls of a fortress. In the distance, they could hear the sound of some huge creature bellowing as it made a kill . . . or perhaps was, itself, killed.

As they approached the flame, Ryana could see that it was certainly not a campfire, but a tall pillar of blue-green fire that seemed to sprout from solid rock.

"How can stone burn?" Korahna asked with wonder as she stared at the flame.

"By magic," said Ryana.

When they reached it, they saw it was the same sort of flame that had pointed out their way across the tablelands and the barrens—the magical flame that had been released by the spell scroll. But it could not possibly have been burning all this time, Ryana thought.

They would have seen it for miles. It seemed to sprout directly from the stone at the base of a large rock out-cropping in front of them. They were hemmed in by this same rock on three sides. The only way out was back the way they had come. Sorak stood back from the pillar of flame, staring at it.

"There is nothing here," Ryana said, looking around. "The trail has come to a dead end."

"If Torian finds us now, we shall be trapped," Korahna said apprehensively. "There is no way out except the way we came."

"We were brought here for a reason," Sorak said.

"What?" Ryana asked. "There is nothing here."

"We were brought here for a reason," Sorak repeated.

"Come," a deep, echoing voice suddenly spoke, the same voice they had heard before, directing them to Nibenay. It came from within the flame.

"Come where?" Ryana asked.

"Come," the voice repeated once again.

Sorak stepped forward.

Ryana grabbed him by the arm. "What are you doing?"

"We must approach the flame," said Sorak.

Ryana stared at the pillar of fire. "I am not anxious to draw any closer than this," she said.

Sorak gently disengaged himself. "We did not come all this way to fail now," he said. "We must do as we are bid."

"Do not get too close," Ryana cautioned him uneasily.

Sorak stepped closer to the flame.

"Come," the voice said once more.

He stepped closer, almost within arm's reach of it.

"Come," the voice spoke, yet again.

Sorak strode forward.

"Sorak!" Ryana shouted.

He was only inches from the flame.

"Come," said the voice.

"Sorak, no!" Ryana shouted, lunging after him.

He stepped into the flame.

Korahna cried out, bringing her hands up to her mouth. Sorak had completely disappeared from view. Ryana froze, staring wide-eyed with disbelief. And then the voice spoke again.

"Come."

"Ryana, we must go back," Korahna said.

Ryana simply stared mutely at the spot where Sorak had entered the fire.

"Ryana, it is too late," Korahna said. "He is gone. We must flee this place."

Ryana turned around to look at her. She simply shook her head.

"Ryana, please . . . come away."

"No," Ryana said. She stepped closer to the flame.

"Ryana!" The princess ran after her and seized her by the arm, trying to pull her away. "Don't! Sorak has killed himself. There is no point to throwing your life away as well!"

"Do you feel the heat, Korahna?"

"What?"

"The *heat*. Do you feel the heat?"

"You shall feel it all too well if you go any closer," said the princess. "Come away, Ryana. Please, I beg you."

"We should be feeling it already," said Ryana, staring at the fire. "Standing as close as we are to a flame of this size, we should be feeling the heat of it. And yet, there is no heat. Is there?"

Korahna simply stared at her.

"*Is* there?"

Korahna blinked. "No," she admitted.

Ryana took her hand. "You said that you had courage," she said. "You said that you would rather die than fail to be the mistress of your fate. The time has come to prove those words."

Korahna swallowed hard and shook her head as Ryana pulled her toward the flame. "No, stop! What are you doing?"

"We must follow Sorak," said Ryana.

Korahna jerked away. "Are you mad? We shall burn, as he did!"

"How does stone burn?" Ryana said. "How does flame fail to give off heat? That is no ordinary fire, Korahna. I do not believe that it shall burn us."

Korahna moistened her lips and swallowed hard. "Ryana . . . I am afraid."

"Sorak went into the fire. Did you hear him scream?"

"No," said the princess, as if realizing it for the first time.

"You told me you had courage," said Ryana. "Take my hand."

Biting her lower lip, Korahna stretched forth her hand.

"Come," said the voice from the flames.

They stepped into the fire.

Miraculously, it felt cool. Korahna marveled as they walked through the flame. Fire was engulfing them on all sides, and yet, they did not burn. It felt almost as if they were walking through a waterfall, except they did not get wet. They stepped out into a grotto illuminated by phosphorescent rock. A greenish light permeated the rock chamber, emanating from the walls. And they heard the dripping sound of water.

"What kept you?" Sorak said.

Korahna laughed. "Water!" she said, seeing the pool at the far end of the grotto. Sorak stood beside it, water dripping from his wet hair.

"Drink your fill," he said. "It is water from a spring that comes up through the rock."

"But . . . where does it go?" Ryana asked, puzzled.

"It flows down this passageway here," said Sorak, indicating a tunnel in the shadows back toward the rear of the grotto. "There must be a cavern farther down."

As Korahna filled their water skins, Ryana came up to stand beside Sorak and looked in the direction he was indicating. Toward the back end of the grotto, on the opposite side of the pool, there was an overhang that partially concealed a tunnel heading back farther into the rock. She could hear the trickling sound of water flowing gently down a portion of that passage. As they walked around the pool, they could see that the tunnel sloped slightly to the right. The water bubbling up from the spring had over the years cut a channel into the rock, and there was a ledge on one side, wide enough to allow passage.

They heard scrabbling sounds behind them and turned to see that the flame covering the entrance had disappeared and the kank had come up to the opening, where some plants grew up out of the rock, their roots sustained by the moisture in the grotto.

"Well, at least the kank shall not go hungry," said Ryana. "We, on the other hand, still have to find food."

"I am grateful that we have found water," Sorak said.

"I was beginning to despair of our chances. Undoubtedly, it was the Sage who led us here."

"If Torian is still on our trail, he will have seen that fire, as well," Ryana said.

"Yes, but it is gone now," Sorak replied. "And without the flame to guide him, he may fail to find this place. It is well concealed."

"I would still feel better if we were on our way after a short rest," Ryana said.

Sorak shook his head. "No. Not yet. I do not think the only reason we were directed to this place was so that we could find water. The flame pillar that covered up the entrance to this place was a test of our resolve. There is something else here for us to find."

Ryana looked around. "I see nothing here except the grotto."

"There, perhaps," said Sorak, indicating the tunnel.

Korahna came up beside them as he spoke. "You are not thinking of going down there, surely?"

"Why not?"

"There is no way of knowing what waits for us down there," the princess said.

"There is one way," Sorak said as he ducked beneath the overhang and started down the tunnel.

"First through fire, now into a black hole," Korahna said. She sighed. "I cannot say this journey has lacked excitement."

Ryana smiled. "Most of that excitement I could easily have done without," she said. "After you, Your Highness."

Korahna grimaced and ducked beneath the overhang to follow Sorak. They went slowly down the passage, which, like the grotto, was dimly illuminated by

phosphorescent rock. The water flowed beside them in
a channel as they started down a gradual incline, feeling their way along the wall of the tunnel. Ryana tried
to listen for the sound of rushing water, which might
indicate a sudden drop-off, but she knew that Sorak
would detect any hazard long before she would. His
hearing was much more acute than hers, and he saw
well in the dark. The slope of the tunnel gradually
increased, and they headed farther underground. The
tunnel ran straight for a while, then turned and turned
again. By that time, Sorak was well ahead of them.

Ryana was not sure how far they had walked when
she heard him call out, "Ryana! Princess! Come
quickly!"

Fearing that something may have happened, Ryana
brushed her way past the princess and hurried ahead,
drawing her sword. The tunnel turned sharply, and
she saw light up ahead. Hearing Korahna behind her,
rushing to keep up, Ryana started running. When she
reached the end of the tunnel, she stopped short and
gasped.

The tunnel opened out into a huge cavern, shot
through with phosphorescent veins that illuminated the
vast expanse as if with moonlight. The water continued
to flow in an undulating stream down a slope and
toward the center of the cavern, where an ancient ruin
stood. It was a keep, with a stone tower rising above the
walls of mortared rock. The stream flowed into an
underground lake, and the keep stood on an island in
the center of it. To their left, an arched stone bridge
spanned the waters of the lake, leading to the island.

Ryana heard the princess gasp as she came out of the
tunnel behind her. "A fortress!" said Korahna. "An

underground fortress! By the design, it must be thousands of years old! But . . . who could have built it?"

"One of the ancient races, about whom only legends exist," Ryana said. "I have heard tales of underground cities and ruins, but I have never known of anyone who actually saw one."

"It is said that spirits inhabit such places," Korahna said uneasily.

"Perhaps," said Sorak. "And yet, we were led here to find this place. I think we may have found the sanctuary of the Sage."

* * * * *

"We shall lose ourselves forever in this maze of rock!" said Rovik.

"We shall do no such thing," said Torian. "I have marked the way, and the trail leads through here. What is more, they cannot be more than an hour or two ahead of us, at most. This kank spoor is still fresh. They came toward that fire we saw last night."

"But there is no fire now," said Rovik. "Whatever it was, it has burned itself out. There is no longer a beacon to follow."

"No, but it is almost dawn, and the trail will be easier to follow," Torian said. "Hand me another torch."

"That was the last one," said Rovik. "The rest have gone with our supplies and those miserable deserters."

"I shall deal with them when we return," said Torian, flinging the sputtering remnants of the last torch to the ground with disgust.

"What could they have found to burn out here?" asked one of the other mercenaries.

"That was no campfire," Torian replied. "It was much too bright a flame."

"And did you mark how it burned blue and green?" the other mercenary said. "It was a witch fire!"

"I doubt a witch would survive out here any better than anything else," said Torian wryly. "Doubtless, it was a volcanic fire, and that was why it burned as it did."

"A volcano?" said the mercenary with alarm. "You mean like the Smoking Crown?"

"Calm yourself," said Torian. "If it was a volcano like the Smoking Crown, we would have seen the cone of the mountain rising up from miles away. And if it had been a full eruption, the entire sky would have glowed red. Doubtless it is but some minor fissure or a sulphur pit that occasionally belches forth some flame. We shall be safe enough."

"As safe as any man can be in this forsaken land," the mercenary said.

"Are one elfling and two women braver than the lot of you?" asked Torian sarcastically. "The princess has lived the pampered life of a royal aristocrat, and she has made it this far, amazingly enough. Has she more fortitude than you?"

"If she lives, perhaps she does, indeed," the mercenary said. "More likely, she has died, and they have merely abandoned her body somewhere in all these rocks."

"If they had, I would have seen some sign of it," said Torian. "No, she lives. They would have no reason to bear her corpse along. And we shall come upon them soon. The chase is almost ended."

"What will you do to the elfling when you find him?"

asked the mercenary.

"I will cut him to ribbons," Torian said, "and take his head for my trophy."

"And the priestess? Will you kill her, as well?"

"I care not what happens to the priestess. You may have her, if you wish."

The mercenaries smiled.

SEVEN

The span of the stone bridge arched high over the lake and was constructed in such a manner that it could be easily defended by anyone in the keep. The bridge was narrow, allowing only two abreast, and there was a barbican at the opposite end. The arch of the bridge had been designed so that any sort of shield carried in advance of an attacking party would be rendered useless, because archers on the barbican could fire over it as the attackers started down the slope of the arch. However, there was no sign that anyone had passed this way in years. The mortar was old and cracked, badly in need of repair, and the low walls on either side of the bridge had lost a number of stones to the lake below.

Sorak started slowly across, testing his footing as he went, unsure how much the structure had weakened over the years. It seemed incredibly old, and there was a thick layer of rock dust on the surface of the span. However, it seemed solid. Sorak was followed by Korahna, then Ryana. As they approached the barbican at the opposite end, they could see that part of the structure had crumbled. Bats nested in the barbican, and a flock of them streamed out on their approach, wheeling around in mad arabesques and emitting high-pitched shrieks as they spiraled up toward the roof of the cavern.

Ryana remained on the alert, her sword held in her hand. Sorak simply held his staff; Galdra hung in its scabbard on his belt, beneath his cloak. Korahna's tension was evident in her bearing. She was clearly frightened, but she said nothing as she followed Sorak, taking care never to fall more than several steps behind.

There must have been, at one time, a thick wooden gate in the barbican, but the wood had long since rotted away due to the moisture in the cavern, and only pieces of it still remained. Sorak used the staff to brush aside several large cobwebs as he went through, followed by the others. The keep was built on solid rock that jutted from the surface of the lake. It was uneven, and the walls had been constructed to accommodate its shape.

They passed through the barbican and approached the outer walls of the keep, which were about forty feet high. The walls, too, had crumbled in places, and the topmost portion of the tower had fallen, but most of the structure still stood. Sorak led them beneath the arched entryway and into a small courtyard set with mortared stone. Inside the courtyard was an old well, from which the residents must have drawn their water, and several smaller structures that may have functioned as guardhouses or small outbuildings separate from the keep itself. The tower of the keep loomed over them—dark, silent, and foreboding. All was hushed, save for the chittering of the bats.

"I suppose that we must go inside," Korahna said.

"You may wait out here if you wish," said Sorak.

"Alone? I think not," the princess said quickly.

As with the barbican and the outer wall, there was no longer any door to the keep itself, and Sorak mounted the stone steps and went through the arched entryway in the darkness. Korahna followed uneasily, and Ryana brought up the rear. They came into a great hall that was dark and covered with dust and cobwebs. There were small droppings on the floor from some creatures that could be heard scurrying away at their approach, and guano was everywhere. The place smelled of decay.

"I cannot see a thing in here," Ryana said, knowing that Sorak's vision in the dark was as good as hers in the daylight.

"There is nothing much to see," he replied, his voice echoing in the darkness from somewhere to her right. "If there were any furnishings in here, they are long since gone. The hall is square-shaped, with a raised stone dais on the side to our left, where the lord of the manor sat during meals or when court was held, hard though it may be to imagine such convocations in a dismal place like this. There are sconces in the walls for torches, and an arched gallery that runs around three sides of the chamber on the upper floor. Looking up at the ceiling, I see rotted beams. The floors, for the most part, are now gone. No one has lived here for countless generations."

No sooner had he spoken, however, than a flickering light suddenly appeared, illuminating the walls of the stone steps leading up to the tower. It was as if someone were coming down the stairs, carrying a candle, except this light was blue.

"Witch light!" said Korahna, her voice scarcely above a whisper. She took hold of Ryana's arm.

As they watched, the light grew brighter, and down the steps, around the curving wall, a figure came. Korahna gasped and drew back fearfully behind Ryana. Ryana's fingers tightened on the sword hilt. As the figure came toward them, descending the stone steps, they could see it was a man in robes. He was not carrying a candle or a lantern. The blue glow emanated from his very body, rendering his features somewhat indistinct.

He had long hair, down past his shoulders. In the blue glow that he cast, it was impossible to tell what color the hair was, but Ryana imagined that it had to be white, for he looked very old. He had a lengthy beard, as well, which obscured much of his face. His proportions were human, and his robes were intricately woven with many decorations. Around his bare head, he wore a circlet of what looked to be either gold or silver—Ryana could not tell because of the glow that emanated from him. The center of the circlet was set with some sort of precious stone, cut into facets. He wore a sword buckled round his waist, with a hilt and pommel that were set with precious stones, as was the scabbard. Around his neck was some sort of chain of office, and wide metal bracelets hung on his wrists.

His soft-booted feet left no tracks in the dust on the stair as he descended. On the last step, he stopped and gazed at each of them in turn, his bright blue aura illuminating the entire chamber.

"Are you the Sage?" asked Sorak, staring intently at the figure.

"I *was* Lord Belloc, Duke of Carador, Lord of the Out-
lands, Keeper of the Seals of Knowledge, vassal to King
Valatrix the First of the Teluri."

"The Forgotten Ones," whispered Korahna. "The old
legends speak of them. They are said to have been the
first to practice sorcery."

"You are a spirit, then?" Ryana said.

"My body has been dead these past three thousand
years," the spirit said.

"And you have dwelt here ever since?" said Sorak.

"There was a time when I dwelt in a palace that
rivaled that of King Valatrix himself," the spirit said.
"It stood several days' ride to the west of here, in the
grassy plains, by a cool spring."

"Silver Spring," said Sorak. "How came you here?"

"Valatrix grew jealous of my knowledge and felt
threatened by my power. He coveted the Seals of
Knowledge, which were given into my safekeeping by
the Holy Sisters of the Order of the Willing Key." He
turned to face Ryana. "Greetings, Sister. It has been a
long time since I have met a priestess of the sacred
order."

Ryana stared at the spirit, uncomprehending at first,
and then it dawned on her. "The Willing Key . . . willing key . . . the *villichi?*"

"Valatrix believed the powers of the Holy Sisters
stemmed from their sacred Seals of Knowledge and not
from within themselves, as it was in truth. He believed
also that my own powers stemmed from these same
Seals, and not from years of arduous and patient study
of the mystic arts. He believed the Seals of Knowledge
held great power, when all they really held was the key
to that power, a power that one had to unlock within

oneself and nurture patiently through many years of dedication. In his jealousy and greed for power, Valatrix made an alliance with the Damites, who lived to the north in their fortress city in the Dragon's Bowl, and together, their forces marched against me.

"I could raise no army capable of defeating such a host," the spirit continued, "and so I was forced to flee, together with those of my loyal retainers and my people who managed to escape. The Holy Sisters scattered to the four quarters, to meet again in a secret place of which only they knew. I came here with my faithful few to build this keep and guard the Seals in this hidden cavern. Here we lived, and here we died, those who chose to stay. I was the last one left, and on my dying bed, I vowed to remain until such time as I could pass the Seals of Knowledge into the hands of one worthy of keeping and protecting them."

"The Seals of Knowledge," said Ryana. "Do you mean the Lost Keys of Wisdom of which villichi legends speak?"

"They are, indeed, the keys to wisdom," said the spirit, nodding, "but they shall give up their secrets only to one who knows their proper use."

"What of the Sage?" asked Sorak.

"Ah, yes, the Wanderer," the spirit said, nodding again. "Once, many years ago, he came, the first living soul to visit this place since my death. He was quite young then, rash, and full of the impetuosity of youth. I saw then that one day, perhaps, he could receive the Seals, but he was not yet ready."

"The Wanderer?" said Sorak with surprise. "You mean the Wanderer and the Sage are one and the same?"

"He has gained much in wisdom since those days," the spirit said, "but he cannot leave his sanctuary now, and I cannot go beyond these walls. It will be for you to take the Seals of Knowledge to him. That is why he sent you, to bring him the Seals and bring me my rest."

"But . . . we do not know where the Sage is to be found," Sorak said. "Where are we to seek him?"

"In your heart," the spirit said, "and in your dreams. The Wanderer shall be your guide, and the Seals shall be your keys to wisdom. Behold. . . ."

The spirit held out his right arm, fingers out-stretched, then turned his hand palm up, raising his arm in a lifting motion. A large stone block in the center of the chamber floor started to move with a loud scraping sound. It slowly rose up out of the floor to a height of about three feet and hovered there. As the spirit moved his arm, the block moved, floated to one side, then fell to the floor with a resounding crash and cracked into several pieces. From the hole once covered by the block, a small chest rose into the air. It seemed to be made of some sort of metal, for it gleamed softly in the light. It floated over to Ryana and hovered before her at the level of her chest.

"It is only fitting that a priestess bear the Seals," the spirit said. Ryana reached out and took the chest. It was fastened with a small iron lock, and as she held it, the lock sprang open . . . and immediately disinte-grated into dust. "My time on this plane has ended," the spirit said with a weary sigh. "I can rest at last."

And as they watched, the blue glow began to fade, and with it, the spirit faded from sight as well. "Remember, to the seeker the one true path is the path to knowledge," the spirit's disembodied voice echoed through the hall. "The Wanderer shall be your guide. The Seals shall be your keys to wisdom. Go now, and go quickly."

A cold wind blew through the hall as it was once again plunged into darkness. Ryana felt Sorak take her arm and lead them back out of the keep. Outside, she stared at the small chest she held in her hands. It was made of solid gold and carved with ancient runes.

Behind them, there was a rumbling sound and, as they turned, they saw the stones of the tower start to crumble.

"Quickly," Sorak said, taking their arms. "We must hurry."

They ran back across the courtyard and through the arched gate in the outer wall as the keep collapsed behind them in an avalanche of rock. They continued running through the barbican and out across the bridge. The span trembled beneath their feet as they ran across it. The mortar cracked, fissures appeared in the stone bridge, and heavy stone blocks fell into the lake below.

Korahna cried out as she tripped and fell, but Sorak caught her and swept her up into his arms. The entire cavern reverberated as the keep crumbled into rubble behind them, sending up a cloud of rock dust. The bats wheeled through the cavern, filling it with their screeching cries.

Sorak dragged his companions to the other side just as the bridge collapsed behind them, sending up gouts of water as the heavy stones fell into the lake. And then the rumbling ceased, and as the dust slowly settled, they could see nothing more than a pile of rubble where the keep had stood.

"Rest, Belloc," Sorak said. "We shall fulfill your charge."

Ryana stared at the small chest in her hands. "I have learned something not even Mistress Varanna knows," she said softly. "I have learned the origin of the villichi sisterhood. They scattered to the four directions to meet again in a secret place of which only they knew: The valley in the Ringing Mountains, where the temple stands today. And in this small chest lie the long-lost Keys to Wisdom . . . the Seals of Knowledge, which no priestess has seen in over three thousand years!"

"And now you may look upon them," Sorak said.

Ryana shook her head. "That I should be the one . . . I, who have broken my villichi vows. . . ." She shook her head again. "I am not worthy."

"Lord Belloc thought you were," said Sorak.

"But he did not know. . . . I did not tell him. . . ."

Sorak placed his hand on her shoulder. "Who am I, an outcast, to bear the magic sword of elven kings?" he asked. "Who are you to bear the Seals of Knowledge? And who is Korahna to go against all her father stands for and ally herself with the preservers? Who are we to question any of these things?"

"Questions are what led us here," Ryana said.

"True," Sorak replied, nodding. "And there are still answers to be found. But we shall not find them here. I had dared to hope our search was ended. I think now it has only just begun."

Korahna stood staring across the lake at the pile of rubble where the keep had stood. "To think, that poor spirit walked those dark and empty halls alone for longer than any of us have lived—or shall ever live. I had always thought that spirits were things to be feared, yet I feel pity for that poor shade, and relief that he may rest at last."

"Yes, now that he has passed his charge to us," Ryana said, staring at the golden chest. "And it is no small burden."

"What are the Seals of Knowledge?" asked Korahna.

Ryana opened the chest. Inside it, resting in slots cut into a block of polished obsidian, were four gold rings, with large, circular faces, like coins, engraved with runic characters. When pressed into hot wax or clay, each ring would make a seal.

"According to villichi legend, these are enchanted rings," Ryana said, "made by a druid sorceress who was the first high mistress of our ancient order. Each ring is said to be a key, one for each of the four quarters, and when all four are used together as seals, the impressions made by them unlock a spell that opens up the doors to wisdom."

"But what does that mean?" the princess asked.

Ryana shook her head. "I do not know. If there was more to the story, it has been lost over the many intervening years. Legend has it that each villichi priestess, when she came of age, departed on a pilgrimage to seek the Keys of Wisdom, which had been lost somehow. That is how our pilgrimages are said to have begun, and we know now how the keys were lost. Belloc kept them hidden in his sanctuary in the cavern while Valatrix, and who knows how many others, must have searched for them. Even if they did not possess the knowledge to use them properly, they would still have been worth a fortune. Now that metals are even more rare, they must be nearly priceless. And the sorcerer-kings would doubtless give anything to have them."

"And now you have them," said Korahna.

Ryana bit her lower lip and grimaced wryly. "And if news of it gets out," she said, "then I shall become a target for every thief, brigand, and defiler on the planet."

"Should you not take them back to your villichi temple in the Ringing Mountains?" asked the princess.

Ryana shook her head. "And give those same thieves, brigands, and defilers a reason to seek out the temple? No. In time, the same thing would only happen all over again. Besides, Belloc was entrusted with them, and it was a trust he held not only through life, but also in death. He believed they should be given to the Sage, and if anyone knows their proper use, the Sage would be that one."

"Then we had best be on our way to Nibenay," said Sorak, "for that is the destination we were given."

They made their way back through the tunnel and came out into the grotto once again. Sorak bent down by the pool and splashed some water on himself. "We should take this last opportunity to refill our skins and refresh ourselves a bit," he said.

"Indeed, you should, for it *shall* be your last opportunity," said Torian from the mouth of the grotto. He stood there, silhouetted in the light from outside, holding his sword and flanked by his mercenaries.

"Torian!" Korahna said.

"My compliments, Your Highness," Torian said, stepping into the grotto. "I never would have dreamt you could survive a trek across the barrens. Clearly, I vastly underestimated your strength of will and spirit. You not only survived, apparently none the worse for wear, but you have managed to find water, too. My men and I are grateful. We had grown very thirsty."

They looked tired and worn out from their journey across the savage barrens, but the determination in their eyes was no less intense for their ordeal. The mercenaries held crossbows drawn with bolts fitted. And they did not take their eyes off Sorak and Ryana for an instant.

"You should not have followed me, Torian," Korahna said. "I shall not go back with you."

"Oh, I have no intention of crossing that miserable, forsaken waste again," said Torian. "We are but two or three days' ride from the mountains, and once across those mountains, we are in my domain. I intend to take you back with me to Gulg, where you shall find a far more comfortable life in my family estate."

"No, Torian," Korahna said. "I am not going to go with you. I am going home, to Nibenay."

"To what?" asked Torian. "To a miserable life of skulking in the shadows with the Veiled Alliance? Living in some hovel in the slums and hiding from the templars? Plotting pointlessly in stinking, filthy little rooms amidst the stench of unwashed, sweaty bodies? Fearing to show your face in the light of day? That is no life for a princess. I can offer you far more than that."

"Perhaps," Korahna said, "but at a price I cannot and will not pay."

"Then I am afraid that you shall have no choice," said Torian. "I did not come all this way for nothing. Four men have died because of you, Korahna, and two more shall die when I catch up with them, provided the barrens have not already done them in. You have caused me a great deal of trouble, Your Highness, more than I would have suffered for any other woman. I intend to be compensated for my efforts, and you, Korahna, shall be that compensation."

"We may have something to say about that," Ryana said.

"You shall have precious little to say about anything, my lady," Torian replied with scorn. "You enjoyed the hospitality of my tent, and you repay me by stealing my property."

"Your *property?*" Korahna said with disbelief.

"Priestess or not, no one plays me for the fool," Torian continued, ignoring Korahna's outrage. He turned toward Sorak and raised his blade, using it to point at him. "And you, elfling—you I shall kill personally."

"Talk won't get it done," said Sorak.

"Then I am done talking," Torian said, raising his blade and leaping toward him.

With a motion so deceptively fast and smooth that it almost looked lazy, Sorak drew Galdra and parried Torian's blade as it came down. The moment Torian's sword came in contact with the elven steel, it split cleanly in two. Torian did not even feel the impact of the parry. His arm continued on with the downward stroke, throwing him off balance, and as the upper half of his sword blade clanged to the rock floor of the grotto, Torian recovered, staring with astonishment at what remained of his sword . . . the hilt and a foot of blade.

"You were saying?" Sorak said, raising one eyebrow.

Torian's eyes grew wide with fury. "Kill him!" he shouted to the mercenaries. "Shoot him down!"

The mercenaries raised their crossbows and shot their bolts, but though no more than fifteen paces separated them from their target, each bolt flew wide of its mark. The mercenaries gaped in astonishment.

Torian sputtered incoherently and screamed at them, spittle flying from his lips. "Idiots! What's the matter with you, can't you even hit a target not twenty feet away? Shoot him, I said! Shoot him! Shoot him!"

The mercenaries reached for fresh bolts, but suddenly all their arrows simply took flight on their own, leaping from their quivers and flying across the grotto to clatter against the far wall and drop into the pool.

Ryana's bolt, however, did not miss its mark. It struck one of the mercenaries in the throat, and he fell, choking and gurgling and clutching at his neck where the arrow penetrated his larynx and poked through to the other side. As he collapsed, Ryana drew her sword. "The rest are mine," she said. Torian gaped as she waded into the remaining mercenaries, swinging her sword with both hands.

With a scream of inarticulate rage, Torian drew his dagger and hurled it at Sorak.

Sorak merely raised his hand, and the dagger stopped in midair as if it had struck an invisible wall.

Torian's jaw dropped in disbelief; the dagger clattered harmlessly to the ground. His hand clawed for his second dagger, but before his fingers could close around the hilt, the knife flew out of its sheath and sailed across the grotto in a high arc over Sorak's head, falling into the waters of the pool behind him.

Seeing Torian disarmed, standing there stunned and apparently helpless, Korahna suddenly rushed toward him in a fit of royal outrage. "Your *property*, am I?" she said, her eyes blazing with fury. "I will show you whose property I am!"

"No, Princess!" Sorak cried out, but it was too late.

She swung to backhand Torian across the face. As her blow fell, Torian took her hand, spun her around, and grabbed her from behind. Seizing her in a power-ful grip, he held her before him, one arm clamped across her throat, the other gripping her by the hair. "Try any more of your tricks, elfling, and I'll break her neck! Drop your sword, priestess!"

The two remaining mercenaries, though seasoned and experienced fighters, had had their hands full with Ryana. Her assault had backed them to the mouth of the grotto, and now, when she saw that Torian had the princess, she hesitated, backing away slightly and holding her sword before her. The two mercenaries took advantage of the respite to spread apart, one to either side of her, ready to move in. Her gaze shifted quickly from them to Torian and back again.

"Drop your sword, I said!" Torian repeated. "Drop it or I'll kill the bitch!"

Ryana hesitated. "Sorak . . ." she said, uncertain, while keeping a wary eye on her two antagonists, who held their ground.

"If you kill her," Sorak said, "then there is nothing to save you from me."

"And if I let her go, I suppose you will graciously allow us to retire and go our way," said Torian sarcasti-cally. He gave a barking laugh. "No, my friend, I think not. You are not that stupid. You know that I would only bide my time and try again. You could not afford to let me live. I advise you to tell the priestess to drop her sword, before I grow impatient."

"Sorak," she said, "what should I do?"

"Don't listen to him, Ryana," Sorak said. "Those men

will kill you the moment you drop your sword."

"I give you my word that they shall not," said Torian.

"You expect me to trust your word?" Sorak replied contemptuously.

"You do not have much choice," said Torian. "But even so, you do not trust me. Consider this: I stand to gain nothing by having the priestess killed. She is of more value to me alive, as a hostage."

"The princess is of more value to you, still," said Sorak, stalling for time as his mind raced to find a way out of the situation. One quick twist and Korahna's neck would be broken. And he felt sure that Torian would not hesitate to do it. "You came all this way for her. Kill her now, and what have you got to show for all your efforts?"

"Clearly, it would be a loss," Torian admitted in an even voice, "and doubtless it would mean my life, as well. However, I would have died denying you your satisfaction, and that would count for something, I suppose. You have some designs of your own for the princess, I'll wager, else you would not have risked so much to bring her with you. The priestess, perhaps, would have helped her out of the goodness of her heart, and as a fellow preserver, but you? I think not. I think there is something in this for you, something that you want. A reward, perhaps, or something else that she has promised you."

Sorak damned the man for his shrewdness. He had hit upon the truth, though he did not know exactly what it was. He did need the princess, quite aside from his concern for her, and Torian knew it.

"If I release her now," said Torian, "then there is, indeed, nothing to save me from you. And if I kill her, then I face death, as well. Either way, conditions would remain the same. I am prepared to meet them, one way or the other. But so long as she remains alive, well then, the game continues. I will take the priestess as my hostage to make sure you do not try any of your tricks. You have demonstrated that you are a master of the Way, and I have no more illusions about my ability to kill you. The priestess shall ensure that *you* do not kill *me*."

"What do you propose?" asked Sorak tensely.

Torian smiled, realizing he had turned things around dramatically and now had the upper hand. "I will make my way to Gulg with the princess *and* the priestess. You shall have the liberty to follow us, but not too closely, for if I see you, the priestess shall suffer for it, understood?"

"Understood."

"Sorak, no!" Ryana cried.

"We have little choice, Ryana," he replied.

"Listen to him, Priestess," Torian said. "Now is not the time for foolish thoughts or noble gestures."

"Go on," said Sorak. "State your terms."

"When I reach the safety of my family estate," said Torian, "I shall release the priestess. Unharmed, so long as you do your part. The princess remains with me. Whatever reward she has promised you, I shall match it so that you shall not walk away with nothing to gain. That will give you an incentive to continue on your way and trouble me no more. I have no desire to watch my back for the remainder of my life. You shall wait outside the gates of Gulg. I will send your reward with the priestess, and you can meet her there. If you set foot within the city gates, I will leave word to have you killed. Even a master of the Way cannot stand against an entire city guard.

"I will even allow you to retain your magic sword, though I am sorely tempted to demand that you surrender it. However, I am a practical man, and have no wish to antagonize you any further. You took something from me, and now I have it back. I am content to leave it at that, and even to pay you for all the trouble you have caused me. I will consider it an investment in the future. So . . . what is it to be? Shall we both be practical? Or shall we conclude this sad affair right here and now, to no good profit for either side?"

"Put down your sword, Ryana," Sorak said.

"Sorak, no! Don't listen to him! You cannot trust him!" she replied.

"I think I can trust him to look after his own interests," Sorak said. "And it is in his interest to keep the bargain in good faith. Put down your sword."

She hesitated, then, with an expression of disgust, threw down her sword.

EIGHT

It wasn't very difficult for Sorak to trail Torian and his mercenaries without being seen. He did not even need to allow the Ranger to the fore to do it. Torian was an experienced tracker, but Sorak was an elfling, and not only did he have the training of the villichi to aid him in his task, he also had certain genetic advantages. He possessed superior senses and greater powers of endurance and could move more silently than a human ever could.

Torian, of course, would know that he was out there. He was no fool. He had threatened to take it out on Ryana if he caught even a glimpse of Sorak, but Sorak was reasonably confident even a man as experienced as Torian would not suspect just how close he could come without alerting them. He never allowed them out of his sight.

He did not trust Torian. What he had told Ryana was the truth: he was sure he could trust Torian to look after his own interests, but Torian's interests did not necessitate leaving them alive. He had tried putting himself in Torian's place in an effort to anticipate what he might do. That task proved as easy as allowing the cynical, self-centered Eyron to the fore.

"*Simple,*" Eyron had said. "*If I were Torian, I would consider the available alternatives and choose whichever course was the most convenient and involved the least risk to myself, and I would act on that.*"

"*And what course would that be?*" asked Sorak.

"*Well, assuming you kept your part of the bargain, of course, then I, being Torian, would do likewise. Up to a point,*" said Eyron. "*I would make my way toward Gulg, taking care to keep a careful watch for you. How far do you suppose it is?*"

"*Four or five days, I would think. Perhaps a little more. If he makes good time, he should reach the mountains in another two or three days. Once there, he said he knew the country. The Barrier Mountains are not very high. It should take him no longer than two days to cross them, and Gulg lies in the valley at their foot.*"

"*Then he will always make certain to leave a guard on watch when he makes camp,*" said Eyron, "*for he has no more reason to trust you than you have to trust him. He will doubtless bind his captives carefully and thoroughly, taking care there is no way they can work their bonds loose, and he will keep a bright fire burning because he knows it would reflect within your eyes should you approach. He will take no chances and make certain Ryana is always close at hand so that he may threaten her should you make any attempt at rescue.*"

"*And if I make no such attempt and allow him to reach Gulg? What then?*" asked Sorak. "*What would you do in his place?*"

"*Why then, the simplest matter would be to proceed directly to my family estate after first issuing orders to the guards at the gate to be on the watch for you. Once I had*

*reached safety with my captives, I would then do exactly as
I had promised. I would release Ryana and give her the
reward I promised you, but first I would make certain a full
complement of guardsmen were stationed at the city gate,
not in full view, of course, and perhaps I would arrange to
have some more concealed outside. The moment Ryana
came out of the city gates and you came forth to meet her,
they would strike. You would both be dead, and my problem
would be neatly solved, with no inconvenience to myself."*

"You have a devious turn of mind, Eyron."

"Well, it is your mind, too," Eyron replied.

"True," said Sorak. "Sometimes I wonder how there is
room for all of us."

"You could always leave," said Eyron. "I would not
object to being the primary."

"Somehow, I suspect the others would have a word or two
to say about that," said Sorak wryly. "Nevertheless, I am
grateful for your presence, oppressive though it may sometimes be."

"Whatever would you do without me?"

"I don't know. Cultivate a brighter outlook upon life?"
said Sorak.

"And go through it trusting people blindly, I suppose."

"I never trusted Torian. But I trust him now to do
exactly as you suppose he will. The question is, will he
expect me to anticipate his plans?"

"If I were Torian, I would weigh matters very carefully
and plan for every possible eventuality," said Eyron.

"And Torian is a clever man," said Sorak. "If we have
anticipated what he shall do, then chances are that he will
have anticipated that, as well. So then, what are we to do
about him?"

"Something very final, I should think," Eyron replied.

"I was hoping for an answer that was somewhat more specific," Sorak said.

"You will have to excuse me," Eyron replied, "you so rarely ask for my opinion about anything, much less my recommendations, that I am unaccustomed to all this sudden attention. The answer is obvious. You must overcome Torian before he reaches Gulg."

"I could have thought of that myself," said Sorak. "The question is, how do I accomplish that without risking the safety of Ryana or the princess?"

"Torian will not harm the princess save as a last resort," said Eyron. "He was quite prepared to kill her in the grotto, for he had nothing left to lose. He had to convince you of the earnestness of his intent, and he knew the only way he could do that was to be prepared to carry out his threat. He gambled that you would be unwilling to gain victory at the cost of her life."

"And he was right," said Sorak.

"Obviously," Eyron replied, "or else we would not now be in this position. Yet Torian knows that all he gained is time . . . and another hostage. And he would strike at Ryana before he would harm the princess."

"If he did that, then nothing could save him," Sorak said.

"Perhaps he knows that," Eyron said. "So he would not kill her, then. However, there are many things that he could do short of killing her. And Torian strikes me as an imaginative man. Therefore, we must plan to strike at him in such a manner that neither he nor his two mercenaries would have the opportunity to act."

"So then speed is of the essence," Sorak said. "But that, too, is obvious. He will expect me to attack, and he will know that swiftness would be my only chance."

"*Precisely,*" Eyron said. "*He will expect you to attack. So the attack must come from someone . . . or something . . . else.*"

* * * * *

"Any sign of him?" asked Torian.

Rovik turned and shook his head. "No. Gorak and I have been keeping careful watch, but there has been no sign that he is following us."

"Oh, he is out there; you may be sure of that," said Torian. "And doubtless closer than you think."

"In this open country, if he was close, we surely would have seen—"

"You would have seen *nothing*," Torian said, his voice a whip crack of authority. "The Nomad is not a man. He is an *elfling*, with all the attributes of both his cursed races! He could find cover in a place that would not conceal a child, and he can move more softly than a shadow. And when he comes at you, if you so much as pause to blink with surprise, he will be on you with dazzling speed. What is more, he is a master of the Way. Do not underestimate him merely because he appears human. Observe. . . ."

He indicated the obsidian blade he had taken from the man slain by Ryana at the grotto. It had a hide thong fastened around its hilt, with a loop through which his hand could fit. "He shall not disarm me quite so easily again," said Torian, "though this blade would be of little use against that cursed sword of his."

"So what is the point, then?" Gorak asked.

"The point, you brainless fool, is not to use it against

him, but against the *priestess*," Torian said scornfully. "He values her. Doubtless, they are lovers."

"But I had heard that villichi priestesses do not take—" Gorak began, but Torian cut him off impatiently.

"She is a woman, is she not?" he said. "And he is a comely-looking bastard, for all his coarseness and roughshod appearance. Indeed, many women are attracted to such things."

"But . . . he is not even of her race!" said Rovik.

"So? You have never heard of a human female being bedded by an elf? Where do you think half-elves come from, you idiot? Fruit is often all the sweeter for its being forbidden. Did you mark the way she looked at him? No, of course not. That is because you are a simpleton. Make no mistake: he will attack us before we reach the city. That is why we must press on with all possible speed and clear the barrens before sundown."

"Not that I would dream of questioning your judgment, my lord," said Gorak, "but why?"

"Do you relish the thought of being out here at night without a fire?" Torian said. "There is nothing out here to burn, and the moons will not be full tonight. The elfling can see in the dark. Can you?"

"Oh," said Gorak lamely.

"Once we clear the barrens near the foothills, there will be scrub to burn," said Torian. "If he approaches, you will see the firelight reflected in his eyes. They will be lambent, like a cat's, and you will see them. That is, you will see them if you remain alert. And by the time you see them, it may already be too late. Still, some warning is better than none at all."

"If I were the elfling, I would wait to make my move until we reached the mountains," Rovik said confidently. "There will be more cover there."

"If *you* were the elfling, I would feel more confident about our chances," Torian replied dryly. "Doubtless, he will deduce that we will think that and try to make his move before then, hoping to take us by surprise."

"You would have made a good general, my lord," said Rovik.

"Generals serve kings," Torian replied. "My ambitions are considerably higher. Yours, if you have any, should be concerned with survival for the present. We were nearly a dozen when we started out. Now, we are only three. And we still have at least four days' journey ahead of us."

"But he is only one," said Gorak. "He can no longer depend on the sword arm of the priestess. Do you truly think he alone can best the three of us, even if he is a master of the Way?"

"Even if he weren't, I would prefer not to take the risk," said Torian.

"What do you really think our chances are, my lord?" asked Rovik, uneasily.

"That would depend on just how badly you two want to live," said Torian. "The priestess is our best chance to make it back alive. Look upon her and remember that she alone is your security. Keep closer to her than her shadow, for so long as there is a chance that she may come to harm, the Nomad will not dare strike."

Ryana heard him, gagged and trussed up as she was, and shot a venomous look in his direction. Torian saw it and grinned.

"Now there's a look!" he said. "If a gaze could burn, I would be incinerated on the spot." He shifted his gaze to Korahna. "And as for you, my princess, I owe you a debt of gratitude. If not for your timely fit of royal temper, this journey would have ended for me at the grotto."

Korahna was both gagged and bound, as Ryana was, but her eyes clearly conveyed her misery and self-recrimination. She recalled what had happened only too well. She had played the incident over and over in her mind, tormenting herself with it, and the guilt she felt was worse because the consequences of her act had fallen not only on her, but on Ryana as well.

Seeing Torian disarmed, she had believed he was defeated. All she could think of were the insults she had suffered from him. When he had referred to her as his property, as *something* that belonged to him, all she could feel was her outrage, all she could think of was backhanding him across the face and humiliating him before his men—as he had humiliated her. It had never occurred to her that he could raise his hand against her, that he would seize her, that he was no less dangerous for having been disarmed. No one had ever laid a hand on her. No one would have dared. She was a princess of the Royal House of Nibenay.

I have been a fool, she thought miserably—a spoiled, pampered, arrogant little fool, and I deserve whatever happens to me. But what has Ryana ever done except offer me her hand in friendship? Even her friends among the Veiled Alliance were her friends only because she was of use to them. She was of use to Sorak, too, though she knew that his motives were not entirely selfish. But Ryana . . . Ryana had nothing to gain from befriending her. Indeed, she had done it at first against her better judgment. Ryana was the only *true* friend she ever had, and after the bond Kether forged between them, she knew no one could ever be as close to her as the villichi priestess. And this was how she had repaid her for her friendship. Korahna knew this was all her fault, and for that, she could not forgive herself.

Tears flowed softly down her cheeks and soaked into her gag. She could not even raise a hand to wipe them away. How far the princess of the Royal House of Nibenay has fallen, she thought. And when they reached Torian's estate, she had no doubts she would fall further still. In the beginning, Torian had treated her with deference as befitted a woman of her station, and had hoped to win her over with solicitude and gentlemanly manners. But now the border had been crossed, and he had laid hands on her. He had shown her his true colors, and there was no longer any point to the facade of his aristocratic charm. She knew him now beyond a doubt for what he was, and he would no longer bother with pretense. She had no doubt that he would now take by force what he could not win the other way.

But what of Ryana? She had seen the way the mercenaries looked at her. She was a beautiful, young villichi priestess—a virgin. And they gazed at her as if she were a piece of meat and they hungry carrion-eaters. So Torian had promised her to them. Whatever untender ministrations she would suffer at the hands of Torian, Ryana would know worse. Korahna couldn't bear the thought. Somehow, she had to *do* something! But what could she do? If Ryana, who was so much stronger and so much more capable than she, could not escape, then what hope did *she* have?

And in her desperation, in her anxiety about her friend, a spark ignited deep within the princess. It was a small spark, barely a glow, but slowly, it began to burn. It was the sort of fire ignited within those who had nothing left to lose. Only those to whom life meant less than some goal, some ideal, would ever feel its flame. As the spark ignited a fire that began to spread within her, Korahna resolved that somehow, even if it was at the cost of her own life, she would find a way to escape her bonds and help Ryana. And as her gaze burned into Torian, who had contemptuously turned his back on her, Korahna swore silently that she would find a way to kill him.

* * * * *

"*They are moving quickly,*" Sorak said.

"*Torian is anxious to be out of the barrens before nightfall,*" Eyron replied. "*He does not wish to risk making camp without a fire.*"

"*You think he will push on instead of making camp?*"

"*I would not, if I were in his place,*" said Eyron. "*The darkness favors you. Making camp will slow him down, but a camp fire would also render your approach more difficult.*"

"*Our approach,*" said Sorak.

"*Well, when it comes to that, then leave me out of it,*" said Eyron. "*I find violence unsettling.*"

"*You mean you find fear unsettling,*" said Sorak.

"*Call it what you will,*" Eyron replied. "*The fact*

remains that I will not be of much use to you if you can feel my . . . unsettlement. You have asked for my advice, shocking as that may seem, and I have given it to the best of my ability. I have done my part. When the time comes, I would much prefer to be asleep and out of your way. I have had quite enough excitement on this journey, thank you."

"Wouldn't you want to know what happens?" Sorak asked.

"If you execute my plan well, I know what will happen," Eyron replied. *"And if you do not, well, I would prefer to die quietly in my sleep."*

"You think the Shade and Kether and the others would allow us to die?" asked Sorak.

"It would take you time to summon Kether, time you may not have," said Eyron pointedly. *"As for the Shade, even he is not invulnerable, fearsome as he may be."*

"You have too strong a sense of your mortality, Eyron," Sorak said.

"And you have too frail a sense of ours," Eyron replied. *"And since your mortality is mine, as well, it seems rather in my interest to remind you of that every now and then."*

"You have a point," admitted Sorak, smiling to himself.

"And do not give me that condescending little smile," said Eyron, irritably. *"I have not always shirked my part whenever we are all in danger. It is just that this time. . . ."*

"You are worried about Ryana," Sorak said with some surprise. *"I had always thought you found her presence irksome."*

"Well . . . in the beginning, perhaps . . ." Eyron replied somewhat hesitantly, as if reluctant to admit he truly cared about anyone except himself. *"I suppose I have grown accustomed to her. And if, by chance, something*

should go wrong . . ."

"*You would rather not be there to see it,*" Sorak completed the thought for him. "*And you think I would? My feelings for Ryana are considerably stronger than yours.*"

"*I know,*" said Eyron sympathetically. "*I suppose I really am a coward, after all.*"

"*If you are, then you are that part of me that is cowardly,*" said Sorak. "*Besides, feeling afraid does not make one a coward. It is allowing fear to become that which controls you in everything you do that makes a coward. Isn't that right, Guardian?*"

"*Everyone feels fear at one time or another,*" she replied. "*It is but the natural way of things.*"

"*Even you?*" asked Eyron.

"*Even me,*" she replied. "*I fear for Ryana's safety as much as you do. I fear also for the princess. She may be a defiler's daughter, but her heart is pure, and she has chosen the Path of the Preserver. A life as Torian's concubine is a fate as bad as death. And I fear for all of us, as well.*"

"*But what of the Shade?*" asked Eyron. "*Surely, the Shade does not know fear.*"

"*I cannot speak for the Shade,*" the Guardian replied. "*He is that part of us that is driven by the elemental, primal force of survival. He is the beast within, and we all know how terrible he is to behold. When he is awake, we tremble. When he slumbers, we are nevertheless grateful for his presence. Yet as powerful as the Shade is, consider the sources from which that power stems. The instinct to survive is, in part, driven by fear. So even though the Shade may appear utterly fearless, to some degree, fear must be a part of that which drives and motivates him. No one is completely without fear, Eyron. Fear is a part of every living creature. It is one of those things that enables us to understand what it truly means to be alive."*

Eyron withdrew for a while to contemplate the Guardian's words, and the Guardian withdrew as well, so as not to intrude on Sorak's thoughts. However, she was never very far beneath the surface, and Sorak knew he could always depend on her protective, maternal strength and on the wisdom of her perceptions. Eyron, too, for all of his contentiousness, was often a source of comfort to him, irritating though he could be. Eyron's negativity and cynicism were valuable to him in that they were traits he lacked himself. In the past, he had found them to be hindrances, but now he understood that Eyron's character traits were essential as a balance to his own and those of all the others—the Ranger, with his strongly pragmatic sensibilities, his stoic self-containment, and his love of and affinity with nature; Lyric, with his childlike sense of wonder and his innocent spirit; the Watcher, whose ever-aware, cautious presence was set off by her almost constant silence; the mysterious and ethereal Kether, who was, in a sense, a part of them and yet was more like some sort of spiritual visitation from another plane; even Kivara, with her amoral impulses and irrepressible desire for sensual stimulation and excitement. Separately, all of them were incomplete, but together, they achieved a balance that preserved the tribe of one.

And now, the delicate balance of the tribe was absolutely essential to the success of Eyron's plan. If Ryana and the princess were to be saved, they would all have to work together, and the timing would be crucial, for they could not all come to the fore at the same time. Even if Sorak could call upon all of their abilities at once, the plan would still be dangerous. But he could not. Much of the plan would depend on the ones among them who were the least humanoid, the ones who were the living embodiments of the animal sides of their nature. And it would all begin with Screech.

* * * * *

Torian stopped and looked around. "We shall make camp here," he said. Wearily, he dismounted and ordered the two mercenaries to start gathering dry scrub brush for the fire. Both Gorak and Rovik looked exhausted, and Torian knew exactly how they felt. As fit as he was, he scarcely had any energy left.

The priestess and the princess looked half dead. For them, bound and gagged as they were, the journey had been still more difficult. No matter, Torian thought. The priestess would survive for the short time still left to her, and Korahna would have time to recover from the journey once they reached his family estate in Gulg. This ordeal would break her rebellious, independent spirit, Torian thought. By the time he brought her home, she would be meek and docile, with no more fight left in her. He smiled to himself as he thought that women were, in many ways, like kanks. By nature unruly and difficult to handle, once they were broken to the saddle they obediently did the master's bidding. Korahna would make a handsome little kank, and he could use her at his pleasure. As for the priestess . . . well, perhaps it *was* bad luck to kill a priestess, but it would not be accomplished by his hand.

At least they were finally quit of the cursed Stony Barrens. Torian felt a great sense of accomplishment. Not only had he trailed the elfling and succeeded in wresting the princess back from him, but he had crossed the barrens and survived, the first man ever to have done so. The mercenaries, of course, did not really count. Besides, they would have turned back long before if he had not been there to instill fear in them and drive them. For generations to come, bards would sing songs about his feat. In fact, as soon as he returned to Gulg, he would commission a bard to compose an appropriate ballad. "The Quest of Lord Torian." Yes, that had a noble ring to it.

As the mercenaries gathered fuel for the campfire from the surrounding countryside, Torian pulled Korahna from her kank and carried her to a nearby pagafa tree. The stunted, blue-green tree with its multiple trunks and scrubby branches provided little in the way of shelter, but it would serve to keep his captives secure. Korahna did not move or protest as he carried her over to the tree and propped her up against one of the trunks. Her eyes were closed, and she uttered only a small moan as he began to tie her to the tree. Once he had her firmly secured, he then went to get the priestess.

She seemed worn out, offering no more resistance than Korahna as he took her down, but as he was carrying her over to the tree, she suddenly began to thrash and squirm furiously in his grasp. Torian lost his balance and fell, dropping her to the ground. However, he instantly regained his feet and, as Ryana was struggling to rise, he rushed up and kicked her in the side. She collapsed with a muffled groan, and

Torian added one more kick for good measure. This time, she lay still.

"I am much too tired to be forbearing, Priestess," Torian said. "And when I am tired, my temper grows quite short. I remind you that you are of use to me alive, but not necessarily in one piece."

He then reached down and grabbed a fistful of her hair, dragging her by it to the tree. Once there, he bent down and took her by the shoulders, then jerked her hard, smashing her head against the trunk. He repeated the process three times more, until her head lolled forward on her chest. Then he bound her securely with her back against the tree trunk, next to the princess.

Straightening up, he breathed deeply several times, rolled his neck and shoulders to get out some of the kinks, then went over to his mount and took a long drink from his water bag.

"Could we have some water, too, my lord?" asked Rovik, coming up behind him.

"Have you gathered enough fuel to keep the fire fed throughout the night?" he asked.

"Not yet, my lord," said Rovik, moistening his lips nervously, "but we have enough to keep it going for a while. We shall gather more, but the work would go easier if our thirst were slaked."

"Very well," said Torian curtly, "but be quick about it. And keep your eyes open. That cursed elfling is sure to be around here somewhere."

Rovik did not like the sound of his voice, but he said nothing as he went over to his mount and untied one of his water skins. He took a long drink as Gorak came up beside him to wait his turn. When Rovik finished drinking, he handed the skin to his companion.

"Lord Torian's nerves are drawn tight as a bow-string," he said softly, watching out of the corner of his eye as Torian went to sit beside his captives, his sword held ready.

Gorak took a pause for breath. When he spoke, he carefully kept his voice low. "If you ask me, we should just slit his throat, take the women for ourselves, and be done with it."

"And be hunted for the remainder of our lives for killing an aristocrat?" said Rovik. "Don't be a fool."

"Who is to know?" asked Gorak. "There are no witnesses save for the women. And they are hardly in a position to give testimony."

"What would you do, kill them?"

"After we have had our pleasure. Why not?"

"And have nothing to show for all that we have gone through? Are a few moments of pleasure enough to make up for all of that? Besides, Torian would not die easily. He has trained throughout his life with master swordsmen. And then, don't forget, there is still the elfling."

"Aye, I have not forgotten," Gorak said, "but there has been no sign of him. How do we know he has not simply given up or been killed by some damn beast?"

"He is much more at home out here than either you or I," said Rovik. "And it is no easy thing to kill a master of the Way. No, our best chance is to stick with Torian. Three are much stronger than two, especially with the women as our hostages. When we reach Gulg, we shall be well rewarded. And then I shall quit Torian's service with no end of pleasure."

"*Enough!*" shouted Torian from his resting place by

the pagafa tree. He waved his sword toward them. "Get back to work! And keep alert for that damned elfling!"

"It would almost be worth it to cut his throat and return the women to the elfling," Gorak said. "It might leave our purses empty, but there would still be satisfaction in the deed!"

"I might be tempted to agree with you," said Rovik, "if I thought the elfling would be satisfied with that and would let us walk away. But I have no illusions about that, my friend. Even if we manage to complete Torian's commission and leave Gulg never to return, we would still be looking over our shoulders for the remainder of our lives. I would rather die a quick death than live a lingering one. One way or another, it ends here."

They returned to collecting more fuel for the fire, all the while keeping a wary eye on the countryside around them.

* * * * *

Sorak had decided not to wait. He would make his move tonight. Three more days at most and Torian would reach Gulg. And the closer he came to his city, the more the odds favored him. Torian had pushed hard to be clear of the barrens by nightfall. He and his mercenaries would be tired, and that worked in Sorak's favor. However, Torian undoubtedly knew that, too, and so he would expect a rescue attempt. Sorak's only chance for success was to perform the rescue in a way that Torian would not expect.

He slipped back slightly and allowed Screech to

come forth. Screech never spoke except to beasts. If he knew the language of humans or elves or halflings, he had never given any sign of it. But Screech knew how to communicate with beasts. On the rare occasions when he came forth, he preferred animal company, speaking only to them and never to any of the others in the tribe. Screech was more animal than humanoid, but he possessed the cunning of a halfling. As Sorak gave way to him, not ducking under completely, but sharing consciousness with Screech, their body underwent a subtle change in attitude.

Screech crouched down very low and began moving on all fours, with a flowing, sinuous, catlike motion. The rocks and boulders of the barrens had given way to desert tableland, rising gradually toward the foothills of the Barrier Mountains, looming in a dramatic silhouette against the night sky. The countryside here consisted of sandy, rocky soil, dotted with desert scrub brush and the occasional small pagafa tree. Here and there, a spreading broom bush or a large barrel cactus offered a place of concealment, but for the most part, it was open country, offering good visibility even in the dim light of the quarter moons. Screech stayed very low, moving with agonizing slowness as he approached the camp, ensuring that their position would not be given away by any swift movements.

A human moving that slowly, in such an uncomfortable position, would have been in acute discomfort from cramped and spasming muscles. His knees would have been sore within moments, and his hands would have been torn and bleeding from being abraded by sand, small rocks, dry thorny twigs, and cactus needles on the desert floor. However, Sorak's hands were hard and thickly callused, and his knees had built up thick layers of skin from years of crawling through the underbrush. He disregarded the tiny insects that crawled up his arms and legs. Their stinging bites would have maddened a mere human, but Sorak was accustomed to them. Screech was not even aware of the little creatures. His attention was focused entirely on the campfire just ahead.

The two mercenaries had built it up with lots of dry scrub brush, so that it was burning very brightly and illuminating the area all around their camp. Most of the fuel that they were using to start the fire, dry as it was, burned very quickly, which necessitated their steadily feeding the flames. But the desert broom bushes they then added had a high resin content and burned hotter and more slowly. In time, as the heat built up and more broom bushes were thrown upon the blaze, it would burn long with plenty of bright light. The mercenaries were not green to the desert. They were both seasoned campaigners, and they knew the art of desert survival.

As Screech approached still closer, he saw where Torian sat under the spreading, twisted, blue-green branches of the small pagafa tree. Ryana was bound tightly to one of its thin, multiple trunks, and the princess was secured to another. Neither of them were moving. The trunks of the pagafa tree were no thicker around than Sorak's thigh, but they were immensely strong. There was no way that either Ryana or the princess, even if they were not weakened and totally exhausted, would have been able to break free.

The three men obviously would sleep in shifts.

Sorak had hoped that two of them would sleep while one kept watch, but he soon saw that Torian was more careful than that. One of the mercenaries stretched out on his bedding roll between the fire and the tree, while his companion remained awake with Torian.

The mercenary that stayed awake paced back and forth to remain alert. Occasionally, he would throw more fuel on the fire, but for the most part, his gaze continually swept the countryside around them, and his hand never strayed from his sword hilt. As he neared, Sorak saw why. The man had fashioned a rawhide thong, attached to his sword hilt, with a loop around his wrist. Any effort to disarm him with the Way would not jerk the sword free from his grasp. These men learned quickly.

Torian remained close to Ryana, between her and the princess, with his back leaning against the tree. His obsidian sword was out and in his lap. With one quick gesture, he could bring it to Ryana's throat. He sat very still, and Sorak might have thought him asleep. Indeed, perhaps that was what Torian wanted him to think. Instead, the man was wide awake, watching and listening intently. Any attempt to circle behind him and attack from that direction would alert the mercenary, who kept passing that position and watching for just such an eventuality. Any attempt to attack the mercenary first would give Torian plenty of time to threaten Ryana. And it would also give the sleeping man a chance to wake and join the fray. Torian was certainly no fool. However, he had never before been up against a tribe of one.

Screech was now down on his belly, like a snake. He had approached so close that if he rose up to his hands and knees, the mercenary would probably spot him. With his excellent night vision, Sorak carefully marked the disposition of the camp and the supplies. The kanks were staked down off to the right, perhaps fifteen or twenty feet away from the tree. The mercenary who walked the perimeter of the camp was armed with a sword and small crossbow, which he carried in one hand, drawn and ready to fire. The sleeping man had a drawn crossbow lying by his side, and he, too, had his sword out, with a thong fastened to it and around his wrist. Torian sat underneath the tree, his legs stretched out before him, one knee bent. He held his sword out in his lap, and his hand rested on a crossbow. He had also rearmed himself with three more daggers. They were not taking any chances.

"*Now, Screech,*" Sorak said.

Screech flattened out on the ground and closed his eyes as he sent out a psionic call. Moments later, it was picked up. From the area all around Torian's camp, small, brightly colored critic lizards began to converge on the pagafa tree. They scurried silently up the slender trunks behind the princess and Ryana, without making the slightest sound, and began to chew upon the ropes that held them. Meanwhile, Screech sent out another psionic call.

About a quarter of a mile away, it was picked up by a colony of desert antloids in their warren. The queen responded to the call and, moments later, the workers began to swarm up out of the huge mound that was the entrance to their underground labyrinth. The giant ants streamed across the desert in parallel lines, one after the other, like infantry trooping through a canyon, moving swiftly and purposefully, unerringly guided by the call Screech sent forth.

Ryana was the first to realize that something was happening. Having been knocked senseless by Torian hammering her head against the tree trunk, she regained consciousness slowly and painfully. Her head seemed enshrouded by a fog. She had the feeling that something was crawling over her hands. She tried to move them and found that she could not. Her eyelids fluttered open, and she saw the blurred image of the campfire. Slowly, it came into focus, and she remembered where she was and in what circumstances—recalled how Torian had kicked and battered her. The lingering effects of pain were banished by cold rage. She felt the tree trunk against her back and realized she was bound to it.

She looked to her left and saw Torian seated next to her, his head lolling forward on his chest. He wasn't quite asleep, but he was close to it. As she watched, he jerked his head up quickly, catching himself, and gazed out beyond the fire. Ryana lowered her head, feigning unconsciousness. Moments later, peeking from barely parted eyelids, she saw Torian's head loll forward once more. Then she felt something crawling on her hands again. She froze. A snake? She was defenseless. And then she felt one of her bonds give slightly. She twisted her head back as far as she could and saw that the entire tree trunk behind her was crawling with brightly colored critic lizards. And they were chewing on her bonds. She looked toward where Korahna was tied up, just beyond where Torian sat, nodding, and saw the tree trunk behind the princess swarming with the lizards, as well. Dozens and dozens of them. And then understanding dawned.

Screech!

If Torian awoke now and turned around, or if the mercenary guard came any closer, either one of them would spot the lizards instantly. But one of the mercenaries slept, while the other was walking back and forth by the fire, peering intently out into the darkness. And Torian was oblivious to the creatures swarming over the tree trunks to either side of him. Ryana felt one of the bonds part. And then another. Slowly, she assisted the lizards by pulling with her hands, careful not to make the slightest sound. She felt one of them crawling up her back and onto her neck, where it started tugging at the gag tied around her mouth. A few moments later, it came free, and she took a deep breath.

Out beyond the campfire, Screech lay flat upon the ground, his ear pressed against the earth. He could now hear the thrumming sound of the approaching antloids. They were coming fast. A few moments more, and their approach would be clearly audible. Sorak knew he would have to move quickly when the time came. He lay still and waited.

Gorak suddenly stopped his pacing, alerted by some sound out in the darkness. Instantly, he scanned the desert beyond the fire for the gleam of lambent eyes, but saw no sign of them. What was it? It was almost like the sound of distant thunder, but not quite. He raised his crossbow and held it ready, his sword dangling from the thong loop around his wrist. It was growing closer now, and louder, a rumbling that sounded like . . . and suddenly, too late, he realized what it was. His eyes grew wide, and he called out, "Rovik! Lord Torian! Wake up, quickly!"

Rovik was on his feet in an instant, grabbing up his crossbow. "What?" he called out, looking around anxiously. "What is it?"

"Antloids!" Gorak said. "Coming this way!"

At Gorak's first alarm, Torian jerked his head up, and the first thing he did was check his captives. As he turned to look at the princess, he saw the lizards swarming over the tree trunk and her bonds.

"Gith's blood!" he swore, leaping to his feet.

In that moment, Ryana pulled free from her bonds, which the lizards had chewed through. Torian lunged at her, but she twisted away and kicked out with her leg as she rolled, sweeping his feet out from under him. As he went down, Torian heard Gorak's agonized scream.

The first of the giant antloids had come barreling out of the darkness into the firelight, and Gorak only had enough time to loose one bolt from his crossbow. It bounced harmlessly off the creature's thick exoskeleton, and then it was on him, closing its huge mandibles around his waist and lifting him high into the air. Gorak's throat-rending screams echoed through the night as the rest of the antloids swarmed into the camp.

Rovik tried to run, but he knew it was hopeless. Only an elf could outrun a full-grown antloid. Four of the creatures converged on him, and he disappeared, screaming, in a tangle of snapping mandibles. The kanks, panicked by the charging antloids, pulled out their stakes and escaped into the night. The antloids did not pursue them.

Torian regained his feet quickly after Ryana had tripped him up. He lunged for the princess, but Ryana made a dive and tackled him.

As he fell once more, Korahna came to her senses. The first thing she saw were the antloids swarming into the camp. She brought her hands up to her face and screamed, not even realizing in her panic that her hands were free. Then she saw all the lizards swarming over the tree trunk behind her. Several of them were still clinging to her arms. She recoiled from the pagafa tree in horror, flailing with her arms to shake the creatures loose.

Torian wrestled with Ryana, kicking free of her grasp and rolling to his feet, but as he turned to the attack, three antloids lumbered toward him. He retreated, leaving Ryana to the creatures, not realizing they were advancing to protect her. He started to move toward the princess, but two more antloids cut him off. Korahna tried to run, but suddenly found herself surrounded by the huge creatures. She screamed again, but suddenly felt a hand clamp over her mouth.

A familiar voice at her shoulder said, "Do not be afraid. They will not harm you."

She turned and saw Sorak and threw her arms around him, sobbing gratefully into his chest.

Torian retreated toward the fire, his head jerking to the left and right as he desperately sought an avenue of escape. But there was nowhere to run. He was encircled by a ring of antloids. Yet, they did not move in for the kill. They simply stood there in a large circle all around the campfire, surrounding him where he stood, their mandibles making ominous clicking sounds like large sticks being struck together. Only then did Torian realize his two mercenaries were dead.

He stood there, holding his useless obsidian sword before him, knowing it was a hopeless weapon to use against these creatures. And even if he could succeed in killing one, the others would tear him to pieces. So he stood and waited for the end.

Then, to his stunned surprise, one of the creatures scuttled slightly to one side, and Sorak came into the circle. Behind him were the princess and Ryana. The antloids made no move to harm them. In a flash, Torian understood that, somehow, the elfling could make the creatures do his bidding. Only then did he truly understand what he was up against, and he cursed himself for ever having trailed the elfling to begin with. He had followed his own death, pursuing it, and now it had caught him.

"Damn you for a sorcerer!" Torian swore, as he raised his sword defiantly.

"What good do you think that will do now?" said Sorak, gazing at the weapon.

"More good than you know," Torian replied. "It will deny you the final victory." And with that, he quickly turned the sword around, grasping it with both hands, and plunged it deep into his stomach.

Sorak was taken completely unprepared. He simply stared, astonished, as Torian grunted with pain and sank to his knees, transfixed by his own blade, blood bubbling forth between his lips. Ryana caught her breath and Korahna gasped as they both stared at the dying man.

Torian raised his head and gazed at the princess. "You were my undoing," he said, forcing the words out. "You and my own . . . ambition. Had you but . . . accepted me . . . I would not have mistreated you. But no . . . you were too good for me. I would have . . . made you a queen. And I . . . could have been . . . a king. . . ."

His eyes glazed over as the light of life left them, and he collapsed onto the ground. Slowly, the antloids dispersed, returning to their warren, leaving Sorak and the two women alone, standing by the fire, looking down at Torian's corpse.

Sorak looked at Ryana. She smiled at him wearily. Then he turned to the princess and took her arm. "Come, Princess," he said. "It is over now and there is time to rest. Tomorrow, we shall take you home."

* * * * *

From the heights of the foothills of the Barrier Mountains, the barrens stretched out toward the western horizon, a seemingly endless sea of broken rock. The three travelers stood on a promontory, a stone cliff extending like a ship's prow over the desolate wasteland below. Behind them, trees dotted the slopes, growing thicker as the mountains rose. It seemed almost like an alien environment now.

"Can we really have crossed all that?" Korahna said, looking out from the cliff as the sun slowly set behind them, causing the shadows of the mountains to lengthen on the ground below. It was the first time she seemed animated in three days.

The Ranger had tracked the soldier kanks Torian and his mercenaries had used, and Screech had called them, soothing the frightened creatures. He had given the beasts a chance to graze on the brush gathered by the mercenaries and, when they left the campsite the next morning, their steeds were fresh.

Now, near the end of their long journey, Korahna looked less like a princess than ever. Dressed in various items of apparel taken from the slain mercenaries, she bore a greater resemblance to a female brigand than a daughter of the Royal House of Nibenay. The too-large moccasins on her feet were now surmounted by a pair of hide breeches and a sleeveless tunic that had been cut by Sorak so that her waist was exposed. The bottom half of the tunic had been stained with blood and torn by mandibles. There was a wide sword belt at her waist, and Torian's obsidian blade, which he had used to take his own life. She swore she would always value it for the service it had performed. She wore a brown, hooded cloak over her tunic, and her long blond hair, combed out with her fingers, no longer gleamed the way it had when she brushed it every night before retiring in her tent while with the caravan. Ryana thought, despite the haphazard nature of her costume, that it was nevertheless an improvement over the way she had looked before.

Ryana had held her sleeping form while they rode the kank, and Korahna had whimpered softly in her arms. Ryana had not awakened her. She would dream unpleasant dreams for a while, and it was best she get beyond it. Later, when it was Ryana's turn to rest, the princess had said nothing, and during the next day and the following one as well, she had remained silent, brooding to herself. Now, finally, a trace of her old self . . . or perhaps it was a new self . . . made its appearance.

"We are, perhaps, the first to cross the barrens since

the Wanderer did it," Sorak said. "Or perhaps, I should say the Sage."

"No, the Wanderer," Ryana said. "He had not yet become the Sage."

"I wonder how long ago it was?" Korahna mused aloud.

Ryana shook her head. "No one knows. No one can even remember when *The Wanderer's Journal* first appeared."

"There was a copy of it in the templar library at the palace," said Korahna. "I must have read it at least a dozen times. It seemed to me, back then, that the Wanderer must have led a wonderful life. Free to roam wherever he chose, to sleep under the stars, to see the entire world, while I was cloistered in the palace, unable even to venture beyond the walls of the compound until I began to sneak out at night in secret. How I longed for the sort of adventures he must have had!"

"Well, you have had your first," said Sorak. "How does it feel?"

Korahna did not reply at once. When she finally spoke, it was in a soft, contemplative tone. "It was, of course, nothing like what I had dreamt of when I was younger. I had dreamt of adventure without the harsh realities. I had imagined traveling across the desert, but I had not added the sweltering heat to my imaginings, nor the horrible feeling of thirst, nor the aching muscles from hours upon hours of unaccustomed riding. I had no way of knowing what it would be like to fear being attacked by predators . . . either animal *or* human. And I could never have imagined that I could be treated as Torian had treated me."

Neither Sorak nor Ryana spoke, waiting for her to continue.

"He had reduced me to something less than human," she said after a moment. "I was merely a means to an end, a thing for him to possess and use to accomplish his aims. And when he called me his property . . . I think that it was only then that I realized just what I was to him, and all my outrage came bursting forth." She looked at Ryana. "I was such a fool. I do not know what came over me."

Ryana nodded. "Sometimes it happens that way, when a person is pushed far enough."

Korahna looked away, out over the barrens once again. "When he plunged his sword into himself . . . I actually enjoyed it. It felt *good*. It made me feel so vindicated, so *alive*. . . ." Her voice trailed off. She took a deep breath and expelled it heavily and shook her head. "What sort of person that does that make me?"

"A normal person," Sorak said, but Ryana realized it wasn't Sorak. The voice still sounded the same, but she knew him well enough to recognize the Guardian in the subtle changes only she could notice. And then, suddenly, she realized that Korahna would notice them as well because of their shared commonality of experience induced by Kether.

"Guardian?" Korahna said, proving what Ryana had suspected.

"Yes."

"We have never met, have we?"

"I have known you, through Sorak," said the Guardian. "But you have not known me."

"*Why*, wise Guardian?" Korahna asked. "Why?

How can it be normal to feel such passion for some-one's death?"

"Because to a normal person, killing is an act of pas-sion," the Guardian replied. "Either that, or an act of desperation, of self-defense. Torian had denied you that which you, like all people, hold most dear and central to the very essence of your being—your own identity. Your needs and your desires. He denied you your free will. And you also knew that he would have killed us, if he could."

"But he could not," Korahna said. "When he real-ized that, he knew he could not win."

"He made his choice," the Guardian replied. "He could take a life, even his own, and not feel anything. And that is why you, Korahna, are a normal person and Torian was not. What you are feeling now, these are all things a normal person feels. If you did *not* feel any of these things, then you would be right to be con-cerned about what sort of person you had become. Except that, if you were such a person, such thoughts would not occur to you, for you would no longer have a conscience."

Korahna looked down at the ground. When she looked back up, there were tears in her eyes. "Thank you, Guardian," she said, softly. "Thank you for help-ing me understand."

That night, they made camp in the mountains and built a fire and slept. As Ryana felt weariness over-come her, she saw Sorak duck under and the Ranger came to the fore. He stood and walked off into the darkness without a word, moving as silently as a mountain cat. With a sigh of resignation, Ryana sat up and took her sword, holding it across her lap while she waited for the Ranger to complete his hunt and return. She gazed at Korahna as she slept, quietly and soundly.

"Rest well, sister," she murmured, under her breath. "Rest well. The healing has begun."

NINE

The Barrier Mountains were a crescent-shaped range, bowed out to the northwest, with the tips of the crescent pointing east and south. At the southernmost end of the mountain range, near the lower tip of the crescent, stood the city of Gulg. At the opposite end of the crescent, separated from Gulg by the wide and verdant valley sheltered between the opposite ends of the range, was the city of Nibenay. From where Sorak stood, on the crest near the upper end of the range, he could see the city down below. The city of Gulg was barely visible in the distance, shrouded in the early morning mist at the far end of the valley.

The two cities were located in one of the few areas of Athas that were still green. The region was sustained by runoff from the mountains and by underground springs that bubbled to the surface, most located near Nibenay. According to *The Wanderer's Journal*, which Sorak had studied while they camped in the mountains, Gulg was not so much a city as a large settlement of hunter-gatherers who depended on the forests of the Barrier Mountains for their sustenance.

The ruler, or oba, of Gulg was the sorcerer-queen,

Lalali-Puy, whose name meant "forest goddess" in the language of her people. She enjoyed the full support of her rather primitive subjects, who worshipped her as if she were a deity. The oba resided in what was perhaps the most unusual palace on Athas, one that was constructed high up in the limbs of an ancient and gigantic agafari tree. Her templars lived in huts constructed in the lower limbs of that same tree.

The palace, wrote the Wanderer, was small, but magnificent—simple, and yet beautiful, reflecting the strong bond the residents of Gulg felt with the trees of the forest. Though she was a defiler, the oba was the closest of all Athasian rulers to the life path of a druid. However, it was a path she had perverted through her pursuit of power in the defiler arts.

Most of the residents of Gulg lived in small, circular thatched huts around the gigantic agafari tree where their queen made her home. Their simple dwellings were protected by a defensive "wall" that was, in reality, a huge hedge of thorny trees planted so close together that not even a halfling could squeeze through without being cut to ribbons. For the most part, the people of Gulg were savage, tribal peasants who hunted in the forests of the mountains and turned over all their game to the oba, who then distributed the food to her simple people through her templars.

The traders of the merchant guilds had to deal with the templars rather than directly with the people, and for this reason: Torian's father, one of the queen's templars, had forged a powerful alliance with the House of Ankhor. He had also raised a son in the warrior tradition of the judaga, the warrior headhunters of Gulg, fierce fighters and deadly archers whose poisoned darts could kill by the slightest scratch. Small wonder, Sorak thought, that Torian had felt so little compassion or regard for human life.

Nibenay, on the other hand, was a more conventional city, at least in the sense that it had buildings made of wood and stone. The architecture of Nibenay, however, was anything but conventional. Sorak had been fascinated by the Wanderer's description of the stone carvings that covered almost every inch of every building in Nibenay. The people of the city were artisans and stonemasons, and justifiably proud of their skills, which they used to embellish buildings with intricate designs and scenes. Some depicted the buildings' owners or the ancestors of the owners, others showed ritual dances, still more displayed carvings of beasts and monsters executed in painstaking detail, as if to placate such creatures and their voracious appetites.

The people of Nibenay had a much more diverse economy than the people of Gulg, who depended on trade with the merchant houses for all their goods. Aside from the small statues, idols, busts, and building decorations carved by the city's stonemasons, for which there was much demand, the city had an agricultural economy, chiefly centered around rice fields irrigated by springs under the nobility's control. But most of all, Nibenay was known for its production of weapons, particularly those fashioned from dense agafari wood, which was almost as hard and durable as bronze.

Agafari trees were slow growing and drought resistant, but when irrigated or when planted in the mountains, where there was a greater supply of water, they grew thicker and faster. War clubs made from agafari wood were capable of bursting almost any type of armor, and agafari spears and fighting staves were incredibly strong, despite their slenderness. They would resist blows from obsidian swords and even the extremely rare iron weapons could do little more than nick them. Agafari wood simply did not break.

As a result, it was difficult to work, and it took skilled craftsmen to make weapons from the wood. Entire teams of foresters sometimes took days to fell a single tree, working with stone spades and axes and controlled burning of the root system. Crafting weapons from agafari wood required special tools and a forge for carefully controlled tempering. A longbow made from agafari wood was not only difficult to draw, but if an archer possessed the necessary strength, it was capable of launching arrows with such force that armor would be penetrated at a distance of fifty yards. The craftsmen of Nibenay were justifiably famous for their agafari weapons, and the demand for them among the merchant guilds was high. There lay the crux of the rivalry between Gulg and Nibenay.

The weapons makers of Nibenay harvested the agafari trees growing in the Crescent Forest, but the hunter-gatherers of Gulg depended on them for their livelihood. The agafari forests sheltered game that fed the city of Gulg, and beneath the spreading canopies of the agafari trees grew kola bushes and pepper shrubs and other vegetation that not only helped feed the citizens of Gulg, but provided them a spice and herb trade. For more years than anyone could count, a bitter rivalry had existed between the two cities, one that had frequently escalated into war over the available natural resources.

"Why do not the people of Nibenay simply plant new agafari trees from seedlings for the ones that they cut down?" Sorak had asked Korahna.

"They do," the princess replied, "but they plant them in groves surrounding the city, where they can easily be irrigated by the springs. They do not bother to replant what they cut down in the Crescent Forest because irrigating those trees would not be practical, and it would require more time and effort to keep bringing the wood down from the slopes of the foothills. Then, too, the templars, who direct these operations, believe that depriving Gulg of its resources over time will weaken the city and make it more vulnerable to attack, or else render it completely dependent on Nibenay, which would require their capitulation."

"And in the meantime, the Crescent Forest is destroyed," Ryana said, "and along with it, the life cycle of the plants and animals supported by the forest."

"True." Korahna nodded. "As a girl, I had never even thought of such things, and I did not even begin to understand them until I started to study the preserver writings in secret and contacted the Veiled Alliance. The people of Nibenay fail to understand that it is not only the people of Gulg who will be hurt by this cruel practice, but themselves, as well. And the templars, if they know, do not seem to care. It is one of the things I hope, somehow, to change one day."

"That will mean aligning yourself against your father," said Ryana.

"I have already done that," said Korahna. "Once I

had taken the preserver vow, I turned my back on him forever."

"And incurred his enmity," said Sorak.

"If he even knows," Korahna said. "Nibenay cares less and less for the affairs of his family, much less his kingdom. Do you know that I have never even seen him?"

"*Never?*" said Ryana with amazement. "Your own father?"

"Not even once," Korahna said. "If he ever gazed at me or held me when I was an infant, I have no memory of it. His subjects never see him, either. For all my life, he has remained cloistered within the central portion of the palace, where no one save the senior templars ever sets foot. As long as I have lived, few of his many wives have ever even laid eyes on him."

"How many wives does he have?" Ryana asked.

"All the templars are his wives," Korahna said. "Or else they are his daughters. The templars of Nibenay are all female, and the senior templars are the oldest of his wives. It is considered a great honor to be made a senior templar. One must first serve within the sacred ranks for a minimum of twenty-five years, then be elected to the office based on merit, which is determined by the other senior templars. Vacancies occur only upon death, and the oath is said to be most arduous. Some have even died in the administering of it."

"Do you know why it is that you have never seen your father?" Sorak asked.

Korahna shook her head. "I have often wondered, but the few times I have asked, I have been told that it was not for me to question such things."

"You have never seen him for the same reason his subjects never see him," Sorak said, "because the Shadow King is no longer a man. It would repel the eye to look upon him now."

"What do you mean?" Korahna asked.

"He has embarked upon the path of dragon metamorphosis," said Sorak.

"My father?" said Korahna.

"All of the remaining sorcerer-kings are already at some stage of the dragon metamorphosis," said Sorak. "Each of them fears the others will complete the transformation first, so they are expending all their efforts on the long and arduous spells involved."

"I never knew," Korahna said, a stricken expression on her face. "Not even my friends in the Veiled Alliance told me."

"They probably sought to spare your feelings," said Ryana.

"My own father," said Korahna in a hollow voice. "It was bad enough when I realized what it meant to be a defiler, but to think that he is in the process of becoming a creature that is the foulest and most evil thing to ever walk this blighted world . . ." She shook her head. "I curse the day that I was born into such a pestilential kinship."

"Now, perhaps, you can understand why the Sage takes such pains to conceal his whereabouts," Ryana said. "There is only one creature that can stand up to a dragon, and that is an avangion. Each of the remaining sorcerer-kings would give almost anything to learn the Sage's hiding place, for he represents the greatest threat to their power."

"And if they can succeed in eliminating him," said

Sorak, "then there will be nothing to stop them. They will complete their transformations, and then they will turn on one another."

"Then they will all destroy each other," said Korahna.

"Perhaps," said Sorak. "But in the end, it is likely that one shall triumph. However, by that time, Athas will be reduced to a blasted, lifeless piece of rock."

"They must be stopped," said Korahna.

"The Sage is the only one who can stand a chance to do that," said Ryana, "unless, somehow, the dragons can be killed before they are able to complete their transformations."

"I will do everything I can to help," Korahna said.

"You shall soon have that chance," said Sorak, looking down toward Nibenay.

* * * * *

They entered the city by its main gate, two giant, stone columns set into the walls, carved in deep relief with the intertwining figures of serpents and fire drakes. The bored-looking half-giant guards passed them through without comment and without bothering to search them. There was a steady stream of people passing in and out, and in Nibenay, as in most cities of Athas, everyone went armed. The sight of a sword and a knife or two excited no comment. Had they known that the three bedraggled-looking pilgrims carried metal swords, the guards might have been much more interested, but the day was hot and they could not be bothered to examine everybody passing through the gates. Troublemakers soon found more than they had bargained for within the city walls. The templars did not tolerate violations of the city's laws, and the half-giants who composed the city's guard and army were usually more than enough to deal with any criminal.

The first thing they did was make their way to the city's central marketplace, where they sold their kanks. Korahna would remain in Nibenay, and Sorak and Ryana had no idea how long they would be staying. When it came time to leave, they could either purchase kanks or book passage with a caravan, or even go on foot, as they had done before. There was little point in expending their limited resources by stabling the kanks. Sorak's practiced negotiation, aided by the Guardian's psionic powers, enabled them to get a good price for the kanks, and the first of the proceeds bought them a good meal in one of the city's taverns.

Korahna did not draw any curious glances. Since she had spent most of her life within the walls of the palace compound, none of the citizens of Nibenay could have known her by sight, save for those she had met in the Alliance, and they never would have recognized her. She looked nothing like a princess now.

Attired in the too-large clothing taken from the mercenaries and dusty from their journey, she looked more like a desert herder than a scion of the royal house of Nibenay. Her long blond hair hung lank and loose and tangled, her face was begrimed, her hands were dirty and now callused, her once-long fingernails bitten short, and she had lost weight on the journey. She now looked lean and hard, and there was something in her face that had not been there before—a look of experience.

What curious looks they received were due less to her appearance than to that of Sorak and Ryana. Unlike most villichi, Ryana's hair was silvery white rather than red, and though she lacked the unnatural elongation of the limbs that characterized villichi, she was unusually tall for a woman. Her height and coloring, together with her lean muscularity, made her an imposing figure.

Sorak was even more uncommon looking. The people of Nibenay had never seen an elfling before. At first glance, Sorak looked human, but still different, somehow. Many of those they passed on the streets turned to stare at him without quite knowing why. Those who were more observant might have noticed his pointed ears when the breeze blew his hair back, or else they might have marked the unusual, elven angularity of his features, or the lustrous thickness of his hair, like a halfling's mane. They might have noted that he, too, was tall, though perhaps not unusually so for a human. But even the least observant of them, if they looked into his face, could not have failed to note his eyes, deeply sunken, and with a gaze so direct and penetrating that most people were forced to look away.

The tavern where they sat, near the central marketplace, was open to the air and covered by an awning, so that they could watch the street and see the bustle of activity as evening approached and the traders began to close up their stalls for the day. Little by little, the marketplace began to empty as the shadows lengthened and people went home or repaired to taverns and other places of amusement. The tavern where they sat soon began to fill up with noisy patrons, looking to wash the dust of the marketplace and the heat of the day from their throats.

"So, how does it feel to be back home?" Ryana asked.

"Strange," replied Korahna, pushing away her dinner plate and looking around. "When I left, I never thought to see the city again. Now, after our journey through the barrens and the mountains, it seems strange to see so many people in one place. It feels . . . oppressive."

Ryana smiled. "I know just how you feel," she said. "There is something about the solitude and beauty of the desert that invades one's soul. It is as if it expands somehow, freed of the confines of a city or a village . . . or even of a villichi temple. Then, when you find yourself among people once again, you feel closed in and crowded."

"Yes," Korahna said, "that is exactly how it feels."

"People were not meant to live in cities," said Ryana. "Cities are artificial things, born of a need, at first, to band together for survival, and then of a convenience in terms of shelter, trade, and industry, and as the population grows more dense, the available space becomes confining, and the soul draws in to compensate for lack of room. People become less open. They are taken over by the faster rhythms that result from overcrowding. Everyone is always in a hurry, everyone is always in someone else's way. People become more agitated, less trusting, more prone to react with violence. Cities are unhealthy things. They do not let people breathe freely.

"When I was a girl, I dreamt of going to a city because it seemed like an adventure. Now, I cannot imagine why anyone would want to live this way, like antloids in a hive. Maybe that is why defilers live in cities. They have forgotten what it is that they defile. They cannot love a world they only rarely see."

"Still, it is my home," Korahna said. "Here I was born, and here I grew up, and here I must make amends for having lived a life of privilege while others suffered. Cities shall never change, Ryana, unless someone works to change them."

"Can a city be something other than what it is?" Ryana asked.

"Perhaps not," the princess replied, "but it can be *more* than what it is. Surely, the effort is worthwhile."

Ryana sighed. "It would be nice to think so."

"It grows dark," said Sorak. "And night is the best time to contact the Alliance. I shall feel better when I know that you are safely in their company."

"Are you so anxious to be rid of me?" Korahna asked.

"No," said Sorak. "Merely anxious to complete the task for which we came here. And I do not even know yet what that task might be."

"And you think the Alliance shall know?"

"If the Alliance elders have contact with the Sage, then he shall let us know through them," said Sorak.

"And if he does not?"

"Then I do not know what we shall do," said Sorak. "The spell scroll bid us come to Nibenay. Well, we are here, at last. We have done our part. Now it is time for the Sage to do his."

"Well, then I shall take you to meet with the Alliance," said Korahna, pushing back her chair and rising to her feet. "You have brought me home, for which I am profoundly grateful. I left a pampered princess, and I have returned a woman who has learned something of her capabilities. For that, too, I am grateful, and more. . . ."

She looked from Sorak to Ryana. "I do not know how Kether did what he has done, but for the bond that he has forged between us, I shall be forever grateful. Ryana, I fear that you received the worst part of the bargain, for I had nothing of significance to offer you. But for what you have given me . . ." She shook her head, words failing her. "I can only say, I thank you, and yet that does not seem sufficient."

"It will do," Ryana said with a smile. "But do not hold yourself so cheaply. What I received from you was of no small value. I know more of how the nobility lives and thinks now than I ever did before, and I also know what it means to discover a sense of purpose in life when one has been lacking before. I was born to mine, but you sought yours and found it, and had the courage to act on your beliefs, when to do so meant to forsake everything you knew. That took no small amount of courage."

"Well . . ." said Korahna, visibly moved. "Coming from a villichi priestess, that is high praise, indeed."

"A villichi, yes, for that is what I was born," Ryana said. "But a priestess? That is a title I can no longer truly claim. I broke my vows."

"I know," Korahna said. "And I also know that causes you distress. But I will repeat your own words to you. To act on your beliefs, when it means forsaking everything you know, takes no small amount of courage."

"If you two are done complimenting one another, perhaps we can go find some entertainment in this town," Sorak suddenly said, and though it was his voice, its pitch had changed completely, and his entire manner had suddenly undergone a dramatic transformation. He stood with one hand on his hip, his head cocked slightly to one side, a look of bored impatience on his face.

"Kivara," said Ryana.

Korahna merely stared at him, stunned at the sudden change. Her communion with Ryana gave her both a knowledge and an understanding of who Kivara was, but actually seeing her manifested still took her aback.

"This is not the time, Kivara," said Ryana.

"I have grown weary of waiting for the proper time," she replied, rolling her eyes and tossing her head in an irate manner. "I have not been out since we left Tyr. There was nothing of interest on the journey, but now that we have reached a city at long last, I deserve some time."

"We have not come here to enjoy ourselves, Kivara," said Ryana. "We must deliver Korahna safely to the Veiled Alliance and then find out what it is we have to do here."

"So? I am not preventing you," Kivara said. "But why does that mean we cannot enjoy some entertainment in the process?"

"We are preservers in a defiler city, Kivara," said Ryana patiently, though her exasperation was beginning to show. "And we have brought back the exiled princess. We are at some risk here."

"Good," Kivara said. "Then that may add a little spice to what has been a dreadfully dreary journey up 'til now."

"Guardian . . ." Ryana said.

"No!" said Kivara, stamping her foot angrily. Several people turned to stare at this rather curious behavior. "I have not been out in *weeks!* I am *not* going back under!"

"*Kivara,*" said the Guardian, though Korahna and Ryana could not hear her, "*you are misbehaving. This is not what we agreed.*"

"I agreed to cooperate; I did not agree to stay under all the time. I have as much right to come out as any of you!"

"*Kivara, this is neither the time nor the place for this discussion. We shall talk about this later.*"

"No! It is not fair! I never have any fun!"

"*Kivara . . .*"

"No, I said!"

Korahna watched, fascinated, as the apparently one-sided conversation took place before her. Sorak's—or Kivara's—features twisted into a grimace as she struggled against the will of the Guardian.

"No . . . no . . . *no!*"

The patrons in the tavern were all staring now. Sorak's body trembled, and his head shook as his mouth twitched, and his hands, clenched into fists, pounded at his thighs. And then his body slumped slightly and relaxed, and a moment later, he straightened and was Sorak once again. The patrons in the tavern were mumbling among themselves.

"We had better leave at once," said Sorak, quickly leading the way out of the tavern.

The people stared after them as they went out into the street. Night had fallen, and the two women hurried to keep pace with Sorak's long strides as he rushed away from the tavern. He stopped some distance away at the corner of a building, and leaned against it wearily.

"Sorak . . ." Ryana said with an expression of concern. "Are you all right?"

He merely nodded. "Forgive me," he said.

"It was not your fault," Ryana said. Korahna stood beside her, watching him and biting her lower lip. She did not know what to think.

Sorak took a deep breath and expelled it heavily. "She has not done anything like that in a long time. The Guardian never had trouble controlling her before. She seems to be growing stronger."

"Can nothing be done?" Korahna asked.

Sorak simply shook his head. "Kivara is a part of who we are," he said. "When I was a boy, with the help of the high mistress of the villichi temple, I was able to effect an agreement between the individuals of the tribe to cooperate with one another for the sake of all. The Guardian has always been the wisest of us, and she has always managed to keep the tribe in balance. Something like this has not happened for a long, long time."

"Will you be able to keep things under control?" Ryana asked anxiously.

"I think so," Sorak replied. "I am merely tired. It has been a long, hard journey, and my weariness allowed Kivara to slip through. I will be more on guard from now on." He took a deep breath and let it out in a sigh. "All right, Princess," he said. "Lead on."

Korahna led them through the dark and winding streets of Nibenay, away from the market district and toward the center of the city. As they drew closer to the palace compound in the inner city, the buildings became larger and more opulent. Almost every house they passed now had large, stone-columned entry-ways, intricately carved with figures. By now the servants had set torches into the outside sconces so that some light illuminated the streets. There were almost no people in the streets here, and those they passed hastened to the opposite side to avoid them.

"We must look a sight," Ryana said as she noticed several people scurrying out of their way.

"The people are afraid of strangers in this part of the city," Korahna explained. "The wealthier people live nearest to the palace, save for the powerful nobles who have estates just beyond the city walls. From time to time, desperate individuals come here in an attempt to rob a home or waylay some passing citizen. We must be on the watch for the half-giant patrols. They shall surely challenge us."

"And if they do?" Ryana asked.

"Let us just say it is best they don't," Korahna replied. "Come, hurry. This way."

They ran across the street and ducked down an alleyway. Moving quickly from alley to alley, hugging the building walls, they soon came to the sprawling palace compound. Rising up above all the other buildings was the palace itself, a huge edifice built entirely of intricately carved stone, and jutting from it, in the center, was a gigantic head. Sorak and Ryana stopped to gaze in wonder at it. The side wings of the palace looked like shoulders, and the central upper stories like a neck. Sunken eyes with flames burning within them gazed out over the city. The huge brow was furrowed, and the jutting chin was proudly set. The head was shaven, and the expression of the gigantic face was at the same time impassive and malevolent.

"By all that's holy, who is *that*?" Ryana asked in a low voice.

"My father," said Korahna.

"That is the Shadow King?" said Sorak.

Korahna nodded. "It took the city's finest stonemasons decades to carve out his countenance from huge blocks of mortared stone. For most of them, it was their life's work. They labored every day, from dawn to dusk, and then they were relieved at night by other stonemasons who continued the work by torchlight. It is said that many of them died in the task. Some fell from the scaffolding; others expired from sheer exhaustion. And while the stonemasons worked on the outside, teams of other artisans worked within, constructing the inner chambers from marble, alabaster, cinnabar, obsidian, and precious stones. And when they were finished, all were put to death."

"Why?" said Ryana.

"So that none could ever speak of what lay within my father's private chambers," said Korahna. "At the completion of the work, Nibenay moved in, and no one has seen him since that day."

"No one at all?" said Sorak.

"Only the senior templars who attend him," said Korahna. She pointed toward the upper part of the face. "Each night, until dawn, the lights burn within those eyes, as if Nibenay were watching over the city that bears his name. There are some who say that he can see all transgressions and sends templars and half-giants to administer his law."

"And you lived for all your life with *that* gazing over

you?" Ryana said.

Korahna smiled. "When I was a little girl, I thought the stone face itself was my father. I used to stand beneath it in the palace courtyard and call out to it. But there was never any answer. Come, we must keep going. The patrols will be along soon."

They hastened toward the opposite end of the city, past the palace compound and toward the area Korahna said was the elven quarter.

"There is a large population of elves in Nibenay?" asked Sorak with surprise.

"Half-elves, mostly," said Korahna, "but among them are many full-blooded elves who have given up the nomadic, tribal life. It is said that more and more elves are gravitating to the cities these days. Life on the tablelands is hard, and the Great Ivory Plain, which lies to the south of the city, is as inhospitable as the barrens.

"Most of the elves in these parts used to live in the Crescent Forest and in the upper reaches of the Barrier Mountains, which we call the Nibenay Mountains here in the city. However, they have been largely driven out by the foresters and the hunters of Gulg. With the foresters cutting down the agafari trees and the hunters cleaning out what little game is left, the elves in the mountains have been left with almost nothing. A few tribes still dwell there, but they are mostly raiders, and their numbers dwindle with each passing year. No one knows how many elves live in the quarter, but their population grows larger each year."

"What do they do here in the city?" Sorak asked.

"Work at what jobs they can," Korahna replied. "Mostly jobs that humans will not take. Some steal, though the penalties are harsh if they are caught. Many of the elven women sell themselves. There is not much of a life for them here, but there is even less of a life for them outside the city."

"They were a once proud people," Sorak said, "and now they have fallen to this."

The streets were darker in this part of town. Few torches burned outside the dilapidated buildings. The scant structures covered with decorative carvings were old and badly in need of repair. The rest were not much different from the ramshackle hovels in the warrens of Tyr. There were more people out on the streets here. As in Tyr, the authorities did not patrol in the poorest sections of the city. They did not much care what happened to the people here.

As they approached a tavern with two torches burning on either side of the entry, several elven prostitutes lounging against the building walls called out to Sorak and beckoned him, making provocative poses. Some were extremely explicit and graphically demonstrative of what they were offering for sale. Sorak and Ryana were both dismayed to see how young some of them were, scarcely more than children, debased by poverty and bigotry and lack of opportunity. No one respected them, and so they did not respect themselves.

"This way," said Korahna. "In here."

They entered the tavern. A faded, painted sign on the wall outside identified the tavern as the Elven Blade. Sorak thought of his own elven blade and made certain it was well covered by his cloak.

Inside, the tavern was little more than a large, cavernous chamber with stone arches and an aging plank floor. People were seated on crude wooden benches at long tables. Most were drinking. A few were gambling with dice. On a small raised stage against one wall, a blind elf musician strummed an elf's harp while two others accompanied him on flute and drum. A baby pterrax in a large cage snapped at food scraps thrown to it by patrons. Barefoot serving girls bore trays among the tables, periodically going back to the bar to refill their earthenware pitchers and fetch fresh bottles and ceramic goblets.

Most of the patrons were half-elves and elves, but they saw some human faces, as well. There would be no dwarves here, for elves and dwarves were not fond of one another, nor would there be any halflings. Halflings were feral, and no halfling would ever be found in a city, though Sorak thought the same could once have been said of elves, as well. A few eyes turned to stare at them as they came in, but for the most part, no one looked directly at them. Directly meeting someone's gaze in such a place could all too easily be taken as a challenge. Korahna glanced toward the bar at the back, then beckoned them to follow as she crossed the room, walking with purposeful strides.

As they passed among the tables, a bench suddenly came crashing down in front of Sorak. Its occupant leapt to his feet, knocking against him. "You lying piece of dung! I'll cut your tongue out for that!"

The elf seated opposite him snarled and sprang up, launching himself across the table. Both of them crashed into Sorak, who was still trying to disentangle himself from the elf who had knocked into him. They all fell to the floor in a jumbled heap, the two elves shouting and screaming at each other.

Suddenly, Sorak felt expert fingers lifting his purse and realized the nature of the game. As several others pulled the two apart and off each other, Sorak got to his feet.

"All right, you two, out!" shouted the burly human tavern keeper, coming around from behind the bar with a large agafari club in his hands. "Settle it outside!"

"Just a moment," Sorak said as the two elves turned to go.

"And what's your interest in this?" the tavern keeper demanded, still holding the club ready.

Sorak pointed at one of the elves. "He has something of mine."

"What?" the tavern keeper demanded.

"My purse," said Sorak.

"He lies!" the elf protested. "I never touched his filthy purse—if he even had one when he came in here!"

"Your quarrel was merely an excuse to enable you to lift it," Sorak said.

"You had best be careful of your accusations, friend," the elf said menacingly while his companion, who moments earlier had seemed intent on killing him, now stood by to back him up. "This purse is mine," the elf said, taking out his purse and shaking it. It rattled with a few ceramic coins. "My friend will testify to that, and so will the serving wench, who saw me pay her out of it. See, it is stitched with my name!"

"I did not mean that purse," Sorak said. "I meant the one you secreted in the pocket of your cloak."

"You're mad."

"Am I?" Sorak said. "Then what do you suppose this is?"

His purse came floating up out of the hidden pocket in the pickpocket's cloak and hovered in front of the thief's face. For a moment, the elf simply gaped at it, then with a cry of fury, he batted it aside and snatched out his blade. As he lunged forward and brought the sword down in a wide, sweeping arc, Sorak smoothly drew Galdra from its scabbard and parried the blow in the same motion. The elf's obsidian blade shattered in an explosion of thousands of tiny slivers.

The thief simply gaped in disbelief as Sorak brought the falchionlike point of Galdra to his throat. "My purse," he said. The thief glanced around behind him in panic, looking for support, only to see Ryana standing with her dagger at his confederate's throat. The entire tavern had fallen completely silent. All eyes were upon them, and the slightest whisper would have carried through the room. The thief's panic-stricken gaze returned to the blade held at his throat, and then he seemed to truly see it for the first time. He marked its unusual shape, the elven steel it was forged of, and the elvish runes inscribed upon the blade. His eyes grew very wide, and he gasped, looking up at Sorak as if he'd seen a ghost.

"Galdra!" he said, in a low voice. He dropped down to his knees and bowed his head. "Forgive me! I did not know!"

An excited murmuring broke out through the tavern.

"Get up," said Sorak.

The thief sprang to obey.

"Now retrieve my purse."

"At once," he said, scampering after it. He picked it up from where it had fallen and brought it to Sorak. "I am but a craven and unworthy thief, my lord. Do with me as you will, but I most humbly beg your pardon."

"Be silent," Sorak said. "You talk too much."

"Yes, my lord, I do. Forgive me."

"Get out of my sight," said Sorak.

"Thank you, my lord, thank you," the elf said, bowing deeply as he backed away. His companion followed with him, also bowing, staring at Sorak and Ryana fearfully. As they left, a number of others slipped out the door, as well.

"Serpent's teeth!" the tavern keeper said. "What was all that about? Are you a nobleman?"

"No," said Sorak. "He must have mistaken me for someone else."

"You are not a nobleman, and yet you carry a blade of rare worth and manufacture. You have the aspect of an elf, yet you are not an elf. And you have the eyes and hair of a halfling. Who are you?"

"He is my friend," Korahna said, approaching the tavern keeper.

"And who might you be?" said the tavern keeper.

Korahna stepped up close to him and lowered her voice to a whisper. "Look closely, Galavan. Do you not recognize me?"

The tavern keeper frowned and stared at her for a moment, then his eyes grew wide and his jaw dropped. "Serpent's teeth!" he whispered. "We thought you were dead!"

"We can discuss that later," she said. "You know why I have come. These two are my friends, and I vouch for them with my life."

"Your word is enough for me," said Galavan. "Come, this way, to the back room."

He led them around behind the bar and through a

curtained archway. "Watch the place," he said to one of his assistants, and then passed through.

It appeared to be no more than a storeroom with a small table, chair, and lantern. The walls were lined with wooden shelves containing spare goblets, pitchers, plateware, bottles, and other supplies. Galavan approached one of the shelves, reached inside and tripped a hidden switch. Then he swung the entire shelf away from the wall, revealing a dark passage.

"This way," he said, picking up the lantern from the table and beckoning them inside. He handed the lantern to Korahna, and after they went in, he closed the hidden door behind them.

"Where does this lead?" Ryana asked the princess.

"You will see," Korahna replied and started to descend the flight of stone steps that led down to a tunnel beneath the street. They walked through the tunnel for a while when they suddenly became aware of greater space around them. The tunnel walls had ended, and they were in an open area, but it was underground.

"What is this place?" Ryana asked, unable to see much past the glow of the lantern.

"Ruins," said Sorak, whose vision in the dark allowed him to see far more than she could. "Underground ruins. We are standing in some sort of courtyard."

"Nibenay is built upon the ruins of another ancient city," said Korahna, "dating back over a thousand years. Neither the templars nor my father know of it, but throughout the city, there are places where access to the ancient city can be found. The Elven Blade is one such place. Galavan is a secret ally of the Veiled Alliance."

"So what happens now?" Ryana asked.

As if in reply, a score of torches suddenly blazed up all around them, illuminating robed and hooded figures standing in a large circle, surrounding them.

"Welcome home, Korahna," one of them said. "We have been expecting you."

TEN

One of the robed figures stepped toward them with his torch. As he approached, they could see that his robe was white, and his face within the hood was covered with a white veil.

"These are my friends," Korahna said. "They helped me to escape captivity and brought me here across the Stony Barrens."

"You crossed the barrens?" said the hooded man with amazement.

"If not for these two, I never would have survived," Korahna said. "I owe them my life."

The hooded figure turned to gaze at Ryana, then at Sorak. "You are the one who is called Sorak, the Nomad?"

"You know me?" Sorak said.

"Your arrival was foretold."

"By whom?" said Sorak. "By the Sage?"

The Guardian tried to probe him, but the hooded figure merely shook his head. "Do not try to use the Way on me, Nomad. It shall not serve you. I am shielded."

"Your magic is strong," said Sorak.

"Yes, but not strong enough," the veiled sorcerer

271

replied. "Regrettably, the Shadow King's is stronger. We are grateful to you, and to you as well, Priestess, for returning Korahna to us. She will be a great help in our struggle. But you had reasons of your own for bringing her with you."

"Yes," said Sorak. "We had hoped that she would help us contact you. We were sent to Nibenay—"

"I know," the sorcerer said. "We were expecting you, though we did not know in what manner you would arrive, or from where. We thought you might come with a caravan or perhaps by the little-traveled northern trail . . . but across the Stony Barrens: that is a feat that shall be told in tales for a long time to come. I look forward to hearing the details of your journey. However, Korahna can supply them. I fear you shall have other things with which to be concerned."

"What do you mean?" Ryana asked.

"The templars have discovered that the Elven Blade is a contact point for the Alliance. They have been sending spies to watch who comes and goes. We did not learn of this until after Korahna had disappeared, so there was no way she could have known.

"Following your . . . encounter, known informers were seen leaving the tavern in a hurry. They will run straight to the templars. It is unlikely that any of them would have recognized Korahna, but you revealed yourself in your exchange with the thief. Soon the Shadow King shall know of you, and then you shall be in gravest danger."

"But how could the Shadow King know of my quest to find the Sage?" asked Sorak.

"Do not underestimate the powers of Nibenay," the

wizard said. "Besides, you carry Galdra, the enchanted sword of ancient elven kings. That alone would make him see you as a rival. No defiler would wish to see the elves unite behind one ruler, unless that ruler were himself."

"But I am not an elven king," protested Sorak. "This sword was given to me by the High Mistress Varanna, and she said nothing of any legacy associated with it. I have no wish to rule or unite anyone. I am not responsible for fanciful stories that grow up around a sword."

"Nevertheless, you will find yourself affected by those stories. Stories that are repeated often enough become legends, and people set great store by legends. Whether the prophecy is a true one or not, there will be those who will try to make it so. They shall either try to cast you in the role, or else take your sword and usurp it for themselves.

"You could, of course, give up the sword, but then you would risk having it fall into the wrong hands. Nibenay could do much with such a blade. If it wins the allegiance of the elves, I would much rather see it in your hands. Either way, you are in danger so long as you remain within the city. It is possible the forces of the Shadow King may find the hidden entrance in the storeroom, but if they do, we are prepared to cave in the tunnel on them. There are other ways into and out of the old ruins, ways they have not yet discovered. There is a branching off point in the tunnel through which you came that will take you up into the alley behind the Elven Blade. It would be best if you were not seen leaving the tavern. You could be followed."

The hooded wizard reached inside his robe and

withdrew a small, rolled up scroll that was banded with a green ribbon. He handed it to Sorak.

"This will tell you what you need to know," he said. "Ask me no more questions, for I have no answers to give you."

The wizard turned to go.

"Wait," said Sorak. "How shall I contact you again?"

"It would be best if you did not," the wizard said. "The longer you remain here, the greater will be the risk to you and anyone who helps you. You have your quest, we have our struggle to wage. In the end, perhaps, our goals may be the same, but we must pursue them by our separate paths. Good luck, Nomad. May you find that which you seek. Come, Korahna."

The princess looked at Sorak and Ryana. "Words are insufficient to express my feelings," she said. "I will always be deeply indebted to you both."

"You owe us nothing," Sorak said.

"No, I owe you a great deal," said Korahna, "and someday, perhaps, I can properly repay it." She hugged Sorak, then Ryana. "Farewell, Sister," she said. "You shall always be in my thoughts."

"And you in mine," Ryana said. "May your feet be steady on the Path."

"And yours," Korahna said. "Farewell."

She handed the lantern to Ryana and went with the others. Their torches receded into the darkness of the underground ruins until they parted, going off into different directions and disappeared from sight. Sorak looked down at the rolled up scroll he held in his hand.

"And so another clue in our long search," he said. "Let us see what this one holds." He untied the green ribbon and unrolled the scroll. It merely said, "Burn in a safe and isolated place."

"Well, this place certainly seems safe and isolated enough," Ryana said. She held up the lantern. Sorak stuck a corner of the scroll into the flame. At once, as the flames licked up the length of the scroll, they began to burn with a blue-green fire. Sorak dropped the scroll onto the ground and they both stood back.

As the edges of the burning scroll curled up and blackened, sparks began to shoot forth, dancing up into the air. More of the scroll burned, and more sparks rose up, only instead of being extinguished as they rose, they grew brighter and swirled around in mad arabesques, like frenzied fireflies going around and around, faster and faster, eventually forming a swirling, sparking column of blue-green light. Within the light, a bare outline of a figure formed, its features indistinguishable but dressed in robes. The figure was a brighter light within the light, sparkling and giving off radiance that lit up the entire underground courtyard. And then it spoke.

"You have done well, my children. You have secured the Seals of Knowledge, corrected an injustice in rescuing the Princess Korahna, and proven your worth and your tenacity in your arduous journey across the Stony Barrens. But greater challenges, and still greater dangers, lie ahead. You must now leave the city of the Shadow King, and leave it quickly, for he has great power, and the time to deal with him has not yet come. Set your feet upon the path to the village of Salt View, across the Great Ivory Plain and beyond the Mekillot Mountains. There you must seek a druid known as the Silent One, who shall guide you to the ancient city of Bodach, where lies the next object of your quest. Guard the Seals of Knowledge with your lives, for together with what you shall find in Bodach, they hold the key that will unlock the final object of your quest."

"But what are we to seek in Bodach?" Sorak asked.

There was no reply. The shimmering figure faded from view as the whirling sparks shot out in all directions and dissipated in the gloom of the underground ruins.

"Gith's blood!" swore Sorak angrily. "He toys with us and poses riddles! Why does he not speak plainly and tell us what we need to know? How many *more* tests must we pass?"

"Perhaps he doles out the information we require in small portions," said Ryana, "so that we cannot reveal all if we should fail and fall into defiler hands."

"Now we must seek something in Bodach," Sorak said in frustration, "and we know not what it is. And after that, he implies that there is yet a *third* object to be found, only we know not what or where."

"Perhaps this druid called the Silent One, who is to be our guide, can tell us," said Ryana.

Sorak sighed with exasperation. "Only to find him, we must first cross the Ivory Plain," he said. "The barrens are nothing but miles of broken rock. The Great Ivory Plain is nothing but a sea of salt. And as if that were not enough, we must then make our way to Bodach, and the Silent One would have to be insane to willingly guide anyone to that evil place."

"How is Bodach evil?" asked Ryana.

Sorak snorted. "How is it *not* evil?" He reached into his pack and pulled out *The Wanderer's Journal*. "Listen to this," he said, opening the book and reading:

> *"Bodach, lying at the tip of a peninsula projecting into one of the great inland silt basins, was undoubtedly one of the mightiest cities of the ancients. Its ruins cover many square miles of the peninsula. When you stand at the edge of the silt basin, you can see its towers rising above the silt for many miles beyond.*
>
> *"Unfortunately, Bodach and the surrounding territories are not good places to linger. As the crimson sun goes down, thousands of undead zombies and skeletons crawl out of the cellars, sewers, and hidden dungeons, then begin scouring the city and the surrounding countryside. If you are here after dark, you will spend the entire night fighting one long, pitched battle.*
>
> *"I have talked to those who say that the undead are controlled by a powerful defiler who is using them to keep treasure hunters away from the city while he systematically loots it. Others claim that the undead are the original inhabitants of the city, and they cannot rest because there is some terrible secret buried in the heart of the ancient city that they do not want discovered. In either case, if you go to Bodach, be prepared for an intense battle against this gruesome army."*

"Oh," said Ryana. "I see."

"Note that nowhere does he say that he himself has been there," Sorak said. "Even the Sage did not dare go to Bodach, and yet he sends *us* there."

"He was not yet the Sage when he was the Wanderer," Ryana reminded him. "And now that he is the Sage, he cannot go himself. The pyreen told you that this quest would not be easy. You seek the Sage to ask a boon and find direction for your life. Well, something gained for nothing is worth exactly what it cost to gain. In any case, before we can think of Bodach and its armies of undead, we must first leave the city safely and reach the village of Salt View. What sort of place is that?"

"The Wanderer describes it as a village of former slaves who now live as raiders and gypsy entertainers. It is governed by a mul who was once a gladiator, and the marauders we have met before make their camp not far from there. Doubtless, they use the village as a base of supply and a place of recreation. In other words, we can expect to find no friends there."

"We should find one in the druid," said Ryana. "Do not be discouraged, Sorak. We embarked on this quest together, and we shall see it through together. You have lived in ignorance of your past for all your life. Surely, you did not expect to find all the answers in a few short weeks?"

He sighed. "I suppose not. It is just that I had hoped. . . . Well, it makes no difference. I chose this path, now I must walk it."

"*We* chose this path," she said.

He looked and her and smiled. "Yes, we did. Together. Forgive me, little sister. And thank you for your strength."

"You are forgiven," she said. "And you are welcome. Now let's get out of this miserable place. The lantern burns low, and I have no wish to stumble around down here in the dark."

They made their way back down the tunnel and found the branching point the wizard had told them about. They turned down it and walked along a short corridor before they came to a flight of stone steps. At the end of the steps they reached only a brick wall.

"Now what?" said Sorak.

"There must be a door somewhere," said Ryana.

After searching for a few moments by the dim, flickering glow of the lantern, she finally found an iron ring set into the wall to their left. As the lantern flickered out, she pulled it. The ring did not give on the first try, but on the second, when she put more strength into it, it pulled out of the wall slightly, and there was a grating sound as the wall swung open. It was a concealed door, pivoting around a central rod that ran through it. It opened out into a wooden storage shed, built against the back wall of the tavern. They cautiously opened the door of the shed and peered outside. The way seemed clear. They stepped out into the alley and breathed the fresh night air.

Almost at the same moment, they heard the solid tramping of feet, a tread far heavier than that of humans, and they flattened themselves against the wall as a squad of half-giants trooped past the mouth of the alley. They were carrying huge agafari war clubs as they marched with great strides around the corner toward the entrance to the Elven Blade.

"The wizard was right," said Sorak. "Doubtless, they have come to look for us."

"Then it would be in our best interests to get elsewhere," said Ryana, "and with all haste."

They ran toward the mouth of the alley and cautiously looked out from the shadows. The street seemed clear. But as they moved out of the alley and quickly started walking back toward the center of the city, someone behind them yelled out, *"There they go! Look! There they are! There!"*

They glanced over their shoulders and saw someone standing in the entrance of the tavern, pointing in their direction. Almost immediately, several half-giants came running out past him, into the street.

"Why can't these good citizens of Nibenay mind their own cursed business, as they do in Tyr?" said Sorak through gritted teeth, as they turned and ran. Behind them, the half-giants thundered on their trail. They could not run as quickly, but their huge strides ate up a lot more ground.

"This way, hurry!" Sorak said as they darted down a dark alley. They ran to the opposite end and into the side street, but could hear the bellowing half-giants still in pursuit—and getting closer. It sounded as if Sorak and Ryana were being chased by a lumbering stampede of mekillots.

"We cannot outrun them!" said Ryana. "They can cover more ground with one stride than we can with three, and they know this city, while we are already lost!"

"Then we shall have to see what we can do to discourage their pursuit," said Sorak. "In here!"

They ducked into a building entryway and pressed themselves against the doors as the half-giants thundered toward them. Ryana fitted a bolt to her crossbow. The half-giants ran past their place of concealment, and she raised the crossbow and took aim.

Suddenly, the looming guards halted. "They did not come this way!" one of them called out. "They must have doubled back!"

Ryana fired. The bolt hissed through the air and struck one of the half-giants in the back of the neck, at the base of his skull. With a bellowing cry, he raised his hands up to the arrow and fell crashing to the street. Ryana was already lifting her bow for a second shot as the half-giants turned back toward them. Her second bolt struck home, hitting one of them between the eyes, and he fell dead in his tracks. Several of the others tripped over him as he went down, and they all crashed down in a tangled heap.

"Now!" said Sorak, and they ran once again, back the way they had come.

There had been slightly fewer than a dozen half-giants chasing them, and now that two of them were slain, the rest were totally enraged. Lights were going on in the windows up above them as people brought candles and lanterns to see what all the racket was about. As Sorak and Ryana ducked from one winding street into another, some of these citizens were obliging enough to call down to the half-giant guard and point out the way they went.

"Do you know which way we're going?" Ryana asked, breathing hard as they ran.

"No. Do you?"

"We have gone up and down so many streets, I have lost track."

"We must be getting somewhere," Sorak said.

They turned a corner and found themselves on a lane that somehow looked familiar. And then, a moment later, they saw why. Almost directly across the street from where they stood was the entrance to the Elven Blade.

"Oh, great!" Ryana said. "We have come right back to where we started from!"

"Well, look on the bright side. At least we know where we are now," Sorak said.

They could hear the half-giants coming up behind them.

"This way," Sorak said, pointing back the way they had first come when Korahna brought them to the tavern. But they had not run halfway down the street when they saw another troop of half-giant guards come round the corner, led by one of the Shadow King's own templars.

"*Those two!*" she called out as they skidded to a halt in the center of the street. "*Stop them!*"

They turned around to run back the other way, but before they could run three paces, they saw their original pursuers come thundering around the corner. They were cut off, hemmed in on both sides.

"We're trapped!" said Ryana, looking both ways.

"I was getting tired of running anyway," said Sorak, drawing Galdra. Ryana fired one more bolt, dropping another half-giant in his tracks, then quickly slung her bow across her back and drew her own sword. They took up position in the center of the street, back to back, each holding a sword in one hand and a dagger in the other.

The half-giants came at them from both sides, bellowing as they charged. The first one to reach Sorak raised his agafari war club and brought it down in a vicious swipe. Sorak parried the blow with Galdra, and the war club was split cleanly in two. He swung his sword again, and the half-giant recoiled, but not quickly enough. Galdra opened up his stomach from side to side, and as the half-giant screamed, his guts came tumbling out into the street.

At the same time, Ryana moved in to meet her attackers. The two who reached her first were over-confident at being confronted by a female, but they soon discovered that the villichi priestess was no ordinary woman. Ryana's blade flashed with dazzling speed as they both raised their clubs, and before they could even bring them down, both half-giants fell, their fatal wounds spouting blood. But more were coming.

As the other half-giants reached Sorak, he suddenly felt himself spinning away, as if he were falling. Consciousness receded, and the Shade came rushing forth like a cold wind from the depths. The half-giants were stunned at the juggernaut that suddenly plowed into them, swinging his sword as if it had a life of its own. The gaze of this new antagonist was as frightening as his blade, for those who met those eyes felt a chill that froze them to the marrow.

Three more half-giants fell in as many seconds, and Galdra dripped with their blood as the blade flashed in search of fresh victims. With one hand the Shade swung Galdra, slicing through a half-giant's waist, while with the other he caught a war club that was coming down, aimed at his head. The half-giant stared, wide-eyed with disbelief that someone so much smaller could so easily catch his blow. He had time for no more reactions: the Shade kicked out with his foot and smashed the half-giant's kneecap even as he parried another blow from yet another half-giant.

Another war club was cut in two, as if it were no more than a twig, and a second later, two more half-giants lay dead in the street.

Meanwhile, Ryana looked to her speed and skill to avoid the blows aimed at her. Moving like a deadly dancer, she twisted and turned, sidestepping attacks and darting between the half-giants that attempted to surround her. She darted among them like a fly buzzing among beasts, stinging painfully with every pass. One half-giant collapsed to the ground, howling in pain as his knee tendons were severed; another saw her poised before him and raised his club only to find that she was not there and that suddenly blood was pouring from the gaping wound in his chest. So quickly had she struck that he never even saw the blade go in. He fell, knocking over one of his comrades, and Ryana dispatched him, also, as he tripped.

The close quarters of the combat now worked against the half-giants as they knocked into one another, trying to get at their opponents, who moved among them with terrifying speed. One half-giant struck out blindly with his war club, hoping to connect, but instead smashed in the ribs of one of his fellow guards. The other, maddened with pain and enraged, caved in his compatriot's skull with his own war club. And then he, too, fell as Ryana plunged her sword into his side.

The templar watched from the far end of the street, amazed as one half-giant after another fell before the furious onslaught. It was impossible, she thought. Who *were* these people? Only a handful of the guards remained now, and as they pressed in their attack, they met with no more success than those who had gone before them. Over the din of the combat and the enraged bellowing of the guards, another sound rose above the fray, a sound that made shivers run down the watching templar's spine.

It was the sound of the Shade howling for blood. It was an animal cry, frightening and inhuman. Two more half-giants fell, and then another, and another, and the Shade had no more opponents confronting him. He turned, then, and ran to help Ryana with the ones remaining. Between the two of them, three more half-giants fell in the blink of an eye. Only four remained. Human guards would have given up and run, but the half-giants were too stupid for that. Motivated only by rage, they smashed their clubs upon the ground with each missed blow, and were too slow to recover. Big as they were, they were no match for their much faster opponents. Moments later, all the half-giants lay bleeding in the street, now littered with the bodies of two full squads.

So astonished was the templar at what she had witnessed that she had simply watched, frozen to the spot. But when the elfling turned toward her and fixed her with his gaze, she was suddenly galvanized into action. At least forty yards separated them, and as fierce a fighter as the elfling was, the templar knew he could not reach her before she summoned up a spell. As she lifted her arms in preparation, she saw the elfling raise his sword. He wasn't even moving toward her. For a moment, she paused and smiled at what she thought was a last, defiant gesture, and then her jaw dropped with amazement as he *hurled* the blade.

She laughed at the pathetic attempt, knowing that it

could not possibly reach her. But the laughter froze in her throat as she saw the deadly blade come flashing at her, spinning end over end, apparently defying gravity as it swooped toward her with a whoosh each time it spun around. It covered twenty yards, then twenty-five, then thirty. . . .

"No," she whispered, staring with horror at the rapidly approaching doom. She turned to run, but Galdra cleaved her right in two before she had taken three steps. Had she still been alive to witness it, she would have been even more amazed to see the sword describe a graceful arc in midair and return to the outstretched hand of its owner.

Sorak found himself standing in the middle of the street surrounded by the corpses of half-giants. The Shade receded, and Sorak quickly looked around to see Ryana right behind him, breathing heavily as she held her dripping sword. She looked at him and smiled weakly, fighting for breath, and then her smile faded as Sorak saw her staring beyond him.

Two more squads of half-giants had appeared at the far end of the street. Sorak and Ryana spun around and saw yet another squad coming up behind them.

"Sorak . . ." said Ryana, staring at him with resignation in her eyes.

"It seems we are not yet finished," he said, feeling the effects of the Shade's exertions.

Ryana simply shook her head. "I fear we are," she said.

"What would Tamura say if she heard you talking like that?" Sorak asked, hoping to brace her up by invoking the name of their old teacher, who had so often pushed them past all limits of endurance.

"I only wish that she were here right now," Ryana replied. "I have no more strength."

"Stay close to me," said Sorak, wondering if there was time to summon Kether. But the half-giants were already charging at them from both sides.

"I always have," she said, as she raised her sword and turned to face her fate.

They stood, shoulder to shoulder, prepared to go down fighting. But as the half-giants converged on them, the darkness of the street was suddenly illuminated with brilliant light as several fireballs exploded around them. One burst right in the midst of an approaching troop of half-giants, sending them scampering for cover or falling to the ground, on fire, bellowing as they rolled in the dirt to put out the flames. The troop coming from the opposite direction was likewise bombarded as fireballs arced through the air and struck them, bursting in explosions of flame as they landed.

"What's happening?" Ryana asked, staring all around at the fireballs that came down on their pursuers.

"The Alliance!" Sorak shouted.

The white-robed figures of the preserver wizards were visible on several of the surrounding rooftops as they hurled fire spells down at the city guard.

"Sorak! Ryana! This way!" Korahna shouted. She stood in the entrance to a building on their right, beckoning to them. "Quickly! Run!"

They ran to the building and ducked inside. Korahna led them down a corridor and out through the back door, then down an alley into an adjoining street.

"Your timing could not have been better," Sorak said.

Korahna turned and grinned at him over her shoulder. "One good rescue deserves another," she said.

"We must get you out of the city with all possible speed. Word has reached us that the templars have ordered the entire city guard to converge on this area. You saw but a small complement of them. The entire elven quarter will soon be swarming with half-giants looking for you."

"Suddenly, I am feeling very anxious to be on our way," Ryana said.

They ran down another alley and out into the street at the opposing end.

"Aren't we are heading away from the city gates?" asked Sorak as they ran.

"There is a hidden tunnel leading underneath the city walls at the far end of the elven quarter," said Korahna. "That will be our chance to get you out of the city safely. The diversion created by my friends should help us. Most of the city guard will be drawn to the fighting in the street outside the tavern."

As they rushed to the end of the lane and turned a corner, they suddenly ran right into another squad of half-giants.

"Well, maybe not all of them," Korahna said, drawing her sword. They were too close to run. Only a dozen yards or so separated them. The half-giants bellowed and charged, brandishing their war clubs.

Ryana felt a sudden shiver run down her spine as Sorak moved quickly past her. He had the lethal grace of some predatory beast, and she realized that Sorak was gone and the primitive entity called the Shade had risen to the fore from deep within his subconscious.

Moving with incredible speed, the Shade met the charging half-giants and waded into them with Galdra flashing. In the blink of an eye, one half-giant was cut completely in two, and his severed torso fell screaming to the ground. Galdra flashed again, and an agafari war club was cut through as if it were no more than a dry stalk of desert grass. Another half-giant toppled, screaming, to the ground. Then Ryana saw a sudden change come over the others.

Several of them recoiled and dropped their clubs, cowering helplessly before their antagonist, while others simply bolted. Ryana abruptly understood why she had felt that shiver run down the entire length of her spine. Each of Sorak's inner personalities had some psionic talent all its own. The Shade's was an aura of unrelenting terror. She had sensed it rising as he passed her, and now she felt it even more strongly as it radiated from him like waves of pure, bestial malevolence. It was stark and primal terror, the hypnotic, gripping fear that strikes tiny mammals when they gaze into serpents' eyes, the involuntary paralysis of the rodent as the winged predator swoops down for the kill.

But even as she realized what was happening, she became overwhelmed by it herself. The Shade was not projecting it only at the half-giants that fell before his flashing blade; it emanated out from him in all directions.

Korahna cried out as she felt it and panicked. She took off, screaming, down the street, running as if her life depended on it. Ryana ran after her, or perhaps with her, some part of her mind trying to tell her it was no threat to her, but she could not help herself. She had to run before she froze in helpless terror and was consumed by it. A block away, she felt the fear ebb and rationality return. Korahna was still running ahead of her, caught up in the momentum of her flight.

"Korahna!" Ryana shouted after her as she ran to catch her. "Korahna, *wait!*"

And then she saw another squad of half-giants, a dozen or so led by a templar, come into the street. Korahna, in her flight, was going to run headlong into them.

"*Korahna!*" Ryana screamed. "*Stop!*"

She ran with all the speed she could muster, closing the distance between them, and then she leapt, tackling the princess from behind. They both fell, sprawling, to the street. Ryana rolled on top of her and pinned her down. Korahna struggled, and Ryana gave her a stinging slap across the face.

"Come out of it!" she cried. "Korahna, for pity's sake!"

She struck her again, and Korahna's head jerked with the blow, and then her eyes seemed to clear. She stared up at Ryana, confused and uncomprehending.

"Korahna, we're in danger! Get up!"

They struggled to their feet, but the half-giants were already upon them. The monstrous guards broke ranks quickly and surrounded them, leering down and slapping huge war clubs into their large and callused hands.

"Well, what have we here?" the templar said, stepping forward. "If it isn't the traitor's daughter, returned to receive her just desserts."

"Narimi!" said Korahna.

"You should have stayed away, Korahna," the older woman said, gazing at her with scorn. "You are a disgrace to the royal house."

"The royal house is a disgrace!" Korahna said. "I am

ashamed to have been born to it!"

"A situation that is easily remedied," the templar said. "You shall not have to live with your shame much longer. You will be executed, as your mother was, but first you will name all your accomplices in the Alliance."

"I will die first!" Korahna said, grabbing for her sword.

But even as she tried to draw it, the templar swept out her hand, and the blade froze in its scabbard. Korahna pulled with all her might but could not free the sword.

Ryana concentrated, focusing her psionic energies upon the club of the half-giant standing behind the templar. He grunted as it twisted from his grasp and flew up into the air, arcing toward the templar's head. But she quickly turned and again flung out her hand. There was a flash of light as the agafari wood was incinerated in midair before it could come down on her.

Then the templar pivoted and swept her arm out toward Ryana. An invisible force struck her in the chest, and she flew backward, landing at the feet of the half-giants behind her. Stunned and with the breath knocked out of her, she could not focus her will.

"A good attempt, Priestess," said the templar, "but psionics are no match for magic. You shall die as well, but first you shall tell me where the elfling is."

"I will tell you nothing, bitch!"

"I think you shall," the templar said, raising her hand once again. "Hold her."

Two of the half-giants bent to pick her up, but as they did, something came whistling through the air over their heads. The templar made a grunting, gasping sound as the knife struck her in the chest. She looked down at it with astonishment, then collapsed to the ground. Instantly, the street was filled with a hail of arrows.

"*Get down!*" Ryana shouted, sweeping Korahna's legs out from under her and rolling over on top of her.

All around them, the half-giants fell, bellowing in pain and fury as arrows seemed to sprout suddenly from their bodies. In seconds, the street was littered with their lifeless bodies.

The hail of arrows ceased, and Ryana looked up. A number of tall figures stepped out of the shadows around them, perhaps a dozen or more, all carrying crossbows. Elves and half-elves. And leading them was a familiar figure.

"You!" Ryana said.

It was the thief from the tavern. And a moment later, Sorak came up beside him. Ryana's eyes grew wide as she saw him. He was completely covered in blood.

"Sorak!"

"It is all right," he said. "The blood is not my own."

"You should have seen him!" said the thief. "He was magnificent! The half-giants fell like chaff before him!" He turned and spoke to his companions. "Did I not tell you, scoffers? Truly, he is the king the legends foretold!"

"I have told you once already, I am no king," said Sorak.

"You carry Galdra, the blade of ancient elven kings."

"A sword does not make one a king!"

"That one does."

"Then *you* take it!"

"Not I," the thief said. "You are the one."

"I tell you, I am *not* the one!"

"Could you two debate this later?" said Korahna. "The quarter is crawling with guards. We haven't much time."

"We will provide escort," said the thief. "It is the very least that I can do to make amends."

"You have already made amends," said Sorak. "Just get us out of here."

"We must reach the north wall, by the stone yards," said Korahna.

"This way, then," said the thief. "I know the shortest route. Trust thieves to know the back streets and alleys."

They ran quickly down twisting lanes and through narrow, refuse-strewn alleys while some of the others hung back to cover their rear. The two women strained to match the pace set by the elves, who were merely jogging by their standards. Before long, they reached the stone yards, a wide and open expanse near the north wall of the city, where the large, quarried blocks were brought to be cut down for use by the city's artisans.

Moving quickly through the moonlit yard, Korahna led the way through the maze of stone blocks piled up all around them. Most of the other elves hung back to cover them in the event of pursuit. Finally, they reached the north wall of the city and ran alongside it until they came to the hovels at the far end of the yard. Korahna paused a moment to get her bearings.

"This way," she said, ducking down a narrow alley. She counted doors. It was not an alley, but a street, though it was scarcely wider than Sorak's shoulders.

They were in the poorest section of the city, where hovels were so crowded together that they made the warrens of Tyr look like the templars' quarter. At the seventh door on their right, Korahna stopped and knocked softly seven times. They waited, tensely, then a moment later, three slow, answering knocks came from within. Korahna knocked once more, and the door swung open.

They entered a room that seemed little more than a closet. A small, cheap lamp cast what little light there was, illuminating a pallet on the floor and several crudely made pieces of furniture assembled from scrap, a low table pegged together from boards, and a small, three-legged stool. There was no room for anything else. The old man who had opened the door was dressed in rags, and his scraggly, gray hair hung limply to his shoulders. Without a word, without even so much as a glance at the stranger who had entered his cramped quarters, he shuffled over to the wood pallet on which he slept, bent over, and with a grunt, pulled it away from the wall, revealing a wooden trapdoor beneath it.

"It is a small and narrow tunnel," said Korahna, "and you will have to crawl. But it leads under the wall and outside the city. From there, you are on your own."

"Then we will say farewell again," said Sorak, giving her a hug. "We owe our lives to you. And to you, as well, friend," he said to the thief, holding out his hand.

Instead of taking it, the thief bowed deeply. "It was a privilege, my lord. I hope that one day, soon, we shall meet again."

"Perhaps," said Sorak. "And do not call me 'my lord!'"

"Yes, my lord."

"Aaah!" said Sorak, throwing up his arms.

The old man opened the trapdoor.

"Hurry," said Korahna. "The longer we remain here, the greater the risk."

Sorak took her hand and kissed it. "Thank you, Your Highness," he said.

"Go on! Hurry!"

He climbed down into the tunnel.

"Farewell again, Sister," said Ryana. "I shall miss you."

"And I, you."

They embraced briefly, and then Ryana followed Sorak down into the hole. The door was closed behind them, and she was plunged into total darkness. She reached out with her hands in front of her and felt a small opening, barely wide enough to crawl through.

"Sorak?"

"Come on," he called back, from inside the tunnel. "But keep your head down."

She squirmed into the opening and started crawling on her hands and knees. She couldn't see a thing. She felt incredibly closed in and wondered what would happen if the tunnel collapsed on them. She swallowed hard and kept on crawling. The thought occurred to her that it seemed like a perfect place for snakes and venomous spiders. Why did that have to occur to her now? She was grateful that Sorak was crawling up ahead, because that meant if there were any spider-webs inside the tunnel, he would break them before she crawled into them headfirst. It was not, perhaps, a very considerate attitude, she thought, but at least it was an honest one.

After what seemed like an incredibly long time, she finally felt the tunnel sloping up slightly. And then she reached the end of it. She found out because she ran into the wall headfirst. With a curse, she pulled back and rubbed her head, then felt around her. A shaft was open above. She crouched, then stood, and felt wooden rungs in front of her. She climbed up perhaps a dozen feet or so and then felt Sorak's hand close around her wrist, helping her out. She breathed in the welcome, cool, night air and felt a soft breeze blowing. They stood in a thicket by what she first thought was a stream, then realized was an irrigation canal. They were about thirty or forty feet beyond the city wall. The distance she had crawled had somehow seemed much longer.

"I *hate* tunnels," she said, brushing the dirt off her clothing before realizing that there wasn't much point to it. After all that they had been through, her clothes were filthy and torn in places. Sorak did not look much better. In fact, he looked even worse. There was dried blood caked all over him, covered with a layer of grime.

"Don't stare," he said. "You do not look much better."

They stood in a grove of agafari trees, sheltered from view. Ryana unslung her crossbow and unbuckled her sword belt, dropped her pack to the ground, and waded into the canal. It felt wonderful to let the cold water caress her face.

"Well?" she said. "Are you coming in, or do you intend to spend the rest of our journey looking like a corpse?"

He grinned, took off his sword belt and his pack,

then waded in beside her. The water came up to their chests and they both submerged themselves, then scrubbed their faces and their clothes.

"It would be just our luck to be caught here, bathing, after all that we have been through," said Ryana.

"I would not tempt fate if I were you," said Sorak.

"Yes, my lord."

He splashed her. "Stop that."

"Yes, my lord." She splashed him back. Suddenly, they were laughing and splashing each other as they had not done since they were both small children, playing in the pool by the temple. After a short while, they climbed out and rested for a moment on the bank, the water dripping from them.

"That felt good," she said, staring up into the trees.

"Enjoy the feeling," Sorak replied. "It is the last water we shall see until we reach the Mekillot Mountains."

She sighed. "I suppose we had best be on our way and put as much distance between us and the city as possible while it is still dark."

Sorak got to his feet and buckled on his sword belt. "If it were not for the fact that I have no other sword, I would be sorely tempted to toss this one into the canal."

"That would be a fine way to treat a gift from the high mistress," said Ryana, shouldering her pack.

He drew the blade and looked at it. "The sword of elven kings," he said dryly, then sighed. "Why does it fall to me?"

"You should be grateful," said Ryana. "It has saved our lives."

"And placed them in jeopardy, in the first place,"

Sorak replied wryly. He sheathed the blade. "Still, it is a fine and wondrous blade."

"And we shall yet have need of it," Ryana said. They started walking, heading through the grove of trees and keeping under their protective cover as long as possible.

"It feels rather strange not to have Korahna along," said Sorak as they walked. "I had grown rather fond of her."

Ryana nodded. "As did I. At first, I disliked her, but she proved to be much more than what her appearance had suggested. Do you think she will be safe?"

"No," said Sorak. "And I do not think she would have it any other way."

Ryana smiled. "At least she will have a chance to get some rest," she said. "Every muscle in my body feels tired and sore."

"We will try to find a sheltered place to rest a while shortly after daybreak," Sorak said. "We have a long walk ahead of us."

"I don't suppose Screech could scare up a kank?"

"In the Ivory Plain? I would not count on it. And it is doubtful we shall find wild kanks this close to the city. No, I am afraid we have no choice but to go on foot."

"Do you think they will pursue us?"

"Perhaps," said Sorak. "But I suspect they will think we have found shelter with the Veiled Alliance. They will search the city for us first. By the time it occurs to them that we have fled beyond the walls, we will be long gone."

They soon reached the end of the grove, beyond which acres of cultivated rice fields spread out before them. They waded through the irrigated fields, past darkened, outlying estates, both of them feeling too tired to do much talking. Soon, they reached ground that was more sparsely covered with vegetation. The ground was sloping slightly, and Ryana knew that it would not be long before they reached the desert once again. They had filled their water skins back at the canal, but she knew she would have to make the water last as long as possible. And chances were it would not be long enough. By daybreak, they had reached a ridge and stopped to rest among the rocks. As the sun came up, she looked out over the ridge and saw, in the distance, a vast expanse of white land, gleaming in the morning sun.

"The Great Ivory Plain," said Sorak.

Far in the distance, Ryana could see the outline of the Mekillot Mountains, their next destination. "Well," she said with an air of resignation, "I had always wanted to go on a long pilgrimage." She sighed. "However, this is not quite what I had in mind."

There was no reply from Sorak. She turned to find him stretched out on the ground in the shadow of the rocks, fast asleep. This time, the Ranger did not come out, nor did any of the others. Their body's weariness had finally caught up with them.

"Sleep well, Nomad," she said, stretching out beside him. "We have both earned our rest."

She closed her eyes and thought of the forests of the Ringing Mountains, of the flowing river and spreading canopy of trees. It seemed to belong to another lifetime now. She wondered, briefly, what life would have been like had she chosen not to follow Sorak, but to remain at the villichi temple. It would have been, she thought, a pleasant, peaceful, and serene life . . . and utterly predictable. She had no regrets. And as she fell asleep, she smiled.

EPILOGUE

The weary travelers looked utterly exhausted as they fell asleep beside each other on the sheltered rock ledge looking out over the plain below. They slept in shadow, protected by the overhanging rock as the dark sun rose above them, reflecting in myriad sparkles off the vast expanse of salt and quartzite crystal that was the Great Ivory Plain. They would have a long, hard journey ahead of them when they awoke, and when they reached the Mekillot Mountains, they would face still greater challenges. With a sigh, the white-robed figure passed a long and bony hand over the surface of the scrying crystal, and it clouded over. The faces of the weary travelers faded from view, as if disappearing into a mist. The large and perfect sphere went as dark as the black velvet on which its silver stand stood.

"Let them rest a while in peace, Kinjara," said the Sage, turning from the scrying crystal. "We shall look in on them another time."

The rare white-and-black striped kirre made a low growling noise, rising in tone. It raised its massive head and its twin ramlike horns and twitched its long,

301

barbed tail.

"What is it, Kinjara? You are hungry?"

The kirre gave an answering growl.

"Well, do not look to me. You know which way the door is. If you are hungry, then you must hunt. That is the way of things."

The kirre growled plaintively.

"Do not give me that. Yes, of course I am still your friend. But you are a wild creature. Simply because I provide you with shelter and companionship, do not expect me to start feeding you, as well. You would only become spoiled."

The kirre grunted and exposed its huge teeth in irritation as it rose up from the floor on its eight muscular legs and moved with lithe grace toward the door.

"That's a good kitty," said the Sage. "And remember our agreement. Do not kill any birds."

The kirre gave an answering grunt.

"No, I am sorry. No birds and that is final. I will not have you looking at me hungrily when my wings begin to sprout. I know your sort."

Grrrrrr.

"And the same to you. Go on now, get."

Another robed and hooded figure approached from across the room. At first glance, it might have been taken for a human, except that it was very large, just over six feet tall, and extremely wide in the shoulders and upper torso. There were other peculiarities about its proportions. The arms seemed unusually long, and the hands had only four clawlike fingers, ending in sharp talons. The feet, too, were very large and bird-like, more like claws than feet. And from beneath the robe, there hung a reptilian tail. As the figure stepped into the light, the face within the hood became visible. It was not even remotely human. The open beak revealed rows of small, very sharp teeth, and the yellow, lizardlike eyes were covered with nictitating membranes. The creature emitted a series of low, clicking sounds.

"Yes, they have secured the Seals," said the Sage, turning toward the pterran. "You see, Tak-ko, you were wrong. They did survive the Stony Barrens, as I knew they would."

The pterran spoke once more in its peculiar, clicking, chirping language.

"Yes, I have sent them to see the Silent One, whose help they will require in the next step of their journey."

The pterran chirruped again.

"No, the Silent One is not crazy. A bit peculiar, perhaps; eccentric, to be sure, but crazy? No, I do not think so."

The pterran clicked.

"What do you mean, am I sure? How can anyone be sure of anything in this world?"

Click-click, click-click-chirp-click, click-click-chirp.

"I am *not* equivocating! Life is merely full of uncertainties, that is all. Even I cannot know everything. For certain, that is."

The pterran spoke once more.

"The pain? The pain is not so bad today, thank you for asking. It is just a general, dull ache. I scarcely notice it. It will grow worse with the next stage of the transformation, but I am not yet quite prepared for that. Our friends shall have to provide a few necessary ingredients, first."

The pterran clicked in an interrogative manner.

"Yes, next they must secure the Breastplate of Argentum."

The pterran clicked again.

"Yes, in Bodach."

The pterran emitted another series of sharp sounds.

"I *know* there are undead in Bodach. What do you want from me? I did not put them there."

The pterran shook its massive head and clicked several more times.

"They will never make it? That's what you said when they went across the Stony Barrens, as I recall, and yet they seemed to have survived that somehow."

The pterran issued a brief response.

"Oh, they were lucky, were they? Well, perhaps they were. But I think that skill, patience, dedication, and perseverance may have had something to do with it, don't you?"

The pterran shrugged and chirped a reply.

"You always find the dark cloud in every silver lining, don't you?" said the Sage. "Well, I think you're wrong."

The pterran spoke.

"Would I care to wager on it? Why, you oversized, insolent, prehistoric sparrow, you have your nerve! A wager! A wager with *me!* What insufferable arrogance! What sort of wager?"

The pterran returned a quick response.

"Hmmm, I see. Interesting. And what if *you* should lose?"

The pterran gave out a raucous caw and clicked again.

"Name my stakes? My, my. Such confidence for someone who cannot even eat without dropping half his food onto the floor. Very well, then. I shall name my stakes. But I shall name them when you lose."

The pterran threw back its massive head and gave out a long, ululating, piercing cry.

"Laugh all you like, my friend," the Sage said. "We shall see who winds up laughing out of the other side of his beak."

Still cawing raucously, the pterran left the chamber.

The Sage grunted irritably, then walked over to the window, moving slowly, a man in pain. He looked out over the landscape toward the rising sun. "Your path is no less arduous than mine, my children," he said as he gazed out the window. "I shall do what little I can to ease your hardship. But the rest, I fear, is up to you. More depends on what you do than you can know. Our fates are linked now. If you fail, I fail. And if I fail, all is lost for our benighted world."

He turned away from the window and hobbled over to his chair, sinking down into it slowly. For a time, the pain of transformation had subsided. But soon, it would return again. He gazed into the mirror at his fading humanity. He had almost grown accustomed to it. As he pondered his reflection, he could no longer see any trace of the young man who had once set out across the world to chronicle the lands and ways of Athas. Now it was for Sorak to follow in his footsteps and go beyond, where he had never dared to go. He fervently hoped the elfling and the priestess would succeed. For now, all he could do was wait. He leaned back in his chair and closed his eyes as the sun's rays warmed him through the open window. After a while, the Wanderer slept.

COMING FALL/WINTER '94

The Ogre's Pact

Book One in the new Twilight Giants Trilogy by Troy Denning, *New York Times* best-selling author

When ogres kidnap Brianna of Hartwick, her father forbids his knights to rescue her. Only a brash peasant, who covets Brianna's hand, has the courage to ignore the duke's orders. To Tavis's surprise, slaying the ogres is the easiest part . . . the challenge has only begun!
Available September 1994
TSR #8546
ISBN 1-56076-891-6

Realms of Infamy

The incredible companion volume to the *Realms of Valor* anthology

From the secret annals of Realms history come never-before-published tales of villains – Artemis Entreri, Manshoon of Zhentil Keep, Elaith Craulnober, and many others – told by your favorite authors: R. A. Salvatore, Ed Greenwood, Troy Denning, Elaine Cunningham, and others.
Available December 1994
TSR #8547
ISBN 1-56076-911-4

Sug. Retail Each $4.95; CAN $5.95; £4.99 U.K.

DragonLance® Saga

THE HISTORIC SAGA OF THE DWARVEN CLANS
Dwarven Nations Trilogy
Dan Parkinson

The Covenant of the Forge   **Volume One**
As the drums of Balladine thunder forth, calling humans to trade
with the dwarves of Thorin, Grayfen, a human struck by the magic of
the Graystone, infiltrates the dwarven stronghold, determined to
annihilate the dwarves and steal their treasure.   ISBN 1-56076-558-5

Hammer and Axe   **Volume Two**
The dwarven clans unite against the threat of encroaching humans
and create the fortress of Thorbardin. But old rivalries are not easily
forgotten, and the resulting political intrigue brings about
catastrophic change.   ISBN 1-56076-627-1

The Swordsheath Scroll   **Volume Three**
Despite the stubborn courage of the dwarves, the Wilderness War
ends as a no-win. The Swordsheath Scroll is signed, and the dwarves
join the elves of Qualinesti to build a symbol of peace among the
races: Pax Tharkas.   ISBN 1-56076-686-7

Sug. Retail Each $4.95; CAN $5.95; £3.99 U.K.

PLANESCAPE™ –
Venturing the planes of power

You've never experienced anything like this before!

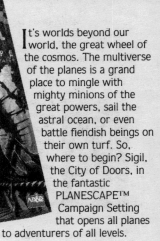

It's worlds beyond our world, the great wheel of the cosmos. The multiverse of the planes is a grand place to mingle with mighty minions of the great powers, sail the astral ocean, or even battle fiendish beings on their own turf. So, where to begin? Sigil, the City of Doors, in the fantastic PLANESCAPE™ Campaign Setting that opens all planes to adventurers of all levels.

AD&D®
2nd Edition

On Sale May 1994
TSR #2600
Sug. Retail $30.00; CAN $42.00; £21.50 U.K. Incl. VAT
ISBN 1-56076-834-7

Composition Interligne.
Impression Société Nouvelle Firmin-Didot
à Mesnil-sur-l'Estrée, le 10 janvier 2008.
Dépôt légal : janvier 2008.
1ᵉʳ dépôt légal : janvier 2003.
Numéro d'imprimeur : 88537.

ISBN 978-2-07-042693-5/Imprimé en France.